DAINTREE
REFLECTIONS

Destiny in Disguise Series

DAINTREE
REFLECTIONS

Living in Crocodile Country
North Queensland

ANTHONY W BUIRCHELL

National Library of Australia Cataloguing-in-Publication
Creator: Buirchell, Anthony W., author.
Title: Daintree Reflections: Journey to Crocodile Country North
     Queensland / Anthony W. Buirchell.
Edition: 2nd edition.
ISBN: 9780995424333 (paperback)
Series: Buirchell, Anthony W. Destiny in Disguise series ; 2.
Subjects: Historical fiction, Australian-Queensland. Daintree
     (Qld.)-History--Fiction.

Printed & Channel Distribution
Cover Design - Laila Savolainen - Pickawoowoo Publishing Group
Publishing Consultants/Interior Design - Pickawoowoo Publishing Group

Publisher
Cric Croc Enterprises, www.criccroc.com
For enquiries, write to: rights and permissions via publisher.
Lightning Source | Ingram (USA/UK/EUROPE/AUS)

To my partner Deb Johnson for all her
encouragement and computer skills and for being
part of the family that this novel is built around.

Johnson Family in the Daintree
L2 R Keith, Madeline, Isobel, Max, Molly, Marion, Eva and Burt

Burton shows the model Ford Tourer Pickup to Marion in passenger's seat holding Marge.
L2R back Twin hiding by driver's door, Eva, Unknown, Twin, George, Burt
Front L2R Isobel, Molly, Madeline, Max

Chapter 1

George Whittaker, aka Ginger, sat on the verandah looking out over the lush verdant pastures and rainforest towards the distant ranges.

It was a far cry from his native England that he had left over six months ago.

It felt like a life time since he had said a teary goodbye to his friend and sponsor Mr Frisworth and caught the steam train into London.

The freezing cold weather had chilled him to the bone, as he hunted for the Australian Agricultural Group, to obtain a ticket to this new world.

Thank the lucky stars he had run into Bevan, the bedraggled urchin. His knowledge of the streets was immeasurable as he not only guided Ginger to the ticket office but found the Jervis Bay, the ship that would sail George halfway around the world to Queensland in Australia.

George smiled as he recalled the ice-bound waters of the Thames. It amazed him how quickly the solid ice broke up as the huge iron ship edged from its mooring.

The trip had been uneventful except for a stowaway who had been found hiding in the lifeboats and the information sessions provided by the first mate.

The adventures in Rockhampton leading to finding the Johnson family flashed through his mind.

George also recalled the family's flight from the town after the unfortunate death of George Sirrat, the kindly but clever farmer, who had taken on Burton Johnson as a share farmer.

The death of the little piglet when Ginger had to plunge into the Fitzroy River in his efforts to catch the parting ship, the Cirrus, brought a tear to his eyes.

He recalled the moment when Burton Johnson had called him son which brought such joy to the red-headed English youth.

Now he was in the Daintree with his adopted family and he was here to stay.

George hoped he didn't have to face any of the dangers that had been pointed out by the captain of the ferry after they had entered the Daintree River. The 18-foot crocodile that flashed so swiftly and viciously to snatch up the dead chicken that had been thrown in its direction. Then there was the 20-foot amethystine python that sun-baked on a branch high in the tree and later the flash flood that had nearly swept Marion and the girls away.

Burton had been shocked and concerned when Marion related the scary adventure walking along the Stewart Creek but had to agree it was the only way they were going to be able to learn to survive in this beautiful but terrifying environment.

Ginger hoped he didn't have to confront these demons but vowed if he ever did he would put life and limb on the line to protect his new and wonderful family.

"Penny for your thoughts," said a female voice and he was jerked back to reality.

It was Madeline the eldest of the girls. She was a plain Jane with her pageboy haircut but her personality stirred Ginger.

"Oh, just thinking about how lucky I've been on my adventures so far. Seems the good Lord is looking after me and has my destiny all mapped out."

"I wish I knew what mine held for me?" said Madeline and she reached out and touched Ginger on the bare upper arm.

It was an innocent gesture on her part but the gentleness and heat of her touch sent tingling throughout his body. He felt himself blush and Madeline saw the reddening and quickly removed her hand. Ginger felt a tinge of regret that she hadn't lingered longer.

"Beautiful spot, don't you think?" said Madeline trying to bring the situation back to normal.

"Yes, it certainly is. Almost idyllic when you look out to the west," replied Ginger.

The house was built on a slight rise that was thirty feet above the flood plain. The gentle slope was 100 yards long and at the bottom of this was a large barn.

To keep the house cool in very hot weather it was built on stilts. Even the slightest breeze would blow under and have a cooling effect. A steep set of stairs had to be negotiated before reaching the verandah and the front door. A lounge room was to the right and the first bedroom to the left and a short hallway led into the kitchen. The main bedroom was to the left. A back door stepped down to another corridor and a third bedroom was to the right. Further on down and a right turn was the bathroom.

A back door led down steps to a separate laundry and storeroom that were ten yards from the main house.

The toilet or thunderbox as it was nicknamed, was a further twenty yards away and stood alone by itself. Pointing directly at the house was the wooden door.

The family exploration of the rooms turned out to be fun although the sibling rivalry raised its ugly head when it came to choosing the sleeping arrangements. The girls wanted the back room because it was close to the bathroom. That way they wouldn't have to go past the boys in their pyjamas.

The boys also wanted the back room as it was more private and well away from the snoring of Burton, their dad.

Eventually the deadlock was broken by their father who decreed that the girls were to sleep in the front bedroom so that they could be on instant hand to help their mother with baby Max or whenever she wanted them. That ended the stalemate.

Burton called a family meeting and outlined the routines on the farm. This involved the important activity of milking the cows then separating the cream from the skim milk.

He explained that once they achieved a smooth routine then other things would be put in place. Bed would be 7 pm as the milking had to start by 4.30 am and be finished before sun up.

Burt, the eldest boy of the family, would row the cream to the Butter Factory until the others got more skill and confidence at rowing and swimming. He would be accompanied by George in case of any mishaps.

There would be no school until Burton thought those attending could get themselves there safely. He would see the headmaster and explain his decisions.

The latter disappointed both Eva and Isobel as they were looking forward to attending school and furthering their education. On the other hand, they were level headed enough to understand the wisdom in what their father had decreed.

Chapter 2

Marion was first to awake in the morning. It was pitch black outside as she shook Burton awake.

He was up in an instance throwing on his overalls, socks, boots and his hat.

Burton went out to light the fire. It took one strike of the match on the edge of the Redhead matchbox for a flame to illuminate the darkness.

The kindling was sitting on the newspaper where Burt, his eleven year old son, had set it last evening.

Burton pushed the flame onto the paper and it ignited and began to crackle and splutter as the thin kindling caught. He added larger pieces of wood from the heap lying on the floor against the stove.

Soon the heat was so intense that any wood added was instantly aflame.

He slid the top of the stove across to cover the hole he was working from and pulled out the flue. A roaring sound told him that the air was flowing through and adding oxygen to the flames.

By the time Marion had fed Max, dressed and entered the kitchen, Burton had opened the stove top and shuffled the red embers into a flat bed.

He was busy toasting a third lot of toast. He made

two pieces at a time using the wire toasting fork that they had found.

He had already knocked on doors and called the other members of the family.

Soon everyone was filing in greeting each other and helping make the breakfast which was fried eggs on toast with a slice of cold spam.

Marion and Keith were left with the dishes as all the others trooped off down the track leading to the barn.

Burt and Ginger ran off into the gloom and began calling the cows.

Burton and the girls found the barn and lit up a hurricane lamp that Burton had carried from the house. Using the light from the lamp they located three other similar lamps hanging on the wall of the barn. These were lit and hung one in each stall. It was possible to have four cows milked at a time in this set-up.

The three girls selected the stall where they wanted to sit to do the milking. They added dry chaff to the feed boxes and found a stool and pail each. Madeline also checked the fourth stall and set it in readiness for her father.

Outside, but a long way away, they could hear the boys calling the cows.

All of a sudden there was a lowing quite near and the first of the herd wandered up and stepped into the first stall.

Madeline was pleased and said, "If they are all this well-trained milking will be a cinch."

The cow poked its head into the chaff and began chewing.

Madeline shoved the yoke across to lock the cow's head into position so that it wouldn't move. She tied a rope around the back leg to stop any sideways movement.

The cow was used to all this and simply went on enjoying the chaff.

Madeline washed her hands in the spare pail that was set aside for that purpose and sat down on her stool.

She took a teat in each of her hands and began to draw down from the top towards the bottom. As she felt the milk flowing she squeezed and the milk shot out into the pail.

She squeezed one teat and then the other rhythmically and at speed.

She was an accomplished milk maid.

As soon as she recognized that the two teats were running out of milk she swapped to the others. Using the same method she filled the pail, stood up and poured the milk she had extracted into the separator.

At this point, Burt would have been back and turning the separator but he seemed to be having a problem out there in the darkness.

Madeline used her initiative and took up the

separator handle. The frothy white cream spun off into one bucket and the skim milk into the other. She expected about one eighth to be cream and the rest skim milk.

As she worked she noted that Isobel and Eva had both started milking, so some of the cows were at the barn.

Madeline returned to her stall just as another cow arrived.

She had to let the first one out before she could accommodate the next.

Cow number one was happy to get its freedom and sauntered off back to the paddock on the other side of the barn.

It was important to load from one paddock and release into another or else confusion would reign.

Finally, Burton and the two boys appeared around the corner of the barn.

They were all muddy up past their knees and their arms were caked with mud. Burton was furious, which was unusual. He let out several expletives about the weather, floods and mud before apologizing to the girls.

"The cows got out of the top paddock and wandered back into the flooded area. Half of them have been bogged up to their teats and we've had to drag them out one at a time. Sorry ladies but you are in for a messy milking session, stay calm."

It was rather an ironic comment coming from Burton who had already lost his normal cool.

The sun came up and they were still at it.

"Just five to go, Come on look lively and we can all go and have a decent cuppa," encouraged their father.

He turned to the older boys and motioned them forward. "We need to find those heifers today. When we released them from the barn, they set off at a merry pace towards the creek."

"I only hope they didn't get caught in the flood. They are very valuable to us," said Burt.

"At least the piglets are safe because Barry Hayden took them home and put them in his sty. He had plenty of skimmed milk for them and thought that was the right thing to do. I really like the way these Daintree folk operate," said Burton.

The final cow was shooed out of the barn and Ginger was whirling the separator handle like his life depended on it. Madeline watched fascinated, but she kept her thoughts to herself.

"Three cans of cream this morning but none last night thanks to the storm. At a shilling a gallon, we will get one pound ten shillings. Not too bad. That means we should get three pounds a day which is a good take. If we keep that up we'll do very well out here. The best I could do at Bray's Creek was a pound seven shillings a day and that was with 30 milkers," said Burton.

Burton was chuffed and thinking into the future.

He should have reflected on yesterday and this morning to bring a sense of reality back.

Burt had been sent ahead so Marion was well prepared for the weary, mud splattered milkers as they came into the kitchen.

"A nice hot cuppa for each of you and a freshly baked scone," she offered.

"I helped mum too," said old Keith dusting the flour from his oversized apron.

"Good boy and these are delicious," said Burton.

After cleaning up and resting, the family decided to look around the home paddock and start fixing up the things that needed attention.

Eva found the remnants of the vegetable garden and was surprised to find silver beet growing.

"Over here," she shouted, "There are the remains of a veggie patch. We could dig it over and plant seeds for our own food just like we did at grandmas."

Burton, being the practical one sauntered over and looked around. "Wild pigs have been in here," he said pointing to a lot of fresh, exposed soil. "We'll need to build a strong fence around where we intend the garden to go. As for seeds, we can pick them up next time we go into town. I remember seeing packets in the Co-op."

Ginger went off with Burt to search for tools to dig with and Burton started looking for timber that could be used for fence posts. He managed to 'kill two birds with one stone' as he explained later.

Down past the outhouse, he found a lot of old posts, as well as 20 yards of chicken wire. This was all entangled in the logs of the wood heap.

Burton arrived back with the six posts over his shoulders to find everyone busy hoeing, raking and digging.

"I've found lots of posts and wire so that's a start. It looks like Ginger and Burt chanced upon tools for gardening," said Burton.

Burt and Ginger planned out the area and then started digging holes for the fence posts.

Madeline, Eva and Isobel took turns clearing the grass from the area and turning over the soil.

Burton walked back to the fence post pile and returned with another six posts.

As he approached the industrious group he puffed his chest and felt really proud of how well his children co-operated together and their willingness to join in and work. They were only children and yet here they were doing a man's job.

Nearly three hours went by before Marion appeared and offered them all sandwiches, scones and a glass of milk for lunch.

"My goodness," she commented, "You have raised a

great garden bed there. I can't wait to plant the seeds."

"It needs a gate," added Burton, "But for the time being we'll leave a gap."

The afternoon was taken as a rest time as they had toiled extremely hard and they needed to build up energy because milking started again at 4.30 pm.

Chapter 3

They all sat on the verandah after milking and reflected on what had happened since they had made their way up the Daintree River in the ferry.

Burton was pleased with their achievements although concerned about the rapidity of the flood that they had experienced.

"We are going to have quite a lot of skim milk every day so we will need to establish a pig sty and bring our little pigs home. Tomorrow after milking that will be our job."

The pig sty developed rather rapidly mainly because the last resident had built quite a cosy one. It had a few broken rails and a sheet of corrugated iron missing from the roof. So fixing these things was relatively easy.

Burton stood back and watched the children put the finishing touches to the sty.

"We need to expand it to take at least twenty pigs in my opinion. We have over twenty gallons of skim milk from each milking session. If mum needs five gallons a day to keep us all fed that will leave, Eva?"

He had a habit of throwing questions at the children

when they least expected them. He said it was his way of improving their education. Marion did a good job helping them with the 3Rs Reading, 'Riting and 'Rithmetic so he felt he had to add to this.

Eva looked up nonplussed and then looked around searching out Isobel hoping she would give a hint. Isobel was the clever one, always reading and first finished when mum gave them a problem to solve.

Isobel mouthed the word, "Fifteen," and Eva thankfully caught the gesture and replied, "Fifteen gallons, dad."

"Correct, we'll make a scholar out of you yet. Fifteen gallons a day will be plenty to fatten twenty pigs. Hopefully, we'll then get a good price when we sell. I'll go over to Barry Hayden tomorrow and see what he recommends and see if we can increase our stock straight away."

While Burton was away talking to Barry Hayden, Marion was surprised to see a horseman approaching from the Stewart Creek. He was leading two other horses.

As they came closer she could make out a pretty bay mare and a huge black and white draught horse. Both animals seemed to be well trained as they kept pace with the horse the rider was on.

Marion walked out to the verandah and waited for the visitor to arrive.

Keith and the girls soon noticed the stranger and they ran to congregate on the verandah.

"Good morning, madam," called the rider, "Mr Lucas-Hughes sent me out with your horses. He said to tell you these are part of the contract. This bay is called Gypsy and the old fella is Brutus, strong as an ox and quiet as a lamb."

"Mr Lucas-Hughes is wonderful," said Marion, "He thinks of everything. Please thank him when you return. Could I offer you a cup of tea and scones?"

"No thanks madam. I need to be moving on as I have other errands to do. Where can I tether these for you?"

Marion pointed to the railing that stood at the bottom of the steps. "Tie them to the hitching rail, for now. When Burton gets home he'll find a permanent shelter for them."

All the while he was speaking the rider had dismounted, tied the horses to the railing and mounted again. He touched his broad brim hat, turned the horse and cantered away.

"Our own horses, that's terrific," commented Madeline.

"Mr Lucas-Hughes also said to let you know that there is a saddle in the laundry and traces in the barn. There is also a slide down the back near the wood shed. If you need a hand with these give Barry Hayden a hoy and he'll help."

Barry Hayden was only too pleased to offer advice and recommended Burton buy five Berkshires from him and then top up the rest of the pigsty numbers from Bill Weinert who lived across the river from the jetty.

Burton was pleased when he arrived back home after his visit to Barry Hayden. He had borrowed a horse and slide from Barry and a couple of crates for carrying pigs.

He had loaded the ones he brought from Rockhampton and the five he had bought from Barry Hayden. The horse pulled the pigs up the slope to the Johnson house.

When Burton saw the bay and the draught horse tethered out the front he thought he had visitors but Marion was quick to come out to greet him and tell him the story.

"Blow me down," said Burton, "The man thinks of everything and is a mile ahead of us."

He geed the horse up and took the pigs up to the sty. He manhandled the crates into the enclosure and closed the gate before releasing the pigs. The pigs ran around squealing like they were delighted to be in their new home.

Soon they calmed down intent on foraging around looking for whatever food might be available.

Burton set about organizing the troughs.

He walked back to the house and re-appeared

with two buckets. One was full of skim milk and the other, water.

He poured the contents of both buckets into separate troughs.

Pigs came from everywhere and nearly knocked him over. They snuffled their snouts in and gulped the milk and water down.

Burton jumped the railing and began to rip up the paspalum grass that had been allowed to grow in a tangled mess along the back of the pigsty. He threw handfuls into the sty where the pigs pushed and shoved each other seeking to eat all they could.

Burton then led the Hayden horse and slide back to where the bay and the draught horse stood patiently. He untied both and walked off with all three horses towards the barn.

He tied the horses that had been delivered to the barn railing and fed them chaff and filled up the water trough. They would be alright until milking time in a few hours.

He mounted the Hayden's horse bareback and rode off at a canter. The slide and the crates bounced behind.

Milking went smoothly that night and most of the cows had dried out as had the mud.

The girls showed their efficiency by only taking an hour and forty minutes to have all the cows milked and the cream separated and in the cans.

Burton was impressed and sent them off home. He asked Burt and Ginger to take four pails of skim milk up to the house. They were to give two to Marion for the house and the others were to go to the pigs.

The boys were excited about this errand as they had not seen the new pigs.

Burton went off to find the six heifers and have them moved to the top paddock. They were proving a handful as they roamed far and wide. Once in the top paddock, Burton was going to inspect the entire fence and fix any breaks.

Burton arrived home just after the lamps had all been extinguished except Marion's.

She was waiting up for him and at the same time taking the quietness to feed Max.

Chapter 4

Swimming and rowing, along with the milking routine, filled the lives of the family for the next six weeks.

Burton and Marion saw how imperative it was for everyone, with the exception of Keith and Max, to learn to swim and to row.

The weather in the Daintree in July and August was at its best. Each day turned out to be clear and warm with little breeze. Every so often a sprinkling of rain would dampen the ground and keep the grass green. Generally, there was so much moisture in the soil and the creeks that the valley rarely dried out.

With such glorious weather and a high humidity, the thought of swimming and rowing was always met with enthusiasm by the Johnsons.

The crossing over the Stewart Creek where Marion and the girls had reached and paddled in proved to be ideal for teaching the skills needed to swim and row.

Water over the crossing was only a foot deep. Further upstream it got deeper and for 50 yards was four feet deep.

Further up, there was a pool that was 25 yards by five yards and over six feet deep. This pool was shaped like a mini swimming pool. The water entered by splashing over three boulders that had been pushed down there in one of the more powerful floods of the last century.

Burton moved the flatties to the crossing and moored them there.

When the family went down to practice rowing the flatties were easy to access and the lessons were easier in the shallow water.

After learning to balance while seated, they were soon being tested standing without holding on.

Many a time one of the children would fall out of the boat followed by raucous laughter.

Burton cut off branches about three feet long that had a V in them. These he hammered into the sand about a yard apart. He inserted the oars in these and had each participant sit on the sandy bottom, take the oars in their hands and row.

"Dip and pull, feather the oar, dip and pull," over and over he would recite these words while the children, in turn, pretended to row.

Once they were able to handle the pretend row boat and they were able to balance they were ready to move into the deeper water with a real boat.

In the meantime, Marion was showing her expertise in swimming and teaching the ones who were not rowing at that given time.

Marion had earned her swimming stripes on the Tweed River near both Murwillumbah and Tyalgum.

The ferry that plied up and down would regularly take the teenagers for picnic cruises.

The captain would pull up along the river and the youths would spend hours diving, bombing and swimming.

Marion taught each of her children individually in the deepest pool.

Ginger assisted as he too was a competent swimmer having learned after finding a row boat on the canal back in England. Every time he fell out, and that was often to start with, he had to grab the tow rope out of the boat and swim to shore.

He had already shown everyone his swimming prowess back in Rockhampton when he swam out to the Cirrus in the Fitzroy River dragging the heifer and the doomed piglet.

After six weeks Burton announced that he was satisfied that the family could swim and row with skill and he was confident they would be safe in the water.

In the meanwhile, the children's education was being neglected.

The local headmaster, Mr Sam Craydon paid a visit to the house. He came cantering, on his horse and pulled up at the hitching rail. Marion was there to greet him as the others were all down at the barn, milking.

"Hello there Mrs Johnson, I'm Sam Craydon the headmaster of the Daintree School number 1073."

Marion said, "Welcome Mr Craydon."

"Do you have time to discuss your children's education with me?"

"I'm afraid my husband is busy with the milking and he is the one to speak to," said Marion.

"No, it's you I would love to talk to Mrs Johnson. I'll tether the horse and come on up if you don't mind," said Mr Craydon.

Marion could see that she was trapped and that the visit had been carefully planned. She would now cope explaining why the children had not started school.

Mr Craydon sat down in the chair that was offered to him and came straight to the point of his visit.

"No doubt you and Mr Johnson value your children's education," he began, "Well I'm the man sent out to the Daintree to ensure they get the best education they can. Of course, that can only happen if they attend school regularly, are punctual and willing to study hard. Do you agree Mrs Johnson?"

"Of course I agree Mr Craydon but it has been a busy time for us so we have postponed the start of school for our children by a little bit. We do intend to send them, in the not too distant future," explained Marion.

"Ah, but there lies my dilemma, Mrs Johnson. You see the Queensland Education Department is only able to keep a school open if it has more than 20 pupils. At the moment we have 19 and the prospect of losing another one next week if the Gray family pulls out. So you can see the school may be closed shortly unless I find at least two more children. How many of your little ones are eligible for school, Mrs Johnson?"

"Just Burt, Eva and Isobel at this time, then in three years it will be Keith's turn. Burt is 12, Eva 9 and Isobel 8," replied Marion. "This would be Burt's last year," she added quickly.

"Ah that would be perfect in every way," said Mr Craydon, "Three extras to save the school and three more to be educated to a point of excellence," he wrung his hands and chuckled.

The family arrived from milking and met Mr Craydon, he was invited to dinner and then Burton agreed it was time for his three children to attend school.

Mr Craydon was in a very happy mood when he rode off into the darkness. He would have the way illuminated by the hurricane lamp jiggling on the side of his saddle.

The following Monday Marion rowed the three schoolies and the cream over to the jetty. After lugging the three cans to the Butter Factory and saying hello to Bryan Poole, the manager, they all ran off to school.

The two girls were dressed in their most fashionable clothes. They both wore a white cotton dress with an embroidered bunch of flowers on the top left pocket. A pretty pink ribbon was tied around Eva's waist while Isobel preferred green. Their bonnets were almost identical except Eva had a brim, Isobel's did not. Both girls had on their black, flat shoes.

Burt was in grey shorts and a brown shirt. He was bare foot.

"Welcome, welcome, welcome," beamed Mr Craydon as he greeted each of the new students. He excused Mrs Johnson and shepherded the three children into the classroom.

It was a one room school with desks all facing the front. Each desk accommodated two students and was bolted to the floor.

At the front, there was a stage and teacher's desk facing the class. All the windows on the right and left walls were high up so no student could look at the scenery outside. The room was austere and everything was black or brown. The colourful array of clothing worn by the 21 children was a pleasant change.

Mr Craydon pointed to a vacant desk at the back of the class and said, "Burt sit," then he pointed to another nearer the front and said, Eva, sit," and finally Isobel received her instruction to take a seat at the front of the room.

The Headmaster reached his own desk and sat down facing the class. He entwined the fingers of his left hand with those in his right hand then pushed them forward. There was a cracking sound that made many of the students jump.

"You have been introduced to the new students. At recess, you might make your acquaintance with them yourselves. In the interim let us start the morning lessons."

Burt was not a scholar but he was a willing trier. His final year of school would not be a happy experience except for Sports' Day at the end of the year.

Eva liked the prospect of making new friends and gossiping to them, outside of course, although she did get into trouble for, 'Talking when asked not to'.

Isobel loved school and everything that it represented. She was quick to catch on, read fluently, knew her tables and combinations and stayed out of trouble.

Her end of year report made Marion and Burton immensely proud.

Ginger was waiting for them when the final bell rang. He had been sent to row them back home as Marion was busy with Max and the others had to get the milking started. By the time the four of them got home they had to run to the barn to help.

The extra responsibility of going to school added a new and exhausting dimension to their lives. In future, they would have to row themselves down the Stewart Creek, out into the Daintree River and unload the cream before trudging off to school. The return journey meant more rowing and walking.

Chapter 5

It was a fine, warm evening early November and the entire family and Ginger were sitting on the verandah looking away to the west.

They could see the green pastures sloping down to the barn. Several cows munched happily and a heifer kicked up its hind legs and buck jumped ten yards before settling.

The barn, with its concrete floor, stood a little above the flood plain.

Behind and to both sides the rainforest grew thickly with its entanglement of vines, palms, ferns and an assortment of huge, old trees.

As you went further towards the creeks the scrub was thicker and almost impenetrable.

They could make out the denser and greener route where the Douglas Creek flowed. Further in the distance were the foothills and then loomed the high mountains of the Dagmar Mountain Range. It was a blissful scene and one that they had not tired of in the five months they had been in the Daintree.

Burton was staring at the scene and seemed to be oblivious to the others who were chatting and pointing out various things that were catching their eyes. He, in fact, was thinking about all the clearing he had to do. The entire farm was 140 acres and more than three quarters was rainforest or scrub, as the Queenslanders like to refer to it. This was difficult to clear and involved back breaking-labour.

Burton, Burt and Ginger were making slow inroads into the clearing. With all the other jobs that had to be done on a daily basis it was hardly possible to get more than a couple of hours of chopping completed.

Burt had gone off to school and that left only Saturday and Sunday for him to help.

Ginger put in a lot of time and effort but he, like Burton, had to do the milking, feed the pigs, teach the swimming and join in the rowing.

"Once the summer holidays arrive it would be a bit easier," reflected Burton. "Burt would leave school and have more time for the clearing job."

Barry Hayden had put a dampener on his comment this morning when they were talking. "Don't plan too much over December through to April as it is the wet season, and I mean WET!" He emphasized wet loudly before continuing, "The Daintree has over 100 inches of rain annually and most of it falls in the five months I mentioned. I would guess that we will get six or more flash floods like the one that greeted you all. We will also expect three or four major floods and this time I'm talking water three feet up your barn wall and your family and mine isolated for days on end. You will need to start planning for these. Stock up your larder and ensure you have plenty of dry wood for your fires. I cut mine and put it under the house. You'll need plenty of kerosene for the lamps."

He paused worried that he may have alarmed Burton but seeing him considering each word he ploughed on. "The biggest concern comes with the dairying because you will still need to milk twice a day and get the cream to the Butter Factory. This is where planning is so important. It's imperative to establish a temporary milking barn up on the high slopes. You will also need to keep the cattle there as well. On the lower areas they get bogged or they get swept away. You've already had one experience and you don't need another one."

Burton grunted and gave a wry smile. "No thanks I believe I've learned my lesson there."

Barry Hayden was in full flight with his suggestions and ploughed on, "Mr Lucas-Hughes planned earlier on that the Butter Factory must have cream every day to remain profitable.

His launch, the one that you were in when you brought the heifers and piglets up to the farm, is used in emergencies such as floods. It will be sent out to all the farms to collect their cream. In your case it will beach near your barn and you will have to be ready. They won't wait as it takes a long time and effort to get all the cans to the Butter Factory. It's also quite dangerous as you can imagine.

The force and varying depths of the floods make it hazardous and you have to dip your hat to Charlie Morrish as he is Mr Lucas-Hughes' manager and driver of the launch. It has a 25 horse power motor so it is only a really vicious flood that will stop him making a pick up. You'll get a jingle if Charlie thinks he needs to pick up, happens twice a year on average. These floods can go on for days though."

"Burton, Burton, are you alright?" Marion was shaking and asking all at the same time.

"I'm sorry, love, I was deep in thought and may have dozed with it too."

"No you had your eyes open but there didn't seem to be any response. Penny for your thoughts? You should share them with all of us," said Marion.

So Burton went over his thought but this time reiterated them into spoken words. Everyone listened intently. There were a few gasps as he spoke about the likelihood of huge floods and the launch battling its way upstream to fetch the cream.

"One hundred inches of rain," gasped Isobel. She was astounded at that amount of water falling in one place. She was mentally calculating what 100 inches were in feet. "That's over eight feet so it will drown me many times over," she shocked everyone with the calculation and her foreboding comment.

"That's so, but we will be safe and dry up here. We are over 30 feet above the flood plain so we don't have to worry. What we need to do is put a plan in place and make sure all our emergency needs are covered. Marion, you draw up a shopping list for the larder that will last three months and include a good first aid kit. We will need a couple of four gallon tins of kerosene so I'll order that through the Co-op."

Madeline was eager to join in so she added, "We need to grow more vegetables and start a decent orchard, that way we'll have fresh vegetables and fruit all year round no matter what the weather."

"Good thinking Madeline, you are more than a pretty face," said Ginger and he smiled.

Madeline blushed and went all coy. Eva screwed up her face but stayed silent and Isobel said, "Oh, you say the nicest things Ginger but please share them around."

Ginger felt the hotness rising into his face, which slowly turned the colour of his flaming red hair.

Marion was quick to take the heat out of an awkward situation, "All to bed, plenty to think about and to do on the morrow. Let me know if you need anything in Port Douglas as I will be on the ferry first light."

Chapter 6

Even before the sun peeked over the mountains to the east Marion had gathered up her notes, her purse and two hessian carry bags that she had sewn handles on and walked down to the barn.

Here Burton had saddled Gypsy ready for Marion to ride to the ferry.

She was an expert rider and preferred to ride astride. To accommodate this style she had made herself a pair of culottes which looked like a dress but in fact had a pair of legs that fell free to the ankles as a dress would.

She had arrived in time to buy a return ticket and to seat herself inside the cabin where it was warmer. As the boat pulled away she moved out to the railing to catch the heat in the sunrise. It was quite crisp sailing down the Daintree so early in the morning.

Port Douglas was a small harbour side town. The wharf was barely 50 yards, and could fit two ships in at a time. Once unloaded, any ship that waited had to anchor up stream in the inlet.

The *Daintree* would not travel back until 4 pm that afternoon so Captain Osborne knew he had to anchor and take his lighter to shore. He would do the shopping and visit old friends.

Marion made straight for the Emporium where she knew from past experiences she would find all she needed. The gentleman behind the counter gave her a cheery hello and asked how he could assist.

"I have a list, could you fill it out and have the things delivered to the *Daintree* ferry by 4 pm?" she asked.

The shopkeeper flicked an eye across the list and politely said, "That will be our pleasure Madam. What name shall I place on the crates?"

"Johnson. J-O-H-N-S-O-N," Marion spelled out the name and the man wrote it down in the order book then added *Daintree* 4 pm today.

"I will return at 3 this afternoon to check everything is in order and pay you," said Marion and then she left.

She was rather excited because she was going to use a large part of her time at a seamstress's house learning to use one of those Singer sewing machines. She had been pleasantly surprised to learn the Sally Hayden had purchased one and was able to use it to make all her own clothes and the men's as well.

It all started when Marion had gone with Burton on a casual ride. They were enjoying each other's company for the first time in ages without the children being around. Marion was riding Gypsy and Burton was astride Brutus when Burton suggested calling in on the Hayden's and saying hello.

Sally was delighted to have their company even for a little while. The Daintree proved to be lonely for women without children at home. Barry was always so busy running the farm and she was not keen on the milking part so she stayed home and kept the fire burning.

Barry arrived a few minutes later because he had seen the Johnsons ride up and thought Burton might need advice. The men excused themselves and went off in the direction of Barry's pigsty.

Marion and Sally were alone and both were full of news they were bursting to share with each other.

They swapped stories and rumours for nearly an hour then Sally got up and suggested they have a cup of tea and a slice of chocolate cake.

Marion was shocked and surprised as she repeated Sally's words, "Chocolate cake?"

"Unlike you Marion, I have plenty of time on my hands so I get to bake and I get to sew. Unfortunately, I don't get to talk to other people all that often."

"Let's put a stop to that then," suggested Marion. "Every Wednesday let's meet here and wile the afternoon away chinwagging. It will do us the world of good. I know, if you agree, let's start up our own Daintree Women's Club. Anyone can come as they wish."

"That's a great idea," said Sally rather excited. "We

could swap ideas and show each other how to do things. I love baking and sewing so that can be my contribution. What about you Marion?"

"I like making cards for birthdays and Christmas and embroidery, so that's what I can contribute. By the way did you make your dress?"

"Ah huh, now I'll show you a special secret that no one else knows in the Daintree," said Sally and she folded and unfolded her pointer finger, beckoning Marion to follow. Marion obliged and soon found herself in the main bedroom.

A double bed was the centre piece and wooden wardrobes one for Barry and one for Sally were against the wall. Between the wardrobes was a dresser with four drawers two on each side of a space for leg room. A small chair with a velvet seat was pushed into the space. A large rectangular mirror was at the back of the dresser.

The only other piece of furniture appeared to be a small table with pretty forged wrought iron legs.

Sally walked over to this table and ran her fingers across the top seductively, "This is my most precious possession. It's a Singer sewing machine and I make all our clothes on it. You can buy or make your own patterns, buy material and then cut out the garment and sew it up. Hey presto a new dress."

Dramatically she snatched a dress hanging from a hanger on the side of the nearest wardrobe and swung it towards Marion.

"That is fantastic," said Marion, "How does it function?"

In the twinkle of an eye, Sally set-up the sewing machine, threaded the needle and sat down on the little chair she had taken from the dresser. She picked up a sewing box from the floor behind the machine and removed two pieces of fabric. These she placed one on top of the other and said, "I sew these together just as if we are joining two sections of a pattern."

She held onto a large wheel on the right of the machine and flicked her wrist anti-clockwise at the same time she began to move her feet. There was a whirring sound as the wheel spun and a needle jumped up and down. The thread zig-zagged across the material as it was fed through. Within seconds Sally stopped and pulled the material from the machine. She cut the thread and held up one piece of material. "There we go all done."

Marion was so enthralled that she decided she must learn to use one of these machines as it would save many hours of hand sewing. When Sally showed her the dresses and blouses she had made "in a matter of a few hours" she was smitten.

So today she had her opportunity and as Sally said, "Mrs Jessie Hitchens in Port Douglas is the one to see. She'll get you started and will be happy to sell you a machine. She works out of her own house at 14

Warner Street, not far from the wharf."

The trip back up the Daintree River was particularly satisfying for Marion. Her thoughts were on all the supplies she had ordered and a brand new Singer sewing machine. It had cost £8 but that wasn't expensive when consideration was given to the money she would save in making all her own clothing. She would teach the girls and the boys if they were keen.

They could be the finest dressed family in the Daintree. She could take them all proudly to the dances everyone keeps talking about but they never seem to happen.

Burt and Ginger were waiting at the Daintree Jetty at 6 pm ready to put all the shopping into the flatties and row Marion home.

They had left Brutus in traces tied to the slide and the huge horse tethered to a fallen tree branch back at the Stewart Creek Crossing.

Apart from continuous questions about the new-fangled machine that Marion had bought everything else went smoothly.

Burton took one look at the Singer sewing machine as the two lads manhandled it off the slide, up the steep steps and into the lounge. He smiled and kept silent. Marion was a woman who knew her own mind and if she had an idea it generally was to everyone's advantage.

And so it did. The sewing lessons from Sally were transferred across the green fields to the Johnson family. Everyone wanted a turn; everyone wanted to make the most complicated but beautiful dress, blouse, suit, whatever. There was no hanging back until reality started to bite.

Ginger got the hang of the contraption way before the others. He was naturally gifted and loved the art and craft areas.

Eva came a distant second then all the rest stumbled along behind. It would take a while but within twelve months the family Johnson was the best dressed at the dances and picnics and they all made their own costumes.

Burton stayed away from the frenetic sewing as did Burt, although he did get a rudimentary idea. Keith and Max were too tiny but even they got the hang of sewing as the years past.

Chapter 7

All the talk at school since mid-October was about the bloke who blew up the English parliament. Apparently, he did this on November 5th so that day got called Guy Fawkes Night.

Burt was not sure whether to believe the story or not, Eva was sure she had heard about this in history lessons but Isobel didn't have the foggiest. The biggest mystery of all to the trio was how a day got to be called a night!

It was Captain Osborne's son Jimmy who raised the thought on a cool, but mild, Tuesday when he announced, "Dad said I could build the biggest bonfire and invite you all. I'm going to build a Guy and put him at the top and fry him. There will be penny bombs for fingers and toes and Catherine Wheels for his eyes. Just before he starts to explode I'll send up sky rockets for you all to see. Anyone who comes gets a sparkler to twirl around. Mum is going to make supper for everyone."

There was an excited buzz around the shelter shed where they all sat munching on their lunches. Most of the swaps had already been consumed while the slow coaches were trying to find another mate to swap with. "Who's got a vegemite sandwich for fairy bread or a mango?" asked Sheryl Walwork.

Burt looked across and was miffed as he had just finished his vegemite sandwich and when Sheryl wanted anything he was always interested. She was one of those leggy twelve year olds, blonde with blue eyes that teenage boys would put a coat across a puddle for.

Jimmy was not to be put off. He had serious invitations to serve plus he had put a lot of planning into his bonfire idea and had to use all his cunning to convince his mum and dad to let him do it.

He had exaggerated a little, well a lot, in that he didn't have permission for others to attend and he didn't, as yet have sparklers or the skyrockets, but he was devising a way to get these.

If he could charge the ones attending threepence each it would be a cinch to get all the crackers he needed.

"What are you on about?" asked Eva, "All this talk of fires and explosives sounds dangerous to me."

"Uh, oh," stammered Jimmy, "Looks like we need a lesson in Guy Fawkes Night for the newbies."

"Johnson, our name is Johnson how many times do we have to tell you before you and your mates stop calling us Newby?"

Everyone laughed but Eva didn't get the joke and she was becoming angry with the way the boys treated new students.

"It was 1605 over 300 years ago when a bloke called Guy Fawkes lived and he didn't like the King a bloke called James just like me. How anyone doesn't love a boy named James is beyond me. Anyhow he wanted a different king. Had a lot to do with which church people went to, Church of England or Catholic, not that I care. So to get his way Guy and a few other blokes on his side put a whole stack of gunpowder under the parliament where King James and his people were sitting in government. They were going to blow them all to Kingdom Come."

At this point Jimmy mimicked a mighty explosion and let out a huge 'bannnnng' from his mouth. His captive audience all laughed and slapped each other on the shoulder. Jimmy could sure be dramatic in his story telling.

"Not quite so funny," came the stern voice of Mr Craydon who had approached quietly. "If he had succeeded there would have been many dead and an entire historical building burnt to the ground. As it was, only Guy Fawkes and his followers felt the wrath of King James. He was hanged. Now we celebrate his demise every 5th November by burning an effigy of Guy Fawkes on top of a bonfire.

Of course I believe there are far more important lessons to be learned from what happened. First don't play with explosives as they are extremely dangerous, second if you have a problem then seek out peaceful means to solve it and third don't follow others blindly – be your own man."

With those lessons ringing in their ears the children ran off to enjoy the rest of the lunch break. Jimmy spent his time running from one group to the other cajoling their support for the Bonfire at his place and getting them to part with their threepences.

As they rowed home Burt, Eva and Isobel swapped all the information they had gleaned from their play friends at lunch about this Guy Fawkes Night. By the time they pulled the flattie up onto the beach at the crossing they were determined to get mum and dad to let them go to Jimmy Osborne's for the big show.

It was Eva who broached the subject with her father. Burton listened intently and was rather proud of his third child as her knowledge was very sound.

At last he spoke up, "The day is important to many people across the world and in particular those of English descent. I think we need to talk to mum and find out how she feels."

Marion was aghast and wanted nothing to do with explosives and fires no matter what. "No child of mine needs to be going off in the middle of the night to burn another human being to death."

That was the last anyone spoke of Guy Fawkes that year. On the night of November 5th the entire valley was covered with huge fires burning and the Johnsons could hear the bangs of penny bombs and watched tiny lights in the blackness as sky rockets reached their zenith and exploded. Jimmy and his crowd must have been having a ball.

No doubt it will be well described and rubbed in tomorrow at school.

Burt looked around and winked at Eva and then Isobel and whispered, "Next year."

December 1926 was a mixed month with showers followed by brilliant sunny days, then showers again.

At school the seniors, three 12 year old boys, were preparing for their graduation from primary school.

Burt was one and he was looking forward to working on the farm and having a life free from lessons.

His mates were Greg Walwork and Bobby Giblin and they were looking to a future away in Cairns at High School.

Mr Craydon had decided he would have a little ceremony to mark the graduation.

Each boy was allowed to invite their parents and one other person.

The ceremony was to be at the school and each boy would receive a certificate and a fountain pen. The latter was to allow them to start high school with a special writing implement.

Burt invited Burton and Marion. He had trouble thinking of a third person and even considered not taking anyone else. In the end he chose Isobel as she was the one who loved school.

The ceremony was pleasant and Mr Craydon wished them all the luck in their new ventures. He shook each of their hands and whispered special messages to them. To Burt he quietly said, "You've been a pleasure to teach and your parents can be proud of your behaviour and willingness to try. I'm disappointed that you are not going on. Make the most of your life."

Three days later the whole school took part in the Annual Sports Carnival.

Chapter 8

The sun rose on a beautiful day that had the promise of lots of fun and fierce competition. There had already been challenges in the school yard, individual against individual and family against family. It was all or nothing for most of these competitors. As much as this rivalry cut through everyone there was a camaraderie that would never be broken.

As the sun rose it was apparent that it had a sting to it and the community expected a stinking hot day with 95% humidity.

Everyone had rowed, rode, walked or been brought by bus but whatever the mode of transport they had all arrived at the water hole. This was a special swimming area and it had a good 120 yards of sand to run on.

It was up the Daintree River about one mile passed where the Stewart Creek came out.

Mr Craydon and several helpers, who were fathers of students, had marked a running track of 100 yards along the sand. They had drawn rough lines for lanes and across these were lines for the 50 yards, 75 yards and 100 yards starting lines.

The crowd spread their blankets on the sand and under the bank and a few under the shade of the trees that towered over the river at intervals along the sand bar.

It wasn't a concern where they placed their things as long as they could see what was happening. Most moved to the finish line when they saw their children about to race.

All the students were gathered by Mr Craydon just past the 100 yard starting line and he sat them in year levels. The infants or babies as most referred to them, sat first with girls then the boys. Placing the girls first was part of the important etiquette at the time.

Once all the children were accounted for and they were sitting in their correct year levels and gender lines Mr Craydon rushed off to ensure the officials were in place.

He checked the place judges to see that they had place cards and an HB pencil.

As he moved among them he kept giving little hints as to how to judge. To the four fathers who had agreed to be judges it was like water off a duck's back as they had done the job before.

Mr Craydon rushed back to where the children sat quietly, up straight and with their arms folded. They had been left with clear, stern instructions that anyone who played up on Sports Day they would get the cuts and be tossed out of their races. No one wanted any of that so even Bevan Fischer, who normally would push the boundaries, was on his perfect behaviour.

Under the watchful eye of Mr Craydon the infant class and the year ones walked to the 50 yard line. Lots of encouragement came from the crowd. The littlies always got the most parent attention. As the ages increased the less the parents showed their interest.

The three girls from the infant class were placed in a lane and Mr Craydon raised his right arm.

One of the judges raised his to signal that all was in readiness. Mr Craydon called the girls to the start at the 50 yard line.

"Take your marks," he paused waiting for them to obey. He had spent copious time teaching all the students how to start in a race so he expected nothing to go wrong. "Get ready, go!"

The little legs started pumping and they ran their hearts out down the sand. It was hard going as each step they would sink in.

Maisie Hitch won and was presented with a blue ribbon that Sally Hayden had made on her Singer sewing machine. The second girl was given a red ribbon and third a green.

The competition throughout the morning continued to be fierce.

After the running races, there were three-legged races where everyone had to find a partner and then tie their right leg to their partner's left leg.

Then came egg and spoon races, eggs were courtesy

of the Fischer family who had boiled a dozen that very morning.

Shuttle relays were next with four teams made up of one student from each year level and where there weren't any, a substitute from elsewhere was put in. The baton had to be carried up the lane and passed to the next member of the team and so on until the last runner finished by running over the finish line.

It was lunch by the time the land races were over, although most of the people had been nibbling and drinking all morning.

The break lasted an hour with Mr Craydon moving from one family group to the next warning that he would not let anyone in the water events if they had not stopped eating at least 20 minutes before the swimming races began. To emphasize his determination he rang the school bell as a warning that no student was to eat after that time.

The water races were more fun than competitive.

There were swimming races or more to the point, dog paddle for the younger ones. The older children were very capable and had a natural flair. Living on the Daintree made learning to swim a priority.

Next came rowing races with four flatties lined up on the beach with the oars stuck in the sand ten yards away.

The idea was to start ten yards back, run to gather the oars, run to the flattie carrying the oars, row across the river which was 50 yards at this point and row back again.

Burton shook his head and looked at Marion and said, "This is way too hard for these little tackers. There's no way they can get across the river and back. I can see a drowning come up."

"Hush dear and let's see what happens. These people know what they are doing and I'm quite sure they wouldn't endanger their children's lives," said Marion.

As they watched the four infants lined up at the start line. Then they saw the mother of each walk over to where the oars were sticking out of the ground.

Finally, four fathers stepped up and walked towards the flatties. They each climbed into one of the boats and lay down so they couldn't be seen.

"Go," called Mr Craydon and the little ones raced off at rapid speed. When they reached their mothers they slapped hands, the mothers grabbed the oars and rushed towards the boats. As the mothers reached the boats the fathers popped up and placed the oars in the rowlocks. The mums started pushing the boats further into the river and the fathers started rowing.

Burton was enthralled and pleased with what he had seen. He began cheering loudly and encouraging the fathers to row faster. Back they came with muscles bulging and aching.

"Now you see what I mean, Burton," chastised Marion. "It will be our turn shortly, so don't let Isobel down.

Burton grinned and said, "Never. With a team like we have we can't be beaten."

The Isobel, Marion and Burton team did well until it was time for Burton to turn the flattie back from the far bank. He dropped an oar and started to go in circles. The boat floated into the mangroves and became stuck.

In the end Burton, dived out, swum back to retrieve the tow rope and began the swim back to the other shore. As much as he was embarrassed he was astounded at the amount of encouragement everyone gave him and the huge cheer that went up when he finally reached the shore.

Eva and Burt were old enough and strong enough swimmers to run the flattie race all by themselves.

Eva came third mainly because she couldn't balance the oars when she had to carry them to the flattie. She spent so much time dropping them and picking them up that the other girls were across and back before she even got into her boat.

Mr Craydon ran forward and insisted that she get in the boat and finish the race, "No one has ever quit on me," he said, "And you will not be the first. Now get in and row."

Eva was miffed by her experience but when the cheering greeted her as she finished she raised both arms and the oars as though she had won an Olympic Gold Medal.

Burt won his race convincingly and all the hard slog he had done on the farm and during rowing lessons certainly showed.

Finally, the competition came to a close and Mr Craydon stood up to make the presentations.

He had already lined the school up in their year levels and every student waited in anticipation of being called forward.

Individuals who had won a race received threepence and the overall champion of the year level was given sixpence.

Eva went home empty handed, but Isobel had a nice shiny threepenny piece in her hand and Burt was all over the moon with a sixpence and three threepenny pieces. He felt like he had won a King's ransom.

All in all, it was a fun day.

The families packed up and made ready to go back to their farms.

There were thanks, all round and invitations to visit.

During all of this camaraderie, Captain Osborne pointed to the sky and announced, "I think we need to scatter and fast. I don't like the look of the clouds that are starting to bank up over Mount Alexandria to the east."

"Looks threatening from the north too,' added Phil Porter, "So I'd better run as I have the furthest to row."

"Don't worry Phil I'll give you and the family a tow in the powerboat," offered Captain Osborne.

"Thanks that would be handy, how long do you reckon we've got?"

"At a guess," said Captain Osborne, "Thirty minutes to the rain, and an hour to the thunder and the storm. I would move the cattle to the high ground as you never know what these storms are going to do nor how long they will last."

Chapter 9

❧

Captain Osborne's prediction was true in every word. Burton, Marion and family all got home before the storm burst on the valley. It was as sudden and ferocious as the first one they experienced.

Ginger had not gone to the Sports Day as he was feeling unwell but he had noticed the cloud build up so struggled out of bed and rounded up the cattle. Burton was pleased to see them all in the high paddock. That was one less job he had to do.

"Well done, Ginger you are proving your worth more and more every day," Burton said. "And as for both of you," he began pointing to Burt and Isobel, "Congratulations on winning your races but don't forget to squirrel your winnings away in your Commonwealth Bank tins."

Burton was a great believer in saving so that the future would be brighter.

"The big wet has begun," said Barry Hayden over the telephone. "The last time we had this start was back in 22 and it rained nonstop for ten days and then just when we thought it was drying out it started again. Everything was ringing wet and we couldn't move in

57

the paddocks. If it wasn't water bursting in every direction it was mud up to your waist. I sure hope you took my advice and stored plenty of food."

Burton nodded and replied, "Yes, we should be able to see out a month or more."

The rain hammered down all night and into the next day. It was an unbelievable display as sheets of water made it impossible to see more than ten yards ahead.

The creeks burst their banks and the water spread across the flood plains. They all watched in awe as the pasture slowly disappeared under water.

"Will it ever stop?" asked Isobel on the fourth day.

"It will my dear," said Marion but there was a lack of surety in her voice.

After five days the clouds began to break up and the sun tried desperately to peer onto the sodden ground.

The family had been able to continue the milking in a temporary shelter that Burton and the two oldest boys had erected. They erected posts and placed canvas over the top.

The cows needed no encouragement to enter the makeshift stalls. They, like the human beings, were only too pleased to be out of the rain even for a few minutes. They were also aware that it was the only place they were going to get a decent feed.

A fascinating part of the otherwise boring days was

watching the launch come up the Stewart Creek. The water was so high that Mr Morrish could zoom over the waterlogged pastures and settle the boat right alongside where Burton, Ginger and Burt waited with the cream cans. They all helped to load them aboard. The trio pushed the launch back into the deeper water and Mr Morrish raced off with a flick of the wrist.

Later they would spy him across the other side of the tree line that marked the Douglas, powering back towards the Butter Factory. It was amazing to see him navigating areas that were actually pasture in dry times.

It took another three days for the water to drop back to the creek banks and a few more for the pastures to dry enough to allow the cattle back down from the high paddock.

Just as they started to feel dry and warm the clouds raced overhead and the rain began again. All hands rushed to move the cattle.

All the while the food in the larder was being used and the wood pile under the house diminished.

There had been great expectations as Christmas Day approached. Burt, Eva and Isobel had been coming home from school with all sorts of stories about how the community celebrated the Birth of Christ. According to the other children, Father Christmas would visit all the children on every farm in a lorry. He would have a whole lot of elf helpers who sang Christmas

Carols while Father Christmas handed out lollies and checked what presents each child wished for.

Marion wasn't pleased with this when she heard all the talk. Her traditional Christmas, since she was a child back in Bray's Creek, was centred on the birth of baby Jesus. A special manger was arranged in the makeshift church on the Stewart farm and everyone came to pray and give thanks to the good Lord for giving Jesus to all to save them from their sins.

Marion intended to maintain that tradition and to date had managed just that. She did not want the commercial side to interfere with the religious side.

She had been thinking desperately what to do to shield her children from the imaginary nonsense of Father Christmas when the Heavens had opened. True to her beliefs she thought God had solved her problem.

Marion created a lovely manager and made a display showing the Nativity.

On Christmas Eve, and again on Christmas Day, the family came together to pray and give thanks. Afterwards, they gave each other simple handmade cards that said, 'Happy Christ's Birthday to you'.

During all of the desperate times to make things function on the wet, sodden farm, there was another memorable time that brought laughter and gaiety to the family that faced an otherwise depressed state.

Keith turned three on the 30th December. Marion

spent considerable time in the kitchen with Madeline, Eva and Isobel preparing goodies.

They were hoping that the day would allow a picnic style birthday outside but that didn't eventuate.

Keith was greeted in the morning with everyone crowding around his bed and singing Happy Birthday. The milking had been finished so the day was going to be fun and frolic.

At lunch time the table was piled high with fairy bread, scones, patty cakes decorated with an assortment of icing colours, sandwiches, almonds, a bowl of boiled lollies, and four large bottles of lemonade.

At each person's place, there was a paper hat to wear that had written on the front Happy Birthday, Keith.

As they all settled into their places Marion emerged from the bedroom carrying a chocolate cake The cake was smothered in whipped cream and on top were three lit candles with flames spluttering.

Everyone stood up and boisterously say Happy Birthday for the second time that day. The cake was placed in front of Keith and Marion said, "Blow out the candles Keith and don't forget to make a wish."

Keith was so excited by all the attention and the scrumptious cake that he couldn't get his lips to blow out the candles. Everyone laughed and Marion helped out with one swift blow.

"Happy Birthday, son," she said.

It was the nicest thing that could have happened at

that time for the family as it lifted their spirits.

In the afternoon they played games with each other including Tic Tac Toe, Blind Man's Bluff, Hide and Seek, Poison Parcel, Old Maid (cards), Oranges and Lemons, London Bridge. They even went onto the verandah to chant rhymes while they skipped over a rope. The rhyme they all loved was All in Together and they sang lustily as each member ran in and began to skip. Ginger and Burt were on the end of the rope as they were the strongest, but worst skippers.

"All in together
This fine weather
When it is your birthday
Please jump in
January, February, March, April, May, June, July, August, September, October, November and December."

There was so much fun that they were all disappointed that it had to end when Burton said, "Milking time, I'm afraid."

Dutifully they all grabbed their wet weather gear and trudged off for the temporary milking stalls.

New Year's Day came and went without a whimper from any of the family. There had been talk of a New

Year's Eve Dance but this was cancelled due to the inclement weather.

The arrival of 1927 was a quiet and sombre affair.

January came and went as did February.

There were small breaks that allowed Marion to take the girls into Port Douglas to top up their supplies. Burton put Burt and Ginger on wood chopping duty and they made such a competition of this that the pile overflowed.

The sewing machine was getting a fair amount of use and all the girls had a least one new dress, beautifully sewn and fitting snuggly. Bonnets were added in the same material and at one stage they paraded just like a beauty contest, pirouettes and all to show the audience all parts of the dresses.

The pigs and piglets loved the wet weather and dived into every muddy patch they could find. They grew fatter by the day as there was plenty of skim milk for them to suck up.

Burton was desperate to find a boar to service the five Berkshires he had bought from Barry Hayden. He needed to get across the river and look at Mr Weinert's pigs.

After one trip down the Daintree River to Port Douglas, Marion and the girls arrived home with an assortment of tropical fruits. There were pineapples, paw paws, mangoes, passionfruit and star fruit. Along with these delicious edibles was also a hessian bag full of vegetables.

Burton was concerned about the cost of all these items and was about to say so when Eva made an interesting suggestion. "Why don't we grow our own fruit like we have with the vegetable patch? At school the other day Gavin Ingham had mangoes and watermelon mixed in a glass jar. I asked him where he got the fruit and he said his parents grow them. I asked him what else and he told me all the things we've bought here plus bananas and rockmelon."

"You know that is clever thinking Eva. It shouldn't be too difficult to plough out an orchard near the house and plant our own fruit trees. The only problem, as I see it, would be to know where we find the seeds or seedlings. I'll have to talk to Barry he might know or maybe we can make inquiries in Port Douglas on our next trip."

There was a general buzz of excitement in the family as they all started to imagine having their own orchard.

Isobel's imagination took her high into a mango tree, hidden from view, eating the delicious yellow flesh that oozed all over her lips and dribbled down her chin to splash on her white cotton dress. She could hear the others calling for her but she was so well hidden that she could stay there all day and never have to do any chores.

Bliss.

Then she caught a movement to her right and thought there was a 20-foot amethystine python sliding ever so quietly towards her. It opened its massive jaws and …

"Isobel, are you alright?" asked Marion, "You look like you've seen a ghost."

"I'm sorry mum just daydreaming, I'm fine."

Chapter 10

Burt was daydreaming too. He was up the highest branch of the fig tree pigging out as he loved fresh squashy figs. He was picking them, peeling back the brownish skin and in one gulp downing each one.

Below he could see the tiny honeyeaters flittering near the wooden crate he had set up. The box was held off the ground at one end by a stick which had a string attached to it. The end of the string was tied around Burt's left wrist. He had mashed up over-ripe figs and oats and laid this sticky mess towards the back of the trap. All he needed now was for one or more of the honey eaters to dash under the box for a suck on the juices. At that point he would tug the string and 'hey presto' he had a bird.

He would then make a cage and teach it tricks. Of course, it had to be a secret because mum and dad would be livered if they knew any of the children were trapping or hurting the wildlife. That is everything except those pesky wild pigs.

"Burt, Burt," repeated Burton, "I need you and Ginger to come with me and we'll plan out this orchard. I think it's got potential and will save us a lot of money. There must be a nursery in the valley growing these fruits or else how did the Inghams establish theirs?"

Burt's dream came to a premature end and he followed his father and Ginger out the door.

It was agreed that the area on the other side of the pigsty would be ideal for the orchard. They stepped out the positions for each fruit and then marked where to run the fence so that the orchard would be protected from the wild pigs and any other wildlife that might want to damage the seedlings.

All the other children followed the trio out to the field beyond the pigsty.

They were all keenly interested in the stepping out and the pointing by Burton, Burt and Ginger.

Soon they would see an orchard growing in this area and they would have ample supplies of fruit.

Ginger was nominated to do the ploughing of the area so that the new trees and vines would not be in competition with the grasses.

Burt was given the job of digging a large hole at each position they were going to grow a fruit and to add plenty of cow manure before backfilling with six inches of soil. The remaining space would be deep enough for the new plant. Once the roots reached the rotting cow manure the tree or vine would get a real boost of nutrients.

Burton walked back to the house and telephoned Barry Hayden.

He was soon dialing the Ingham number and spoke briefly to Gavin Ingham.

He put the receiver back in its cradle and turned to Marion who was the only one left in the house. "Well that was fruitful," he chuckled, "If you'll excuse the pun. Gavin has got an orchard and tells me he got all his seedlings from Phil Porter who lives over to the north. Apparently, he started his own nursery when he had other farmers asking how to start up their own orchards. Anyway he grows the seedlings in half cut out kerosene tins and you can buy these from him or order them and he'll deliver through the ferry."

Within a fortnight the Johnson orchard was a reality. Not only did Gavin Ingham supply the seedlings but made a special trip along the river to give advice.

The total cost was over eight pounds but Burton could see that the future savings and added healthiness to his family the orchard would repay a hundred fold.

The climate, soils and an abundance of water saw the tropical fruits grow vigorously and it was not too long before they would savour the fruits of their labour.

March turned out to be better than expected. Barry Hayden had warned them that March could spring a few nasty surprises.

For March 1927 apart from drenchings that were short and sharp all else flittered by.

One scary incident shook up four year old Keith. He was always out looking for new adventures and wandering here and there.

It was an overcast day when he was sitting on top of the wood pile and he saw a strange man standing stock still not more than five yards away. He was tall, dark skinned and his long greying hair was unkempt. Around his head he had a dirty, mud splattered bandana. He was almost naked except for what to Keith looked like a nappy made out of an animal's skin. In his hand he held a long spear that had lots of sharp looking barbs at the top. His right leg was bent and the sole rested on the knee of his left. He had white and yellow paint on his face and his chest.

Keith was so shocked that he couldn't move. He was perplexed as to whether this person was going to harm him or ask a question. Slowly it dawned on Keith that this was one of those aborigines that mum and dad talked about. They said they were harmless but why would this one have a long, sharp spear and be looking at him in such a fierce way?

Keith bolted.

He scrambled across the wood heap, scratching and scrapping his little body on the cut logs. Splinters jabbed at him and cuts opened up. By the time he hit the ground redness was welling out of the cuts and tears.

Keith's little legs pumped hard as he ran.

He was half way to the house when he found his

voice, "Dad, help, help!" he screamed. He didn't slow but barged up the steps and through the back door.

"Whatever is the matter," called Marion as she dropped the kettle she was filling and ran towards the screams.

Burton came running from the front of the house and continued up the steps to the back door following Keith's anguished cries.

Keith ran smack into his mother, nearly knocking her to the ground. He was out of breath and his heart was pounding. Marion could get nothing from him in the state he was in so she sat him down.

Burton charged in and grabbed Keith from his sitting position, "What's happened son?" he asked anxiously.

The boy was still unable to communicate so Burton began searching for signs of snake bite and deep lacerations. He found nothing except a lot of blood on the arms and legs.

After a time Keith started to settle and they began to extract what had happened.

Eventually, Burton began to laugh and Marion soon joined in. "It seems our boy has met King Billy and didn't like the experience," said Burton.

He hugged Keith to him and began to walk out of the house.

At first Keith was relieved to be in the comforting arms of his father, but when he saw that they were headed for the wood heap he began to panic.

He fought, kicked, hit and eventually bit Burton in a desperate effort to escape.

Burton decided that fighting an out of control four year old wasn't worth it so he dropped the boy. Keith made good his escape and it would be hours before he crept home asking for his supper.

Burton looked across the wood pile and sure enough, there was King Billy all painted in his tribal ochre colours.

Burton had never had the privilege of meeting him but had heard enough from the other farmers.

Every once in a while King Billy would take his tribe on a walkabout. They would come from up the Stewart Creek and walk through the farmlands and disappear into their sacred lands high in the mountains.

A few weeks later they would return.

Burton had decided that if King Billy was moving through his land he would be civil and treat the man with the respect he deserved.

Things had not started too well and he hoped that the tribal leader would not be offended by his son's wild overreaction.

Chapter 11

As Burton approached the still figure he tried to greet him in pigeon English, "How you do, me ok Burton," he said pointing to himself.

King Billy smiled and held out the hand that was free and replied in perfect English, "Hello Mr Johnson, I'm King Billy." He took Burton's hand and shook it firmly and vigorously. "I know about you and your lovely family. Welcome to the Daintree. I am sorry I scared your little one, maybe one day I can make it up to him."

"He'll be alright, don't worry about him. What can I do for you?"

"As you may know I'm the leader of my tribe and I must look out for them. We are from the ancient clan of the Kuku Yalanji people. My tribe is camping on the sandbar below your farm," at this he pointed to the crossing on the Stewart Creek and Burton could see smoke from fires lazily drifting into the still air. "We are on our way to sacred sites up on the far mountain range and to have a corroboree with other tribes from surrounding areas. I need to replenish our stores so that we can make the journey safely. To do this we have visited farms along the way and offered to do odd jobs for the owners. They, in turn, get us to help out and then pay in goods like flour and sugar. We hope you are a kind man who can help us as others before you have assisted."

Burton was taking all this in and was only too pleased to offer what he could to this original Australian.

He was eager to get answers to questions that kept springing to mind but, before he could articulate his thoughts, King Billy said, "Let me try to answer the queries you have about me. I speak English because as a very young boy my family was taken to the mission that is down river.

"Here we were looked after and gained a white man's education.

"At the age of 13, I was taken by the elders of my tribe to be initiated as a man. This was done in the sacred grounds that we are travelling to. The rites are only for male tribal warriors and are secret to them alone. I can see that you are interested in the scars on my chest and back and the ochre on my body. These are all part of the rites and I carry these as they are related to my tribe and my tribal name. Does that help you know me, Mr Johnson?"

Burton was ashamed that he didn't take the tall aborigine for who he was and show the respect one who was head of a tribe deserved.

"No more questions, you and your people are most welcome. I will give you whatever you need for your walkabout. Please tell me and I will seek these out in our larder and you can be off."

King Billy waggled his index finger towards Burton and said, "Thank you kindly, Mr Johnson, but we must never take something for nothing."

At that Burton again felt a tingling at the back of his neck and the hairs began to rise there.

Something for nothing seemed to him what the white man had been doing to these ancient people ever since Captain Phillips sailed through Sydney Heads.

"We must work for the things that you offer to us and it will be to the worth of the job done."

Burton thought for a while and then recalled Barry Hayden mentioning King Billy and chopping wood. "Well," said Burton, "I do have this pile of wood that needs cutting. No wood, no fire, no tucker."

"Done," said King Billy eagerly. "I will chop until the sun goes behind the horizon and you can see the heap I have made and offer what you believe is a fair price.

Burton returned just as the sun set with a number of bags partly full of goods from the larder.

"You have done well, King Billy, and I will pay you with the following things. Here is a bag of flour, half a bag of sugar, packet of tea, plug of tobacco. Is that enough to cover all you have done?"

King Billy was delighted with the bargain he had struck. So taking the empty sugar bag that had been neatly folded around his waist, like a belt, he packed all the goods, slung it over his shoulder.

"Thank you see you in a few weeks

Next morning there was no sign of the tribe. They had awakened early and continued their journey towards the mountains and their sacred sites.

Keith had a nightmare, being revisited by King Billy and then out of the forest rushed the whole tribe brandishing spears and boomerangs all screaming "Kill the naughty boy who ran from our chief." He awoke to his own yelling with perspiration pouring down his face.

Burton had to spend the rest of the night with him assuring him that all was well and that the aboriginal people were kind and friendly.

April saw the scrub bashing start in earnest by Burton, Burt and Ginger.

The youngsters had honed their cutting skills on the wood pile and reduced it to half its massive size.

They would each select a log of similar size and stand on it, legs astride and balanced. At the command of go called by one or the other they would begin their wood chopping competition.

Burton had spent time with each of them during the wet season explaining and showing them the easiest and most efficient way to use an axe.

The most important lesson was to do with the axe.

"Any fool can swing an axe but only a genius can

make it sing," he would say. "It has to be sharpened so that you can shave yourself with it. A blunt axe and you will expend too much energy going nowhere. As soon as you feel the blade needs sharpening stop and check it. You'll save a lot of time and energy. By the way don't spend too much time on testing it out shaving or that too will waste a lot of time," he joked.

He taught them to heft the axe to check weight and balance.

A heavy axe easily got away from a tiring chopper and that's when accidents happened.

Too light and you spent all day chipping away. Just right and the blade could be made to bite out chunks of wood on a rhythm of top; one, two three, under; one, two, three. He would demonstrate this by standing on a log and swing the blade calling, "Top." The blade hit the log at a 45-degree angle, "One." The head would bite in nearly three inches and he pulled it out and swung at the exact spot again, "Two." Again the axe bit in following the first cut and adding another three inches. He'd pull the axe out and swing calling, "Three." The blade followed the same line and cut a further inch. He then changed the angle of his swing, coming up into the area he was cutting. This time the blade attacked the wood eight inches below the other cuts. "Under, one, two, three." On each blow a large chunk of wood would fly from the log and spin through the air landing softly several yards away.

Burton would then stop and roll the log over and go through the same rhythmic sequence. Most times the log fell apart on the final blow.

"When you are chopping a bigger tree you will soon realize it takes more blows than that and you have to judge how far apart you need your first lot of cuts. You should get to half way through the trunk before you go around to the other side. Don't forget what I've been telling you about checking which way the tree will fall. Always finish on the side away from the fall line."

Both boys would listen intently to all the advice. They had however, a lot of trouble copying Burton who had years more experience than they did.

Now they were ready for the real job.

It was after breakfast and the sun was peeking above the horizon when they reached the first bit of scrub or rain forest just beyond the barn.

Burton explained to the youths that they would hit the smaller timber first day, then heavier trees the following day. They would follow this sequence so that they wouldn't get too tired just whacking into the huge, tough old trees.

Burton placed Burt to his left about fifteen yards away and Ginger to his right the same distance. This way he could watch each and advise them as they went along.

The smaller palms, vines and undergrowth looked

easy enough but the major problem was getting enough room to swing the axe.

As they went along each found their own strategies to cope.

Madeline and Eva arrived at eleven o'clock with sandwiches and scones backed up by a hot billy of tea and a bottle of milk.

All five sat down to replenish themselves and to discuss their progress.

The girls were soon on their way home and the men began clearing the scrub, splinters of wood flying in all directions.

At lunch time they took a complete break and went back home where Marion had ham and salad for them and a thick slice of bread spread with butter. A cup of tea washed everything down.

"Thanks love," said Burton as the three timber cutters went off to the next session of scrub bashing.

At four o'clock Burton called a halt because it was milking time. He stood at the barn and looked back at where the three of them had been slaving for over eight hours. He could hardly make out any change.

Tree cutting was entirely different to tackling the small vegetation. In fact it was extremely tiring from all angles.

The boles of the trees were enormous with many

over four feet in diameter. One ancient stringy bark proved to be impossible for all three to join out-stretched arms all the way around.

The wood of the iron bark was so solid that axes had to be sharpened every hour. Removing the roots was another matter altogether. Digging, burning and having Brutus pulling often budged them but some took months to be entirely removed.

One of the fascinations of this clearing was coming across the most exquisite orchids that grew both at ground level and high in the trees.

Many of the ancient trees had bright flowering orchids clinging to the branches. One of the prettiest was the Dove orchid which when in bloom was supposed to be a rain predictor.

Slowly the bottom paddock became denuded of rainforest and Burton then gave Ginger instructions to plough it and spread the ash far and wide.

Brutus was a good plough horse and Ginger had learned the trade well back in England. It wasn't long before the newly planted paspalum grass began to put down deeper roots and soon covered the entire paddock.

"Well that's one field and many months gone, let's start the next," said Burton.

During the bush cutting, Easter came along.

Chapter 12

Easter was a time when Marion came to the fore.

Although she no longer had a church that she could take everyone to worship in she had maintained her stance that religion was important. So on the important Christian calendar days she insisted on their recognition. Good Friday was celebrated with fish only and the reading from the bible about the trial and death of Jesus. On Easter Sunday she read the rest of the story of how Jesus rose from the dead and ascended into Heaven.

There were no Easter eggs, chocolates, neither Easter Egg Hunts nor Easter Bunnies. These were not seen to be relevant to the solemnity of the occasion.

King Billy returned a few days into May and again left his tribe on the sandbar and visited the Johnson family.

He laughed raucously when Burton related the dream that poor Keith had had the night after he saw King Billy.

There was a patching up when King Billy managed to coax Keith from his hiding place to take the block of Cadburys chocolate that he proffered.

Keith was soon all smiles and listening to the stories

that the aboriginal chief was relating to the family.

King Billy left with a farewell and disappeared back to his people.

The weather had been unusually dry across May and into June with only 28 points falling. The grass was green and luxurious because the soil held the moisture exceptionally well and the hillsides seeped water all year round.

There was quite a display from the butterflies that swarmed across the valley at that time of the year.

The beautiful blue of the Ulysses fascinated the children and the brilliant red of the Redwing took their breaths away.

They spent many hours chasing and trying to catch these giant butterflies. Burton scolded them and insisted they leave 'God's gifts to planet Earth alone or else.' When Burton said, 'Or else,' everyone sat up, took note and did exactly as they were told.

He was a severe disciplinarian but a fair one.

Frogs began their croaking in all parts of the farm.

Once nightfall arrived they began their chorusing. Calling each other and calling for a mate. It sounded like the entire world was alive with the croak, croak booming across the land.

Night was a difficult time to sleep but exhaustion helped the cause.

Max celebrated his first birthday on June 4th, 1927. He was no longer the bubble blowing baby with the shock of wavy black hair. He was now toddling and into all sorts of mischief. He was talking with "mumma" and "dada" being called constantly.

Marion was relieved to find that Eva had taken him under her wing. Everywhere she went she either carried him or encouraged him to follow walking.

Marion made a vanilla cake that had lemon icing. It had one candle and Max needed help blowing this out.

They all sang Happy Birthday before Eva helped extinguish the flame then everyone took their slice of cake and commented on the tangy taste of the lemon icing.

While all the simple things of life went on so did the hard yakka, as Burton called it.

The three timber cutters kept up a steady pace removing the trees and undergrowth in the Lower paddock. Day after day they toiled come rain, hail or sunshine. The only things that put a temporary stop to proceedings were emergencies and floods. Luckily neither occurred so the back breaking grind went on unabated.

One day they tackled the lower canopy trees and vines then the next the huge trees that had stood like sentinels for hundreds of years. Nothing was allowed to stand in the way of progress. Land had to be cleared for dairying.

Once the trees crashed to the ground there was a flurry of effort to clean off the branches and pile all these over the stump with vines and vegetation. Once this dried out it would be fired and burnt to ash.

Another birthday was celebrated on 17th July when Burt turned into a teenager.

He had a chocolate cake with 13 candles and creamy white icing. The rendition of Happy Birthday was followed by a hurricane strength blow that extinguished all the flames instantly. Everyone loved the fluffy, white, sweet icing and the contrasting taste of the chocolate.

The valley came alive as different butterflies hatched from their chrysalises and flew off into the sky. The most striking was the Union Jack with their yellow and white bodies and black wings fringed with red.

Strangler figs were loaded with fruit and these attracted the fig birds with their striking yellow breasts, olive wings, bright orange eyes and black pupils.

Burton was standing near a fig tree that was full of chirping fig birds and he said absent minded, "Ah, it's great to be alive."

More birthdays followed the previous as everyone's was recognized by the family.

This time it was Eva's eleventh on the 4[th,] August.

She was blossoming into a lovely lady with a ready smile.

Her mothering instincts were being honed looking after baby Max.

Her birthday cake preference was a 1-2-3-4 cake smothered with the creamy icing. She requested that the icing be flavoured with passionfruit.

Marion had a tough time finding passionfruit essence but luckily Mrs Ingham had preserved a jar full last year and this was conveyed to the Lodging House where Marion was able to pick it up from.

Chapter 13

October 1927 was proving to be cool but glorious.

The mornings were crisp and heavy dew covered the grass. There were little funnels everywhere where spiders made their funnel-shaped webs that collected all the water droplets.

As the day warmed the grass would dry out and maintain the rich green that it always had.

During the day they began to see the giant Cairns Birdwing Butterfly. This beautiful creature was the largest of Australia's butterflies. It fluttered its black and green striped wings in little jumping motion as it flew. Its bright orange abdomen made it easy for the children to see it in the denser forested areas.

Sitting on the verandah at night Burton would stretch out, put his hands behind his head and remark, "This is the place to be, it is so peaceful and so beautiful."

He would point at the sky where a million stars twinkled, "Where else would you see such a bright display of stars?"

One evening the subject of astronomy arose so Ginger suggested they all go down the steps and lie on the warm grass and look up at the sky.

Off they all trooped and spent a dazzling hour trying to name the different stars and constellations.

"See that's the Milky Way and the cloudy parts are actually millions of suns," pointed out Ginger.

"Look I can see the Southern Cross, over there low to the horizon. See the pointers, and the main stars make a cross shape," said Isobel.

Not to be outdone Madeline found the Big Dipper, "There it is just like an upside down pot, handle and all."

They wiled away the evening, and at the same time added to everyone's astronomical knowledge and interest.

One day Burton went into the Daintree Village riding Gypsy to see Ted Hitch the manager of the saw mill. He had a bright idea and needed to see if Ted could supply him with timber. He hitched Gypsy to the railing outside the mill and wandered in.

He could see Ted struggling to place a large log into the circular saw and heard the high-pitched sound as the blades bit into the wood. He gave a wave and beckoned to Ted.

After seeing the piece of timber fall away from the log he gestured to his assistant to use the cant hook to flip the log 90-degree. Leaving him to accomplish this task he walked over to talk to his visitor, "Hello there Burton, how's that farm coming?"

"Exceptionally well Ted," Burton replied. "I need help with a project I have in mind. Do you have about eight pieces of timber 6 by 1 and about ten feet long?"

Ted Hitch took off his khaki hat and scratched his thinning brown hair, "Well I do but it depends on what you are going to do with it. You see I'd hate to see these boards I've got used on a fence or a pig sty. I cut them from one of the last red cedars in the valley and so I would dearly love to see them on a piece of furniture. The grain of a red cedar is special and I've always admired those trees. The timber cutters of last century sort them out and cleaned the lot out of the valley. They used to call them the Red Gold Tree that's how much they were worth to the English boat builders."

Burton winked and leaned forward to whisper into Ted's ear.

After a while Ted Hitch straightened up and put out his hand. "It's a deal," he said as the men shook hands.

The next day Burton announced that he had to go back to the Daintree Village and make a collection. He was going to need Ginger and Burt because they would have to row the flatties across to the jetty.

While the boys launched the boats and set off in competition to see who would reach the jetty first, Burton rode the bay, Gypsy, into town.

Ted Hitch greeted Burton at the entry to the saw mill and touched his nose. Burton returned the gesture as one conspirator to another. It was their big secret.

Ted pointed to the eight pieces of timber leaning against the wall. Burton selected the first four and hoisted these onto his broad shoulders.

He strode off for the jetty, reaching it just as he spied the two boys come flying out of the Stewart Creek and into the Daintree River proper.

He chuckled to himself as he noted that the youngsters were flat out trying to beat each other and the fact that for the first time ever Burt was in the lead.

Burton turned away to go and fetch the other four pieces of timber.

Burt and Ginger arrived almost together and there was much squabbling over who had won.

Burton put paid to the argument by saying, "Hold up the race is only half way through. You have to get your four pieces of timber back to the barn. First one there will be the winner. Meet you both in an hour."

With this challenge, Burton turned and strode away. He would be home before the boys even reached the junction of the Stewart Creek.

Before leaving the Village he approached Ted Hitch again with a question. "Ted," he began, "You cut a lot of timber but where do the logs come from?"

"Off the local farms mainly. When a farmer is clearing they float their big logs in here and I do a deal with them. Usually, we come to a deal based on 50/50. I cut up the timber into planks for the farmer to use as fence posts or planks for a barn or pigsty. They take half of it. I keep the other 50% and cut it the way I think I can sell it to a buyer. If it is a lot of timber I will on sell it for them for 60%. Either way you can make a handy amount of money from timber."

"You see we have been clearing the bottom paddock down the Douglas Creek and there are ten massive tree trunks sitting there. If I get them to you, can you use them?" asked Burton.

"I most assuredly can and will Burton. It is easier to deal with if you can cut them to 12 feet as this is the longest cut my saw can take. You get them here we will winch them up from the river and cut them," said Ted.

Eight planks of a cherry red wood stood leaning up against the barn wall, with Burt breathlessly asking, "What are you going to do with these?"

"Make a surprise for the whole family," said Burton. "It will be my Christmas present to you all."

Burt knew his father was clever with his hands and could turn anything into something valuable but he had his doubts about eight planks of wood.

At the side of the barn the previous owners had built a comfortable and quite a large lean-to. Here they had established a Blacksmith workshop. It had a kiln with bellows, a rough table, an anvil and numerous tools stuck on nails hammered into the wall of the barn.

Burton often used this space to fashion an idea into reality.

Now he placed the eight pieces of timber side by side on the rickety table and sized them up.

He needed the finest grain to be facing up so he lifted each plank and turned it over and over. Finally, he took his carpenter's pencil and wrote a B on the side he liked. He did this with each piece of wood.

From the wall, he selected a wood plane and checked the sharpness of the blade. It was clear it was brand new and never been used so this was mighty helpful. He selected the first plank and began long strokes with the plane, moving along the grain, watching the fine shavings accumulate under the table.

The call of, "Milking time," by Burt broke his concentration.

He stopped planing the fifth plank and threw four hessian bags over the timber to keep his secret from prying eyes.

The boys had been sworn to secrecy so they wouldn't tell what he was up to.

Chapter 14

While the family was eating dinner that evening Burton told them of his conversation with Ted Hitch regarding the logs in the bottom paddock. "Ted says he will take them if we can deliver them on the water at lengths of twelve feet. That will mean lots of cross-cut sawing and clever ability to float the logs on the creek. The bargain he is offering is too good to let go. However, it will take a lot of time and effort so who says yes?"

There was no one who held back and they all chorused, "Yes," even little Max who was starting to talk and toddle.

So began the massive task of cutting the huge logs into twelve feet lengths and then getting them to the Stewart Creek.

Burton, Burt, Ginger and Madeline all joined into use the crosscut saw. One pulled the other pushed the saw so the teeth cut into the timber. Then they reversed roles as the saw went back the other way.

Unfortunately, they didn't have a saw pit to get the saw all the way through to the other side of the log. Burton devised another method. It was slower but worked.

At the half way point they would stop sawing and three wedges made of wood were hammered into the saw cut. These would keep the saw mark open while the other side was dealt with. If it wasn't for these wedges the hole would close up and jam the saw. It would then be impossible to use the saw and so it would take hours to cut it out. This would also ruin the section of timber.

The work progressed slowly without any mishaps.

In the meantime, they were all trying to devise a plan so they could float the logs downstream. Brutus, the giant Clydesdale, would be used to slide each log to the creek's edge then…

It was Eva who thought of a way.

She suggested hammering an iron peg into the log near the front and tying a rope from this to the flattie. Up to four logs could be tied to each other thus having a long snake-like object floating behind the flattie.

Burton went to the smithy workshop and came up with four large nails with holes at the top like a darning needle.

On the first day they tried the floating snake trick all went well until Ginger got the flattie to the Daintree River. They had forgotten to include the tide in their calculations.

As Ginger manoeuvred the boat out of the Stewart Creek the incoming tide pushed the logs sideways and away they all went.

There were logs tangled in every mangrove over a 25 yard distance.

Burton had trailed along the bank on Gypsy and although he was ten yards back from the water's edge he could hear Ginger's plaintiff cries as he struggled to retrieve the logs.

Burton tethered the horse and hacked his way to the water.

He then swam out until he could see Ginger 50 yards ahead. He was doing a marvellous job getting the logs out of the mangroves but it was clear he was losing strength.

Burton swam to the last log in the line and man-handled it back away from the tangle of roots at the water's edge. He sat astride this log and grabbed the rope that tied it to the third log. With a mighty heave, he had that one back on track.

Ginger saw with relief that Burton had not only arrived but had cleared the last two logs.

Ginger sat and grabbed the oars he had dropped in the bottom of the boat. He pulled hard aiming to go upstream.

At first, Burton was confused thinking Ginger had lost his bearings but then discovered he was using the incoming tide to float the logs into the middle of the river. The logs followed one behind the other with Burton sitting pretty on the last log kicking his legs and shouting words of encouragement.

Ginger changed course once all the logs were clear of the mangroves and did a half circle before lining up with the jetty that was 400 yards away. Burton saw his chance to catch the boat so he slid into the water and swam.

Ginger slackened off and waited to haul Burton into the boat. Once on board they took an oar each and made good time to the jetty.

Ted Hitch had been alerted by the cries of others who had seen the strange goings on at the mouth of the Stewart Creek.

He soon realized it was Burton trying to float his first consignment of logs to the saw mill.

He went back to organize getting the logs up from the river.

Burton and Ginger returned to the farm mighty pleased with their day's labour and the reward that Ted Hitch had given them.

"Timber is rather profitable," said Burton to Marion as they trooped through into the kitchen. "This little lot will boost the bank account in Port Douglas," and he proffered a wad of one pound notes towards Marion.

"Have you paid the boys for their toil?" asked Marion.

"Here Burt and you too Ginger, this is your bonus for today's work. Make sure you add plenty of it to your Commonwealth Bank accounts too. Remember that saving for the future or that rainy day, that will assuredly come along is important."

With that advice still in the air, Burton stripped off two-pound notes and gave one to each. The grins told that they were receiving far more than they had expected. They thumped each other on their backs and Burt said, "When's the next flotilla going down the creek?"

Chapter 15

Every now and again Burton would find a half an hour where he would disappear to the blacksmith lean-to and busy himself with making the table top. He had managed to acquire pig hooves from Bill Weinert at the abattoirs and he had boiled these in water for hours on end. The resulting glutinous liquid was animal glue and it had extraordinary strength. Once he had all the planks smoothed to the correct thickness he smeared the animal glue along the edges and tied them in pairs. He used eight gauge wire and twitched this pulling the planks tightly together. At the end of the time, he had four pairs joined.

The next time he went working on the table top he joined two pairs together thus resulting in two lots of four planks glued and clamped using the wire. Finally, he glued them together and sat back with a large sigh of relief and satisfaction.

Now he devised a way to round off each end. He marked the centre of the end and drew a line. He measured the width of the table top and halved this to discover that this was 24 inches. He marked down each side at 24 inches and joined the dots. Where the line intersected the centre line was going to be the centre of a semicircle. He hammered a nail at this point and using a piece of string and a pencil he was able to draw the half circle.

Burton repeated the same at the other end and then using a crossbow saw began to cut pieces off as close to the line as possible. At last he had rough semicircles at either end. The tricky part was now to smooth these off using a spoke shave.

Burton gripped the handles on either side of the spoke shave and pushed the tool forward. The sharp blade acted like a plane and dug into the wood stripping shavings off as it was pushed up and down.

Burton regularly checked how close to the pencil mark he was coming. Once the mark was only a shave away he moved onto another section.

Within an hour he had one end complete and was mighty pleased with the result.

He soldiered onto the other end and was about ten minutes in when he heard Madeline calling out, "Milking time. Dad, you there?"

One morning they were all at breakfast except Isobel when they heard her calling out, "Oh come here you've got to see this!"

They all scrambled out of the chairs and ran outside to the verandah.

There was Isobel pointing out towards the Douglas

Creek. The new growth on the bottom paddock now stood three feet high and dotted in amongst this was a number of wallabies and their joeys.

"Well I never thought we had wallabies here," said Burton as they all crowded to the railing to get the clearest view.

The entire family watched, mesmerized by these beautiful, fluffy creatures. Every now and again one would disappear from sight by ducking down, then suddenly it would spring up and bound off for several yards. They were not only grazing on the grass but having lots of fun too.

As the sun began to appear in the east and the darkness dissipated it was a signal for them all to seek the safety and shelter of the forest. As if called together they all jumped off and out of sight.

"Now wasn't that just so exciting," said Isobel rather chuffed because she had discovered the wallabies.

The next day after milking and a hearty breakfast Burton announced, "Well I've got to get into town today so I'll catch you all at lunch." He gave Marion a light kiss on her cheek.

It was a few minutes later they heard him cantering Gypsy out onto the track leading to the crossing.

He reached town in less than half an hour and went straight to the jetty.

Here he borrowed a flattie from one of the lads that were employed at the saw mill and rowed across to the Weinert farm.

Bill Weinert wasn't surprised by his visit as there was always people coming and going to his farm and the abattoir that he helped run.

"Good morning Burton nice to have you finally visit," Bill Weinert called out as Burton strode through the gate. "What business are you in for?"

"Want to buy a boar that will cover my sows," replied Burton.

"Sure, come and you can take your pick. What breed are we looking at here?"

As they walked Burton filled Bill Weinert into his piggery, telling him he had half Berkshire and half Large Whites. He was hoping to breed them and sell them at the Mossman market.

"That's the spirit Burton, pigs and dairying are a good mixture. Can I make a couple of suggestions while we are walking?"

Burton was always astute enough to listen to advice from anyone but especially those who had been successful. "Most certainly Bill you have been here longer than I so your knowledge will be invaluable to me."

Rather pleased with such a positive reply Bill Weinert launched into his suggestions with gusto. "First I would buy a couple of boars one of each of the breeds. If you have boars in the two litters you can sell them to another farmer, as breeding within litters produces poor quality. Second I would add a poultry section to the farm, that is, a chook run with lots of hens and one rooster. I recommend White Leghorns as the finest breed out here and for both egg production and poultry meat. The man to get those from would be Don Heale."

Burton nodded his agreement on every word that Bill Weinert had uttered. By the time he had finished his ideas they had reached the pigsty. It was huge, over an acre of pigs, troughs, shelter sheds and wooden railing. There would have been over a hundred squealing, grunting shuffling pigs of all breeds.

"Over here," pointed Bill Weinert, "You can see the five Berkshire boars I have for sale and further across are the two Large White boars. Take your time and I don't mind giving you advice if you need it."

Burton eyed the five boars that ranged from a large old one to a weanling. He settled on one of the other three that had a lot of black in his coat. "What about the one with the hairy end of his tail?" asked Burton.

"Sold," shouted Bill Weinert, "That's a great pick by far. Thought you looked like a pig man to me as soon as I saw you. You can select from the Large Whites. It won't matter all that much which one you choose as they are equally as good as breeders."

Burton arrived back at the jetty full in the knowledge that he had bought the breeding boars for less than he expected to pay and that they would be delivered to the crossing that afternoon by launch. All he had to do was to get the slide down to pick up the crates.

For now he had to pay a visit to Ted Hitch at the saw mill and then ride home to organize Brutus and the slide.

Ted was waiting at the door of the saw mill and the sawing noise was still for once.

"Not busy?" queried Burton when he found Ted.

"No just having a siesta before we tackle the heavy stuff. Young James is sharpening the teeth in readiness. You can't expect the teeth to keep sawing without maintenance. How can I help you?"

Burton placed his pointer finger to his lips and made a sssh sound. Ted acknowledged this gesture by tapping his nose with the same finger of his right hand.

"Do you know where I can get varnish for the project? You see I've nearly got it finished and everything is looking grand. That red cedar grain is amazing to behold."

"I told you so didn't I?" said Ted and winked. "Now I've got something even better than varnish that will enhance that grain and give the project a real professional finish. It's called French Polish and I just happen to have half a bottle left over from many years ago."

"You are an absolute marvel Ted Hitch, thank you ever so much. I must invite you to dinner one evening to show you the finished project so you can be as proud as I am," said Burton

The launch came racing up the Stewart Creek with Bill Weinert himself at the wheel. He waved to Burton and cut the motor.

The launch slowed and glided into the shallow water before nosing up onto the sand. "Here we go, Burton, these randy boars all yours," called Bill.

They unloaded the crates and put them on the slide.

Burton thanked Bill and waved goodbye.

He walked over to Brutus and gave a gee up and away the huge horse trotted. He loved his job and the more he did the more he wanted to do.

The boars were put in pens by themselves to allow them to acclimate and tomorrow they would be moved closer to, but not in the same pen, as the sows. On the third, day they would be allowed to mix but a wary eye would need to be kept on both boars in case they turned on the sows. This final assimilation was the trickiest.

Luckily all went well and Burton and all the family were looking forward to lots of little squealing piglets.

Now was the time to organize a chook run and buy those White Leghorns as suggested by Bill Weinert.

Ginger and Burton were given all the information they needed and instructions to get the poultry section up and running.

It took them less than 48 hours to have a chook coop built. The addition of a rooster and twelve hens completed the project.

The younger children delighted in rushing to the chook pen every afternoon either after school or just before evening milking to collect the white eggs that lay in the straw nests.

Chapter 16

The timber clearing continued to progress on the lower paddock.

The only time it stopped was to float four logs down to the saw mill.

This they managed to do on three separate occasions much to the delight of Ted Hitch who paid handsomely for the logs.

As they continued to cut and bash the undergrowth and slash off the branches from the trees, Burton started to form an idea. He instructed the other youths that he wanted them to stack the fallen timber and undergrowth into piles. These were to be in the form of huge tepees. He encouraged them to stack the piles as high as they could, even suggesting throwing the lighter wood to the top.

Burt and Ginger scratched their heads at this change in instructions as before they simply fired the smaller piles up and later scattered the ashes.

They knew Burton was up to something but just couldn't quite figure it out.

A fortnight later after the boars had been welcomed to the Johnson farm Burton was carrying two buckets of skim milk towards the pigsty.

There was quite a rumpus going on ahead of him so he hurried his footsteps.

The noise was from the far pen where the Large Whites were housed.

Burton bounded over the fences, carrying the buckets until he arrived at the pen where the squealing was loudest.

Here he was surprised to find the boar and a wild pig toe to toe and biting at each other.

The wild pig was a tusker but Burton didn't twig as he was intent on getting the interloper away from his pigs.

He jumped the final railings with the intention of racing forward and whopping the strange pig across the snout with the bucket of skim milk. This was to be followed up by the second bucket and at that point he envisaged the wild pig taking off for the hills.

Burton should have looked to the left field because he had been there many times before but alas he didn't.

As he landed in full flight, the greasy, muddy ground gave way and he slipped then slid on his back directly into the fighting pigs.

At the last fraction of a second, he saw the tusks and knew he was in for a fight, a fight for his own survival.

Burton was a tall man and tough as nails but he was at a distinct disadvantage. He was lower than the pigs and they were in a mean mood.

He cannoned into the pigs and all hell broke loose.

As he tried to regain his feet he saw the pigs were gnashing at each other with their sharp teeth. The tusker was throwing his head around so Burton tried to protect his face. Teeth, tusks and hooves hammered into Burton as he grabbed one of the buckets and tried to force this between himself and the pigs.

Suddenly the pigs took on a more ferocious attitude and both turned their attention to Burton.

A quick glance made him aware that he was bleeding profusely from his right arm where a tusk had ripped it open. They were baying for his blood.

His only chance was to roll away and get under the railing that was three yards away. As Burton rolled, the pigs kept up their attack trying to get to the blood and to bite off other bits of his body.

He pulled the bucket over his head and this protected his face but not his arms and legs.

After what he thought was an agonizing minute he hit the railing and felt his legs go underneath. He wriggled furiously to get his body clear but then he seemed to be stuck.

The attack had lessened although the pigs were charging at his body.

It finally struck home to a semi-conscious, Burton, that the bucket was stuck on the railing!

He let it go and with great relief dragged his head clear.

He looked down at his body and could see large chunks of missing flesh and blood oozing out of numerous wounds.

He tried to stand but the whole world spun and he felt nauseous. He sunk to the ground on all fours and began to vomit.

Through his semi-consciousness he thought he could hear voices but they were far away, too far to save him. "What could he do as he couldn't find the energy to move nor to call out?"

Then there were strong arms gathered around him, more than one pair, and he was lifted off the ground. At that point, he lost consciousness.

When he came to he was in a strange room all painted white and there were gadgets around the bed he was laying in.

A number of strange noises came from different parts of the room and one was a voice and he slowly recognized it as Marion's.

"Welcome back my love'" she said and he noticed tears streaming down her bloodshot eyes. "We thought we'd lost you."

He lay in the Port Douglas Hospital for over sixteen days before he was allowed to go home.

He was a sore and sorry sight for many more days after but finally, his toughness shone through and he recovered to be his old self.

As for the wild pig, it served as bacon for a number of the farming families after Barry Hayden dispensed with it.

The Large White boar was given a pardon by Burton on the condition it made lots of piglets and never attacked anyone again.

The accident put paid to Burton's surprise that he had intended for November 5th.

He was, however, able to convey to both Burt and Ginger that they were not to do any burning off until he returned. He explained that if a fire was to get away and he, the owner, was absent it would not look good.

So the Ginger and Burt concurred and when Burton finally arrived home by launch and slide the first thing he noted was the ten bonfires all ready to be fired.

Several days later he was feeling much improved and was excited about the reaction he would get from the family when he disclosed his surprise to them.

He took Burt and Ginger aside and told them what he was going to do and what he expected their roles to be. The youths were pleased that Burton had included them in his idea and excited to put everything in place.

Burton called everyone onto the verandah at sunset and told them he had a special story for them.

"This is a story about your Great Grandfather,

Ambrose, who none of us met. I was only three years old when he died in Bathurst of heart failure.

"My story was told to me by Fritz, your grandfather and he was barely four at the time but said it was forever etched into his mind.

"Ambrose had migrated from Denmark with his wife, Margherita and daughter Bertha in 1851.

"They went first to Georgia in the United States of America. Ambrose was a qualified mining surveyor and he found a placement on the Georgia goldfields.

"After four years he heard about the gold rushes in Victoria, Australia.

"He packed his family up and sailed from New York in the ship, Tartar.

"When he reached Melbourne they caught a Cobb and Co stagecoach to Jim Crow Creek near Daylesford.

"Here he fossicked for alluvial gold and when this played out and deep mining started he decided to go back to being a mining surveyor. He was so well qualified that the Hepburn Shire accepted him as their surveyor and so did the Victorian Government."

Burton paused at that point waiting for them to appreciate the heritage that he had just divulged to them.

"In 1859 your grandfather Fritz was born and then another boy they called Ambrose Junior in 1860. This was the whole family and they are all your great grandparents, great uncles and aunt.

"The one thing that Ambrose held dear to his heart

was his motherland. Denmark.

"In 1862 he heard about the Royal Princess Alexandra of Denmark's marriage to the Prince of Wales. He was so thrilled and he wanted to share this with all his friends and associates.

"He called on the Mayor of Daylesford, a Mr Peter Miller and asked him if he would be part of a parade to the top of Wombat Hill where each would plant an English oak to commemorate the wedding.

"The parade went ahead and Ambrose, Margherita, Bertha, Fritz and Ambrose Junior led the procession. They danced and sang on the way encouraging others to join in and offering them a barbeque and drinks after the planting.

"Peter Miller and Ambrose planted their saplings near each other on a denuded hilltop. All around them was tons of fallen trees and undergrowth that the prospectors had laid to waste in their search for the yellow riches.

"Wombat Hill was to become a botanical garden as the years went by.

"What followed was considered by many to be the most spectacular scene ever. The entire 1 000 tons of fire wood was torched as if it was Guy Fawkes Night. The fires burnt brightly for hours lighting the entire hillside and could be seen for miles around Daylesford."

At this point, Burton paused and winked at Burt and then Ginger.

Both youths stood up, excused themselves and went out the back as if to go to bed. Instead, they snuck around the house and bolted for the lower paddock.

Meanwhile, Burton was fielding questions about the family ancestors and what they all did. He was happy telling the different stories but became rather solemn when asked about Great Uncle Ambrose Junior. "That's a story that will have to wait until later, this is too happier a time."

He left it at that but Isobel stored the thought away and intended to ask again what the story of Ambrose Junior entailed.

Eva inquired after Burton's brothers and sisters and he readily told them of Ruby, his sister who had married Francis Holt and they lived near Murwillumbah.

Suddenly he stood up and started off down the front steps, "Now we shall see what the Ambrose Johnson family saw all those years ago at Wombat Hill in Daylesford. Keep looking out towards the lower paddock."

Burton had reached the front fence that surrounded the house and here he picked up what looked like a firm stick with a bulge at the top.

He fiddled in his pants' pocket and produced a box of matches. He lit one and held the flame to the bulging end of the stick. It roared into flame making it into a flaming torch. Burton held the burning torch up and began waving it in looping arcs, clockwise then anticlockwise.

Down in the low paddock Burt and Ginger had waited patiently for Burton's signal.

Even though they were over one hundred yards apart they saw the flame of the torch simultaneously.

Both lit their own torch that Burton had made and left by the heaps. As if only one person was lighting the bonfires the outside two burst into flame. Half a minute later the next two and so on.

Back on the verandah the children and Marion stood transfixed as they watched each pile burst into flame.

They got to trying to guess when the next bonfire would start to burn.

Finally, all ten bonfires were lighting up the sky.

"Gosh, isn't this fantastic," said Isobel, "Now we know why dad told us the story about Great Grand-dad Ambrose. His fires would have been even bigger than ours."

Burton called, "This is my Guy Fawkes Night surprise to you all. I hope you like it."

"Yes dad, thank you," they replied.

About ten minutes elapsed before Burt and Ginger came running up the steps. They were puffing and blowing hard having raced each other home.

"Did you like it?" asked Ginger.

Before anyone else could answer Madeline replied, "It was brilliant, you're brilliant...," then she stopped abruptly and began to blush.

"Loved it," said Eva, who then glared towards Madeline.

"That was the most explosive Guy Fawkes Night we've ever had," said Keith.

Max, who was in Marion's hands and bouncing his feet up and down on the verandah railings, let out a delighted scream.

"Seems even Maxy boy approves," said Burton as he rejoined the family.

Next morning as they were on their way to do the milking they could see smouldering embers in each area that the bonfires had been.

"That was so beautiful last night and also served a very practical cause in burning all the unwanted trees and under growth," said Eva.

Behind the wisps of smoke, they could see several large logs that had to be cut up ready to be floated to the timber mill. That would be on the agenda over the next fortnight if the rainy season held off.

Chapter 17

For Eva and Isobel school was fast coming to an end
for the year. Eva had received average marks in most
of her subjects but had struggled with sums. Isobel, on
the other hand, had excelled in all areas. Mr Craydon
was full of praise for her intelligence and her study
habits. He was even talking of Isobel being a likely
Scholarship winner in three years' time. Isobel was so
proud but knew that her chances of going on to high
school were nil.

All of the students were now more interested in the
coming sport's day and then, of course, Christmas time.

The School Sport's day was again held on the sandbar opposite the Stewart Creek. The day turned out to
be lovely and warm with little prospect of rain.

The competition in all the running races was rather
fierce. Eva came second this time and Isobel had the
unfortunate and embarrassing time of falling over.
She landed face first and had a mouthful of sand to
contend with.

In the three-legged race, Eva combined with Olga
Claus and they won convincingly. Isobel had to run
with one of the boys and this proved disastrous as she

couldn't keep up with him and eventually, they over balanced just before the finish line.

In the boat race across the river, both girls did well and came in second in their respective races. It was a much better result for both compared to their disasters of the year before. They had practised hard most of the year with Ginger as their coach and it showed.

Ginger ran down to hug them both much to Eva's delight.

Mr Craydon gave out the threepenny and sixpenny prizes to winners and champions. Eva and Isobel each came away with a couple of shiny new threepenny coins.

Madeline and Burt had not gone to the Sport's day and spent their time doing odd jobs around the farm.

Madeline missed seeing the hug that Eva got from Ginger and just as well.

Christmas was approaching and Burton had been trying to convince Marion to allow the children a bit more freedom that year.

He was happy for the Nativity display to be put up in the lounge room and this pleased Marion.

He then suggested they invite the lorry carrying Father Christmas and the choir singing Christmas Carols to visit.

Marion was against this mainly because she didn't agree with the Father Christmas nonsense. There should be no place for make-believe figures in her children's lives.

There was quite a debate about what was make-belief and real with Burton pointing out that the children missed out on a lot that other children received. The Easter Bunny, Tooth Fairy, Guy Fawkes Night, Father Christmas, these were all exciting times and make-belief characters. He could see no harm in the children enjoying themselves through these characters.

When Burton added that God and Jesus were not materially able to be seen he hit a raw nerve with Marion. She turned on him and said dismissively, "God is real, Jesus is real, end of discussion."

Marion must have thought long and hard about their debate because a few days later Burton walked into the kitchen to hear Marion on the telephone. "Yes dear, that's right we would love the carol singers to drop by this year. (Pause). Yes and you can tell Father Christmas that the children would love to see him. (Pause). Yes my husband is quite in agreement as I have convinced him that it will lift all their spirits."

Burton smiled to himself.

Marion came through to where Burton was sitting in the lounge room and said, "I've decided that you are right and so I've arranged for the Christmas lorry to visit this year. It should be fun."

Burton stood up walked over to her and bent down and kissed her forehead. "Thank you my sweet," he said.

Unfortunately, Burton was not at the farm when the Christmas lorry arrived. He was back in hospital due to a very painful incident.

It was the morning of the 24th December and Burton was watching the family finish the milking. One of the calves that they had brought with them from the Sirrat farm was hanging around the barn, trying to get to the chaff in the feeding lots. Burton decided to chase it off back into the bottom paddock.

Burton called to Burt to give him a hand by covering the escape route to the home paddock. Burt obliged and stood with his arms out shouting at the calf.

The poor heifer looked bewildered as to what it was supposed to be doing. It would have preferred to be left alone to find the chaff.

Burton was waiting impatiently further hoping all Burt's antics would move the calf towards him and then he would be able to shoo it around the barn and back into the pasture.

The heifer turned and began to move towards Burton. The gate to the paddock started to close so Burton ran to prop it open. As this all happened, the heifer saw it had a means of escape.

Under Burt's persuasion and sudden rushing, the calf took off at full speed, head down and determined to get out the gate.

It rounded the corner where Burton had just been and headed flat out for the gate that Burton was presently propping open.

Burton heard the beat of fast running hooves but didn't have time to straighten up.

The heifer cannoned into him and its left horn tore into Burton's lower leg. The wound opened as if a can opener had been used. Burton fell screaming to the ground clutching his badly bleeding leg.

"No not again," he kept repeating while everyone else was rushing here and there getting help and applying first aid.

The launch came rushing up the Stewart Creek, Brutus carried Burton down to the crossing on the slide. The ferry *Daintree* was radioed to turn around due to an emergency and the Port Douglas Hospital staff were put on standby to expect a badly gored farmer within the next hour.

Burton missed the best Christmas Eve the Johnson children ever had.

Marion had placed the Nativity scene in the lounge room and everyone had gathered around while she prayed and read about the birth of Jesus to them all.

Next, she asked them all to wait on the verandah for a surprise.

What a surprise it turned out to be.

First, they heard bells ringing from the direction of the crossing and then a large lorry came into sight. On the back tray were a number of people dressed in red and white and they were all ringing bells like the one at school.

As the lorry came closer they saw Father Christmas riding on the back. He was sitting in a large red chair and there were presents scattered around. The children, especially Max and Keith, were jumping up and down and shouting out to Father Christmas.

The huge lorry came to a halt right near the verandah and Father Christmas climbed down.

"Ho, ho, ho," he called out, "How are all the Johnson children and Mrs Johnson?"

Everyone called back, "Well thank you."

"I've come visiting to see if you all have been good this year. If you think you have been well behaved put your hand up and I'll give you a treat."

Up went every hand except Marion's. "You've been good too mum," said Keith, and everyone laughed.

Marion sheepishly raised her hand.

Father Christmas went from one to another asking their name and then giving them a boiled lolly and saying, "I'm very pleased with you (name) this year."

At last Father Christmas was finished giving out the lollies so he climbed back on the lorry.

All the other people, who were dressed like Father

Christmas's helpers all stood up and began to sing Christmas Carols.

Over the next ten minutes, they sang Silent Night, Come All Ye Faithful (which pleased Marion) and The Little Drummer Boy.

The children clapped each rendition.

At last the lorry driver pressed the starter motor and the lorry lumbered off down the track headed for the Hayden farm. Everyone waved and shouted good-byes and come again.

When Burton was told what had happened he was so pleased and he winked at Marion and said, "Was it worth it to see all those smiles and feelings of delight?"

Marion agreed saying, "You were right once again my wonderful man but can you please stay out of the wars!"

The wet season began in earnest on Keith's birthday. They all awoke to the steady drumming of the down-pour on the corrugated iron roof. The rhythmic sound had a calming effect that did not presage the flooding that was to follow.

Keith had his fourth birthday in almost silence as the noise from the torrential down pour made it impossible to hear each other speak.

The chocolate cake was coated with chocolate icing and to make it really special Madeline had decorated the top with lollies that spelled out Happy 4th Birthday

Keith. She had carefully and cleverly cut up lolly mint leaves to make the letters.

The four candles were blown out in one go by Keith and he was thrilled to get the first slice and a piece of mint leaf.

"Yummy," he said chewing the green sweet and finding it sticking to his teeth. He spent the next ten minutes swirling his tongue this way and that trying to dislodge the sticky lolly but to no avail. In the end, he gave up and waited for the mint leaf to dissolve.

He amused everyone by poking his green tongue out and pulling faces.

The rain persisted for days and everyone watched with dread as the Douglas and Stewart Creeks overflowed their banks and then slowly the fields were inundated.

There was no way Burton was coming home soon.

In fact, Burton had already been released from hospital and was staying at the Port Douglas Hotel awaiting good news that the rain had stopped over the Daintree and the flood waters had subsided.

Chapter 18

Nineteen twenty eight dawned grey and miserable.

The rain continued to tumble down. All through January and into February it was wet, wet, wet.

The musty smell began to waft through every room and Marion and the children longed for a spot of warm weather to dry everything out.

Burton had finally given up waiting for the rain to stop and took a chance on making it upstream through his own endeavours.

He caught the ferry to the Daintree jetty where he hit a change in his luck.

Ted Hitch was sitting at the door of the saw mill looking as forlorn as the day.

He saw Burton alight from the ferry and scratched his head thinking, "How does he expect to get up the Stewart and home with the flooding that has been occurring?"

Burton saw Ted and gave him a half-hearted wave.

Ted, on the other hand, called a hello and beckoned him to come up.

Burton obliged and ran through the drizzling rain. "What's up Ted?" he asked.

"More my question than yours," said Ted. "You thinking about going up river in a flattie or are you going to wade and swim all the way there?" he chuckled to himself while waiting for an answer.

"Actually I have no idea what I am going to do. All I know is I am bored sitting around and I miss the wife and children. How to get there is another thing altogether."

"I believe I can fix that if you're daring enough. I'll borrow the launch from Bill Weinert and see if we can reach your farm. She'll be a bit hairy as the water is rather high at the junction of the Stewart and Douglas Creeks."

"I'll give anything a try," replied Burton, "As long as it doesn't cause you any anguish."

Ted went off to telephone through to Bill Weinert who had his farm directly opposite the jetty.

Within half an hour a launch came whizzing across the turbulent waters towards them.

Ted touched Burton on the arm and said, "Come on here's your lift."

They both ran down the slippery slope and onto the jetty.

Bill Weinert was edging the launch towards a mooring pole. The boat was riding high because of the flooding but Bill was doing a marvellous job keeping it steady.

"Climb aboard and I'll take you home," called Bill.

Burton turned back to Ted and said, "You coming or is Bill going to help me out."

"He's a very experienced river man so you'll be safe with him. Good luck and I'll see you when the river drops," said Ted.

Burton clambered aboard, Ted pushed the nose of the launch back into the river and Bill turned the steering wheel before pushing the accelerator forward. The launch spun around and shot off towards the Stewart Creek mouth.

Within a few minutes, they were zooming over water that covered what was normally farmland.

At last, Bill eased the throttle and the boat slid onto the edge of the water and slushy grassland.

He motioned to Burton to jump out and gave a cheery wave.

The launch turned about and Bill Weinert made all haste back to his farm.

Burton was three hundred yards from home and in the low paddock.

As he started to drag his feet through the clinging slush he saw a rider coming hell for leather from the house. It was young Burt.

Horse and rider soon pulled up and Burt called excitedly, "Dad how are you, welcome home, climb up and I'll take you up to the house."

Burton was pleased to be home and was even over the

moon at the greeting he got from the rest of the family.

One morning the girls awoke and Isobel was the first to ask what the others were thinking. "What's that noise?"

They all looked at each other and listened intently but no one spoke.

"It's not a sound it's silence," said Eva, "The rain has stopped."

They clambered out of bed, dressed and happily skipped to do the milking.

The cows were already at the makeshift dairy because they hardly had any pasture to roam around. It was easy to shunt them into the stalls and start milking.

Soon the boys and Burton arrived. Everyone was so much more cheery than they had been for the last month and a half.

As the sun rose they all exclaimed how beautiful it looked. Madeline said, "I hope the sun intends to keep coming out for the next one hundred days at least." They all laughed and agreed.

The warm sunny days were a blessing and continued on for several weeks.

The creeks returned to normal height and the grasses grew and flourished with all the moisture and the warm sun.

The milk production increased as the cows could roam further to eat the lush grass.

As March progressed the days became hotter.

One day after breakfast they were all lounging around when Burton walked in and announced, "I'm going swimming, who's with me?" He was in his bathers with a brightly coloured towel drooped over his shoulder.

The children scattered and all called out, "Me."

Within a few minutes, the whole family was in bathers and ready to walk to the swimming hole. Burton sprung a surprise by saying, "We are going to the Town Pool just past where the Douglas meets the Stewart. I hear it's got a flying fox and a diving platform so let's go have fun."

The pool was hidden behind a layer of rainforest that had been left untouched.

As they approached they could hear the excited chatter of voices and the splashing of water. Others had decided that the day was hot enough for a swim.

A short trail led the family through the scrub and there in front of them was a peaceful pool 40 yards long and eight yards wide. On the far side was a small sand bar that was barely wide enough to lay and sunbake without your toes getting wet.

About ten people splashed and cavorted in the cool waters. Many of them called a welcome as they saw the Johnson family arriving.

To get to the sand bar the family waded across at the shallow end and then selected a place to sit down.

Within seconds Ginger and Burt were splashing in the water calling the girls to come and join them.

Several youths were standing on a large log that had fallen parallel to the edge of the creek. This formed a natural diving platform and was five feet off the water. The first two lads at the end of the log challenged each other to make the biggest splash. One jumped and held his right leg with his right arm. As he hit the water a mighty splash shot water into the air. "Not bad," called Burt, "Let's see what you can do Macca."

Macca as Burt called him threw himself towards the surface and then pulled his arms and legs into his body. He hit the water with a sickening slapping sound.

"Bit of a fizzog," called Burt, "Looks like Dave won that round."

Further along, there was a rope that had been tied onto trees at both sides of the pool. One side was higher than the other. This was the flying fox. You climbed up the tree which had the rope tied highest, there you found another rope looped over the first. At the bottom of the loop was a strong stick tied on and a lighter rope hung from the stick.

Ginger clambered up to the highest rope and grabbed the stick with two hands. He pulled down on the stick to get his balance correct and then pushed off. He flew through the air for six yards before his feet touched the water and he began to slow down. By lifting his legs he could go further but eventually, he stopped and let go.

Ginger fell into the water and started swimming back to the tree that Burt now occupied.

Burt tugged on the thin rope that was tied to the stick in the loop and both slid back towards him. Eventually, he was able to hold the stick in the same way Ginger did.

He launched himself and the loop ran forward dragging him. As his legs kicked forward he let go of the stick and he literally flew through the air four yards and landed in the pool feet first. The momentum carried him to the bottom where he bent his knees until he felt his feet hit the rocky bottom. Then he propelled himself upwards popping out like a cork.

"That was terrific," called Macca, "Do it again."

The girls were more intent on lying on the sand in the cool of the shade of the trees or paddling in the shallows up stream.

Marion kept a stern eye on Max who wanted to catch the minnows that flicked little tails about in the shallows.

The day was fun and so relaxing.

A picnic lunch materialized from the big wicker basket that Burton had carried on his shoulder all the way to the pool. There were scrumptious ham and pickle sandwiches, curried egg sandwiches, bread spread with vegemite or sprinkled with hundreds and thousands, cup-cakes with an assortment of icing colours and of course bottles of lemonade.

By three o'clock they had all had lots of fun and a lovely cooling off. Burton stopped the festivities by calling loudly, "Johnson family prepare to be leaving in five minutes sharp."

Chapter 19

It was getting towards the end of March and Burton was in the blacksmith workshop using the spoke shave to finish the table top he was making. He was within a few days of carrying the finished product up to the house and showing everyone what he had made.

As he swept the spoke shave forward he caught a movement in his peripheral vision. He stopped and stared at the position where the movement occurred. There was nothing there, not even a shaving from the table top.

He continued on with his planing when he clearly saw an animal to his right and it was moving fast. He kicked at the movement and then looked down. Again there was nothing. He was completely mystified but let it go.

Later that evening he asked the others if they'd seen a mouse, or rat down at the barn. No one had.

Two days later Burton was ready to carry the table top up to the house. He had brought Brutus down to the shed attached to the slide. The tough, old horse waited patiently for Burton to strap the table top onto the slide as well as a small wicker basket that acted as a tool box.

As Burton led the horse up the hill he noticed a movement again in the peripheral vision of his right eye. He pulled the horse up and blinked. There was nothing there. He was about to move on when he realized that there was a shimmering coming off the track. It wasn't hot so it was unusual to see that kind of mirage.

Burton looked up to the sky only to see the same shimmering and it seemed to be getting bigger.

He shut his eyes, shook his head. Everything behind his eye lids was blood red and the shimmering was swirling over the redness.

He opened his eyes and the red disappeared but the swirling, shimmering image continued. It grew until it covered all of his vision.

Burton tried to focus on the track ahead and the house but he couldn't see any of these things.

"What is happening?" he asked out loud.

His next thought was he was having a stroke or had burst a vein in his brain. He knelt on the ground and placed his left hand over his eyes. The sunlight was too bright and he wanted to shut it out.

A few minutes elapsed and Burton noted that the redness was no longer swirling. He opened his eyes and found his vision was covered by a grey cloud that made him blind to all objects.

He was frightened and worried. This could be the

end of dairy farming or at worst he might die.

Slowly, ever so slowly, the cloud lifted and he began to catch glimpses of the house and the track ahead.

He had to decide to wait the whole episode out or push on and be guided by the trusty draught horse.

He waited and waited.

Finally and to his relief, his vision cleared. It was as though nothing had happened.

Then like a fork of lightning, a hammering headache struck. It beat to his heart beat and made him feel nauseous. Again he buckled and kneeled on the ground.

Brutus snorted as though impatient or concerned for what was happening to his master.

A voice called out from ahead, "You alright, dad?" It was Burt who had seen his father start his journey from the barn but had not arrived.

He had gone off to do a few odd jobs and then wondered where his father had gotten to over the last half an hour.

Burton tried to stand but his head was pounding. He felt giddy and wanted to throw up.

A strong arm reached around him and a concerned voice said, "What's happening dad, you look dreadful. Where are you hurting?"

Burton managed to blurt out, "Head, it's aching, get me home."

Burt guided his father onto the slide and slid in beside him so he could keep him from falling off.

"Gee up boy, home," he called to Brutus.

The huge horse was only too happy to oblige and moved off at a gentle trot towards the house.

As they neared the front Burt began to shout out, "Help, dad's taken a turn."

Marion was the first down the steps followed by Ginger and then here was a scramble of bodies.

"Get him inside to the bedroom," instructed Marion and a number of helpers lugged the big frame of Burton up the steps, through the front door and into the bedroom.

Burton must have slept for quite a while because when he woke all was quiet in the house and Marion was sleeping restlessly next to him.

She stirred as he sat up and she asked, "How are you feeling love?"

"Much better, the headache has abated thank goodness. I've never had one that severe, ever."

"I think you and I will take the ferry in the morning and visit your favourite doctors in Port Douglas. Now get to sleep, milking is in two hours."

Doctor Shoemaker flashed the light into Burton's right eye and then quickly away. He watched with satisfaction as the blackness of the pupil dilated. He switched to the left eye and carried out the same procedure and got the same result.

"You say you get a shimmering across your vision?" reiterated the doctor.

"That's what I said doc. It starts small and then grows to cover the entire vision. Looks like the heat shimmer you get looking across a wheat field on a hot summer's day," said Burton.

"How many times would you say this has happened?" asked the doctor as he prised the top eye-lid of the right eye open with his thumb. While waiting for an answer he held down the lower eye-lid and noted the clean whiteness of the cornea and the tiny red capillaries.

Burton replied, "Only the once full on but I've felt strange things happening to my eye-sight over the past fortnight."

The doctor had moved to the left eye and lifted the eye-lid to check for any abnormalities.

"I can't see any problems with the physical make up of your eyes. I'll just be a while as I'll consult my colleague, Dr Razzac, he may have come across a similar case."

A few minutes past and Dr Shoemaker returned shaking his head.

"We are mystified and our only possible diagnosis is a trauma to the optic nerve. This is the nerve that links your eyes to the brain so that what you see can be interpreted. Often a blow to the brain area that deals with vision or a blow near the eyes can confuse one area or the other. Often the trauma will not be observable, such as a burst capillary or vein behind the eyes that may upset the vision. All of these things can only be relieved through rest and care."

"The other possibility is an infection has irritated the membranes that cover parts of the eyes or the brain. These also need time for the body to fight them off. Now, I can admit you and we'll observe you for a few days to a week and see if we can get a better diagnosis or I can prescribe laudanum that you take to lessen the pain from the headache. If you have another attack you need to return immediately. What's it to be?"

Marion was very concerned and wanted Burton to stay in hospital.

Burton made his decision, "I'll go home as there is too much to be done and besides I can't keep expecting the children to accept responsibility for milking and getting the cream to the Butter Factory."

The doctor wrote out a prescription for the chemist to fill and gave one last piece of advice, "As soon as you feel another vision loss you are to get here as quickly as you can."

Marion and Burton arrived back at the farm where all the family waited most concerned for Burton's health and welfare. They all agreed to keep an eye on him and that he must go back to the hospital at the next attack if it was to occur.

Chapter 20

The routine of farm life soon took over and with milking, tree felling, pigs and chooks to be fed the problem with Burton's eyes slowly drifted into the background. The next project was to start breeding so that the numbers of cattle, pigs and fowl increased.

Burton took care of the cattle by doing a deal with Barry Hayden. He would borrow Barry's bull and put him to cover the six heifers that had now grown into cows and Barry was to send six of his cows over for agistment. So the lucky bull would have a dozen cows while they all grazed happily together in the top side paddock. Barry was in agreement and the deal was sealed.

The boars took care of the breeding in the pigsty and it soon became obvious that several of the sows were pregnant.

Burton, Ginger and Burt ordered several planks through Ted Hitch so that they could make breeder pens. These would keep the little piglets safe once they were born. Without shelter from a rolling mother, many piglets would get squashed to death.

Marion was in charge of the chook pen ever since Burt and Ginger had finished setting it up. She made sure she had a half an hour every day to check the water and feed.

She took Max and Keith with her and they carefully collected the lovely white eggs. It was a game of great excitement as the two small boys ran from one nest to the next finding the eggs and placing them carefully in the cane baskets Marion had given them.

One day, as Keith was collecting eggs, he found a hen sitting on the nest.

He could see at least two shiny white eggs under her so he pushed his pudgy little hand to get them.

The hen let out a cackling sound then jabbed her beak into Keith's hand. Although it didn't hurt it frightened the boy and he let out an almighty scream.

Marion dropped the bucket of water she was holding and ran towards the noise. Her first thought was a snake had been seen or worse had bitten Keith.

Marion saw what had happened and began to laugh.

She called Max over and he came reluctantly as he didn't want to meet whatever had hurt his big brother.

Marion showed them both the hen on the eggs and showed how she pecked at them and asked, "Why do you think she does that?"

Both Keith and Max shook their heads, so Marion explained, "The females of most animals and birds like to have babies and with birds, the babies are made inside the eggs. This hen has decided she wants to have chickens so she needs to lay about ten eggs and then sit on them to keep them warm. The yellow yolk inside will develop into a chicken and when it is fully developed it will peck its way out and be a real chicken."

"But why did she peck me?" asked Keith.

"Because she thought you were taking her eggs and then she wouldn't have any chickens. So what we need to do is move her to a nest away from all the other chooks and put ten eggs under her and in a few weeks' time we should have ten fluffy, yellow chickens running around."

Burton needed to finish the tabletop that had been left on the slide the last he had seen of it.

He located it and got the two youths to help him carry the top into the house.

He called all the family into the kitchen and proudly showed them his idea.

"I've made a large table top that will fit over our present table and give us a lot more room. If we have any more children…" He paused and winked at Marion, "Then we'll need the extra space. The top I've made fits over this one and I'll screw it so it doesn't move."

With the help of Burt and Ginger, the kitchen table was turned upside down and placed on the redwood table top. Burton made several holes using his brace and bit and then screwed in wood screws. The trio then put the table right way up.

"There, how does that look?" asked Burton puffing his chest out proudly.

The new table was much bigger than the original and the beautiful grain on top was lovely to see.

Burton then added two props, one at either end to stop the table toppling.

At this point, he said, "Now I need lots of helpers to finish the job."

He opened the wicker basket and produced blocks of wood covered in sandpaper. He showed them all how to move the sandpaper along the grain to smooth the wood.

Everyone eagerly accepted their sandpaper block and began their part of the job.

After about quarter of an hour, Burton was pleased with the progress and called a halt.

All the blocks were put away.

Burton used a broom to brush away all the sawdust that had accumulated from the sandpapering.

He took out a number of rags and a bottle of French polish. He upended the polish onto one of the rags and showed the children how to rub the liquid into the wood making the beautiful grain patterns stand out. He took out another piece of rag, wet it with polish and handed it to Keith. He continued to do the same until everyone had a polishing rag and they all began busily wiping and polishing.

The final result was stunning.

"Beautiful job, family," he said, "Now we wait for the table to dry and then we can use it."

The side paddock became the next to be cleared and it took the greater part of the year 1928.

In between everything else that had to happen, Burton, Burt and Ginger chipped away at the entanglement of undergrowth and huge trees.

The material was piled up into heaps and all talk was again on a Guy Fawkes Night like none other. Burton's mind ticked away, as he tried to see if he could come up with an idea. He needed one that would beat last year's Guy Fawkes celebration.

The trees were left separate on the ground so that they could be cut into 12-foot lengths and then floated down to the saw mill. Burton knew that Ted Hitch would be pleased to see these.

Easter was on the calendar for late April and Burton had convinced Marion to add a little bit of excitement by giving small chocolates to each of the family. His reasoning was that they had all toiled so long and so hard that they deserved such a reward.

He was also angling in later years to give Easter eggs and maybe even have an Easter egg hunt.

For now, he was satisfied that Marion was comfortable with telling the story of the Crucifixion of Jesus and His resurrection plus giving the chocolates.

The children were delighted with the chocolates and ate these very slowly making sure they lasted a long time so they savoured every bit.

Burton was feeling rather generous one evening in May and he was telling Marion about his invite of Ted Hitch to come and see the new table top.

He asked her, "My love do you think we could have him stay to dinner. You select the night and I'll give him a buzz."

Marion was not all that keen on having extras and especially important community members but she could see that it was important to Burton so she said, "Yes that will be fine, what about next Wednesday?"

"Good," said Burton. "I'll give him a buzz."

He jumped up from the comfortable lounge chair and walked into the kitchen to the telephone. He picked up the receiver and wound the handle. "Ted Hitch, please, number 27, thanks."

A minute later the strong voice of Ted Hitch came on. Burton extended the invitation and Ted accepted. They said their goodbyes and Burton put down the receiver and began to walk back to Marion.

He bumped heavily into the door jamb and cracked his head.

"Are you alright, Burton?" asked Marion as she got up to come to his aid.

"Oh no," he said, "My vision has gone all wonky again. The shimmering has started and I need to sit down."

Chapter 21

Next morning Burton and Marion caught the ferry back to Port Douglas and this time Burton was persuaded to stay in hospital for a month.

Max missed his dad on his second birthday. He was sobbing and pleading for his dad to come home. Between sobs, he asked Marion if they could take the vanilla cake, all decorated with lollies, into the hospital so dad could sing Happy Birthday to him.

Madeline decided to try to placate Max by starting to sing Happy Birthday. Everyone else joined in and at the end, they all gave three rousing cheers.

Max stopped crying and tried to blow out the two candles. One continued to burn brightly and this caused more tears so Madeline came to the rescue a second time and blew it out.

She then said, "Max gets the first slice of the yummy cake."

That did it and for the rest of the celebration Max was happy and joined in all the fun.

At the Port Douglas Hospital all was not going as well as the doctors had hoped.

Burton had a number of bouts where he lost his vision and developed the mind blowing headaches. All of the remedies they tried only gave partial relief. They began to suspect that there may have been bleeding somewhere inside the skull possibly along the optic nerve.

Several telephone calls were made to a specialist in Brisbane and eventually it was decided that the patient had to be transferred through to the Brisbane Hospital.

This was organized almost immediately and Burton was on the next ship south with a nurse in attendance.

Marion was telephoned by the Port Douglas Hospital and she tearily passed the message on to the rest of the family. "We'll all have to pull our weight and help each other until your father recovers," she said. "He will be away for at least another month."

Isobel missed her father at her tenth birthday although she didn't cry she was sad. "I just hope dad would get better," she said.

She blew out the ten candles in one go and said to them all, "I know you aren't supposed to tell what your wish is for but I'll tell you mine. I wished the doctors in Brisbane will find a cure for our dad."

Everyone cheered and then gave Isobel an extra three more cheers.

In between Isobel and Burt's birthday, the hen had her batch of chickens.

It was Keith who discovered the mother and her brood and came rushing into the house yelling, "The chickens have hatched come and see them."

Marion corrected him saying, "The eggs have hatched not the chickens," and she untied her apron and hurriedly picked Max out of his high chair.

She walked off after all the others for the chook pen.

There was the mother hen clucking and scratching and all around her were little bundles of fluffy yellow feathers.

"Aren't they so cute," said Eva.

Marion put Max on the ground and he toddled forward to the wire on the pen.

He looked at the chickens and began to jig up and down. Madeline picked him up and told him all about the chickens.

She then said, "Can we count them all?"

Max said, "One, one, one…" he had at least mastered the first number. All the others were busy calling out their own numbers. The general consensus came to nine.

"That's strange," said Marion, "We put ten eggs under her. Burt, go in and see what's happened to number ten."

Burt opened the gate and walked to the nesting box and peered in. "Uh oh," he said sadly, "The last one is not a pretty sight. I'll bury it later when you've all gone."

"No that won't do son," said Marion, "We are farmers and life and death is what we must learn to live with and understand. We can't afford to be squeamish. Now bring the egg and remains out and we can all see what has happened."

Burt carefully picked up the half developed chicken and the remains of the egg and placed them in the palm of his hand.

He approached the fence where everyone was crowded around.

Marion moved forward and explained what had happened. "Sometimes a few eggs do not hatch at all so no chicken develops. Other times the chicken will start to form but for one reason or another, it stops growing and dies. This poor little blighter developed and even tried to peck its way out of the egg like all its brothers and sisters but something stopped it short. More likely the mother hen has stepped on it and it has stopped breathing. Thank you Burt, now you and Ginger may take it away and bury it. Say a nice pray, too."

Mother hen and her nine chickens continued to cluck and scratch as they weren't interested in the goings on around them.

Burton was finally coming home after nearly five weeks in the Brisbane Hospital.

He had been released by the doctors and caught

a ship to Port Douglas and Captain Osborne was to bring him home in the ferry *Daintree*.

There were several Daintree people on the jetty waiting to board and they all enquired how he was feeling.

The bush telegraph had let everyone in the community know that Burton had been unwell and was in the Brisbane Hospital.

Many times over the five weeks Marion had received a telephone call or a visitor asking after Burton's health and offering to help out on the farm.

Burton felt weak and he had headaches but they were nowhere as debilitating as the ones he used to get. The doctors told him to take things easy and build up his strength slowly. That way he should recuperate within two months.

Marion was over the moon when she saw her husband arriving.

She had received a telephone call from Captain Osborne who was in Port Douglas waiting to sail the ferry back to the Daintree Village.

He had told her that Burton was sitting on the wharf waiting to be taken home.

She put down the receiver and ran to tell the family that their father was finally on his way home.

She then made arrangements for Burt and Ginger to meet Burton on the jetty and to row him home to the crossing and then bring him by slide to the house.

Now he was here and she felt his thin body against hers as they embraced. "Welcome home my love," she said. She stepped back and looked at him. He had lost weight and looked drawn and weak.

"We'll get through this," she said, "We always do."

At least Burt got to have his father home for his fourteenth birthday.

Chapter 22

Chickens were chirping and scratching and all happy so the sows must have got a little jealous because the next positive thing that bucked Burton up was the arrival of piglets. Not one litter nor two but seven litters with a varying number of piglets in each.

Burton had thought all his luck had changed in one swoop.

He could fatten this lot up in a matter of months and then make a killing at the Mossman sales come November.

A full census was finally able to be taken by Burt and Ginger with both agreeing there were 43 piglets altogether.

Keith went around trying to name them all but when he went back to a litter he couldn't remember the names he had given them. In the end, he decided that there were too many so he settled for 'Piggy' for each one.

In September the valley was almost overrun by wild pigs.

Wild pigs had always been a problem in the Daintree and wild pig hunting was a favourite pastime among the local farmers.

With the heavy rain of the wet season and the

lovely warm weather since the grasses were lush, the rainforest was growing, vegetable gardens were flourishing and the wild pigs had been breeding. Now they roamed here and there. Eventually, the farmers decided that they would need to deal with the pests.

A meeting in the Butter Factory in September determined three hunting parties, one for the Stewart and Douglas Creeks, another for the Upper Daintree River and the third for the North Daintree River.

Burton, who had slowly regained his health and was starting to take on more responsibilities around the farm decided that he was not strong enough to join the Stewart and Douglas Creek party.

Most of the upper reaches of these creeks were very steep and strewn with rocks and boulders.

At the prompting of Barry Hayden, Burton did allow Burt and Ginger to go along as beaters.

"Beaters?" asked Burt, "What does that mean?"

Barry Hayden was happy to explain how a pig hunt was conducted.

"Most of the time the wild pigs stay hidden in the rainforest or as we call it the scrub. Lazy blighters don't like to go too deep so during the day they lie around, sleeping and resting.

"As soon as the sun dies behind the horizon they are on the move searching for food. To do this easily and to move from one source of food to another they come into the clearings.

"We take advantage of their habits by flushing them out into the clearings where the shooters can see them.

"They also need to know where all the members of the hunting party are located so that no one gets shot. The beaters walk about five yards apart through the scrub with the deepest beater at 45-degree to the first one. The first one is on the edge of the scrub and he makes sure each member of the beating party stays in touch.

"Getting lost in the scrub is very scary. If you ever feel as though you are lost sit down and give a coo-ee. Wait and listen for a return call and then walk towards the call continuing to call and listen. That way you will be 'talked out'. If you don't hear a coo-ee, stay where you are and count to 100 and call again. Keep doing this until you are found. If it gets dark find the warmest shelter but don't go too far from where you are. We will know within a few hundred yards of where you were last seen so it will be reasonably easy to locate you."

Burton began to look concerned while Barry Hayden was offering this advice.

He said, "When you get back remind me to sit all the family down to tell them about the three little boys in Daylesford down in Victoria."

Barry Hayden looked a little confused.

He decided to ignore Burton's interruption and continued, "The beaters carry two sticks to bang together and they also shout out. This noise will flush out any wild pigs and a variety of other wild life. We cover about 100 yards each sweep and rotate the beaters. Are you ready to go?"

Barry Hayden led them to the lorry that was waiting. Ted Hitch was driving, he was a man who could do everything, and on the tray sat five other men all holding a variety of guns. Three youths were sitting on the very back with their legs dangling over.

Burt and Ginger joined the younger ones of the party.

Ted started the lorry and crunched it into first gear before the truck moved away along the track out of the house paddock.

"We'll be back for lunch Mrs Johnson," called Barry Hayden as the heavy lorry made a slow right turn and accelerated towards the crossing.

Burton nodded knowingly. They were off to try the Stewart Creek first and in the afternoon they would wander up the Douglas Creek.

Burton wondered if he would feel like joining them.

The ride was only short but the track was so bumpy that by the time Ted Hitch applied the brakes all the lads at the back were squirming around as backsides got a hammering. They were so relieved to stop and jump off. Each rubbed and scratched their posteriors to stop the hurt and to get the circulation going.

"Right," said Ted Hitch, taking command, "Shooters

will walk five yards apart at twenty yards from the scrub. We only shoot forward or to the right ensuring no one is in your sight. We need to let the pigs run well into the clearing and that way we can see them and hunt them safely."

He turned to the five youngsters who were all chaffing at the bit to get going, "Don. You'll start at point. You walk into the scrub twenty yards. Wait for Trevor to come. He stays five yards away and five yards behind. You are making a 45-degree line to the edge of the scrub while each beater is five yards away from the other. Try to keep within sight of those nearest to you and in hearing at all times. Greg, you're next, followed by Burt, and Ginger you can keep them all in contact. You walk on the edge of the scrub and try to call to each as we go so that no one will ever get lost. They are not to be my famous last words".

The boys were all nodding their understanding.

"Now you will pull on these red beanies so that we are very clear that you are not a pig. Do not at any time run nor come rushing out of the scrub. Here are your beating sticks so grab two and let's away for roast pork awaits. Off you go," chuckled Ted Hitch.

Ginger walked to the edge of the scrub and called Burt. He sent him on an angle to be five yards in and called him to halt. Each of the others was placed in position and Ginger called loudly to each before yelling, "Let's go flush out lots of pigs."

The shooters, who were in a line ten yards ahead began at a slow walk, guns at the ready.

The racket from the scrub was enough to awaken every pig in Australia. Shouting and drumming as they moved along, the beaters were having the fun of a life time.

A hundred yards on, nothing had stirred from the scrub. Ted Hitch called a halt and swung his arm in circles indicating the beaters were to rotate. He waited until Don emerged from the scrub and began calling to the other beaters. "Forward," he yelled.

Seven times they rotated, covering 700 yards and still nothing.

The terrain was getting steeper and the scrub was getting closer to the edge of the creek. The amount of open cleared land was diminishing quickly.

"One more and we'll go back to the truck," called Ted Hitch.

No sooner had his cry stopped echoing across the valley than a huge black and white boar came charging out of the undergrowth barely twenty yards ahead. Behind was a smaller sow of like colouring. Behind her were seven piglets of varying sizes.

The boar seemed to sense that he was trapped so he turned on the nearest threat.

He had two long, sharp tusks and knew how to use these to rip flesh from his enemies.

He swerved and lowered his head.

The noise from the frightened piglets was deafening.

Greg stood transfixed not realizing he was the boar's intended target. The distance between pig and youth diminished at incredible speed. With less than six yards separating them Greg realized his fate was at hand. He screamed and began throwing his beating sticks at the oncoming boar.

Chapter 23

There was a mighty bang that was extra loud as it was trapped in the V-shaped valley. The charging boar seemed to stop in mid-air, its legs no longer pumping and its eyes glassed over. It slid across the ground and then somersaulted to a halt at Greg's feet.

Ted Hitch stood perfectly still, gun pointing at the pig and a wisp of smoke coming from the barrel. "Well that's number one shall we round up the others?" he asked nonchalantly.

The sun was directly overhead when they finally reached the lorry. It took all their combined strength to carry a boar, a sow and seven piglets all the way down the valley.

They were all chuffed as it had been a successful hunt.

Burton and Marion were waiting anxiously at the farm and were relieved when they saw Burt and Ginger waving a piglet each from the back of the lorry.

Lunch of mixed sandwiches was served to everyone and the stories of the hunt were told and retold around the verandah.

The afternoon hunt proved to be even better than the first.

Everyone was now conversant with their roles and so the number of pigs flushed out increased three-fold. There were so many pigs charging out of the scrub that it became difficult to decide which one to shoot at first.

The clearings were also much smaller so the pigs found escape routes readily.

Overall though the party brought home more bacon they did in the morning. Four boars, three sows and eleven piglets in total had been shot.

The most exciting part of the hunt for the beaters came towards the end of the outing.

They had flushed out a sow and three weaners and Ted Hitch had asked the shooters to 'shoulder arms', which meant they were to place the guns over one shoulder with the barrel pointing to the sky.

The sow sensed that the shooting had ceased so she stopped and flopped down trying to hide in the long grasses.

Ted Hitch then called the beaters out of the scrub and one at a time they were given a gun and instructions as to how to use it.

Each lad then got to decide on their target and to try to shoot their first pig.

Ginger was punching the air with one hand and

holding a weaner up in the other as the lorry came up the track to the Johnson house.

"I shot a pig, my very first pig," he cried out.

Ginger was an instant hero to all the family and he never tired of telling anyone who would listen about the day he took steady aim and shot a wild pig clean through its beady little eyes.

The district was pleased to learn over the next few days that the three wild pig hunting parties had successfully removed dozens of pigs. Pork was on offer through the butcher at special prices for the following month and a half.

October was delightful with clear skies and warm days.

Burton began to get his old self back and eventually made his way with Burt and Ginger to the lower paddock to help with the clearing.

He had spent part of his recuperation setting out where he wanted the fences to run, measuring and costing the number of fence posts and wire.

The fencing would wait until after the clearing but needed to be done so he could carefully rotate the cows through the pastures. Overgrazing was a danger and where it occurred the cattle would lose milk capacity and erosion became a constant problem. He needed to avoid these curses.

Burton had also been planning a more exciting

Guy Fawkes Night for the children.

When you have so much time on your hands you can either wile away the hours or you can put them to use through careful planning.

This year there would be an explosive new idea that should make the children cry out in awe. They didn't know what he was up to and no one had found his secret hiding place in the blacksmith lean-to.

On November 2nd Burton received a telephone call from the matron at the Port Douglas Hospital. "Mr Johnson?" she asked over the line.

"Yes, this is Burton Johnson speaking," replied Burton.

"This is Matron Kath Binningham from the Port Douglas Hospital ringing on behalf of Dr Shoemaker. He has asked me to organize an appointment for you for tomorrow morning at 11 am. He says it is important and it concerns your eyes."

Burton was dismayed and immediately went on the defensive, "Surely it can't be that much of a problem. I haven't had an attack for nearly seven weeks."

"I'm sorry Mr Johnson but he did tell me to assure you it was urgent so please be available," she said and then abruptly stopped the conversation with, "Thank you and goodbye."

Burton stood holding the receiver and in shock. "Had they found an incurable disease in his optic nerve?" he wondered.

Marion came in and saw the look on Burton's face. She gently took the receiver from his hand, put it up to her own ear and heard the engaged signal so she put it in the cradle. "What was that all about?" she asked.

Burton whispered to her, "The doc wants to see me, tomorrow."

"Then that's what happens, go get yourself ready for dinner and stop worrying. All will be revealed in good time and I'm sure it will be alright," she assured him.

The ferry trip in was a blur and sitting in the hospital waiting room was uncomfortable.

Burton kept playing silly deadly diseases over and over in his head.

He said sadly to Marion, "Now I know how poor Grandfather Ambrose must have felt when he was told his son Ambrose Junior had diphtheria and then my own father Fritz when told his son Keith had blood poisoning. Both children died in agony over several days."

"Now let's not think so negatively," encouraged Marion.

"Come in please Mr and Mrs Johnson, so glad you could make it," invited Dr Shoemaker.

After everyone was seated the doctor examined Burton's eyes much the same as he had in previous times.

"Seems that the symptoms that we are used to seeing are abating which is good news. My colleagues in Brisbane have been having a conference concerning you and have declared that there is inflammation along the optic nerve. When the bleeding begins it warns you through the shimmering. As the bleeding increases, the cloudiness happens and the headaches start and continue until the blood flow stops. Now don't be alarmed because the bleeding is extremely light and is not going to do much harm except exert pressure on the optic nerve.

"My colleagues believe that the way to bring instant relief for you is to take an anti-inflammatory pill. As soon as you see the shimmering you pop a pill and this will stop any further blood flow and that stops the shimmering, cloudiness and no headache."

"That sounds fantastic," said Marion, "Doesn't it dear?"

Dr Shoemaker had not quite finished so he ignored Marion and went on, "What I need to determine is if there is likely to be a nasty reaction to the pill, Burton. We will need you to stay for a few hours while we get you to take one of these pills. We monitor your vital signs and watch for any adverse reactions if there isn't any you will be free to catch the ferry home. If there is we will need to keep you in while we adjust the dosage."

Burton went through the pill trial and thankfully passed with flying colours. He and Marion were on the ferry *Daintree* headed home by four o'clock in the afternoon.

Chapter 24

The crickets and frogs came out in force on the evening of the 5th November and drowned out the conversation on the verandah. Burton was trying to explain to Eva why this year Guy Fawkes Night was going to be quieter than the previous years.

"Oh, dad that's not fair. I thought you would have set the world on fire again for us'" suggested Eva.

"Well if you look out into the gloom what do you see," asked Burton.

"Nothing but darkness," said Eva disappointed.

"Are you sure now I don't want you to miss anything," replied Burton.

Suddenly Keith jumped up and down and he pointed out into the darkness and yelled, "Fire, there's a fire, look, look, over there."

Everyone followed his pointing and sure enough, there was a fire starting to leap into the black sky. As they watched another further away flickered into life.

"Well come on we'd better go down and see what's going on," suggested Burton, "We can't have the pasture burnt out."

They all ran together towards where the flames were flaring higher and higher. It was a good three hundred yards to the fires but they got there in what seemed like seconds. As they came nearer they could make out figures dancing around the flames.

"Dad you are a trickster," said Eva, "That's Ginger and Burt again up to their fire lighting tricks isn't it?"

Burton didn't reply to the question but said, "Now we need to go further towards the creek for the real surprise."

Ahead of them, they could make out a third pile that was illuminated by the first two fires. On the top of the pile was a scarecrow dressed like a man.

His fingers, thumbs and toes were thick and red coloured. His eyes had pieces of wire sticking out from them and the buttons on his shirt looked like large spirals of an assorted colour.

Burt and Ginger had reached the scarecrow topped pile first and were grinning from ear to ear.

In their hands they both held burning torches.

Burton stopped the family ten yards short and said, "We mustn't get too close as the heat will scorch you. If you feel too hot fall back and shield your eyes. Now I am giving you each a sparkler that Ginger and Burt will help you light. You hold these by the bottom of the wire and watch them throw off stars or you can whirl them around and create special effects. Please be careful not to burn anyone."

Burton handed out the sparklers then called to Ginger and Burt, "Light him up boys, it's time for Guy Fawkes to receive his comeuppance."

Ginger and Burt threw their torches into the pile and there was an instant crackling as the dry leaves caught fire and then swoosh the pile was burning ferociously.

As the fire licked at the guy's toes there was a loud bang and then another and another. Ten terrific bangs echoed into the night. "Dad you put penny bombs for his toes," squealed Isobel all so excited.

The poor guy was now covered with flames up to his waist. As the flames licked at his fingers another lot of penny bombs began exploding. Bang, bang until all ten had detonated.

"Look. Look the buttons on his shirt are spinning around and shooting off streams of sparks," called Madeline, "They are Catherine Wheels. Oh, how beautiful is that? Look there is more," she continued. All four Catherine wheels were rotating rapidly sending sparks in all directions.

The flames continued even higher to the head. No one had noticed that the hat he was wearing had feathers sticking out of the top.

Suddenly one of the feathers started to fizz and shot up into the night sky. A second later a loud bang was followed by pretty sparks cascading down towards them

Before anyone could catch their breath another rocket sped into the sky followed by the same coloured lights show, then another and another. Burton had planted ten skyrockets in the guy's hat all disguised as feathers.

As the last rocket fizzed out Ginger and Burt rushed forward and lit the sparklers. Some of the children just stood watching them fizz and sparkle, others whirled them around.

Little Max ran for Marion wailing in fright. She gave him a cuddle and assured him all was well.

She was in awe of what she had just witnessed.

Burton had won round one.

December came rushing upon them all and it was going to be a hectic month.

The major issue for all the Daintree folk was when would the wet hit. With luck, and in a lot of cases lots of praying, they hoped it would not begin until the New Year.

For the Johnson family, they were gearing up for the School Sport's Day and Eva's graduation.

Then there was Christmas Eve and Christmas Day and of course, they couldn't forget Keith's birthday.

Eva and Isobel had been busily practising for the sports. They challenged each other to running races and begged Ginger to take them to the crossing pool to compete against each other in rowing races.

When the big day finally dawned they were the first out the gate and running for the flatties beached at the crossing.

Burton, carrying Keith, and Marion, carrying Max, walked behind.

Burt, Ginger and Madeline had all decided to stay behind and complete odd jobs that needed catching up on.

Mr Craydon was organized by the time the first family arrived on the sandbank. The area looked spotless with lanes drawn, starting lines marked and flatties lined up on the beach. He had been ever so keen to have everything ready as it was his last hurrah at the Daintree.

He had applied for a transfer back to his home town of Gladstone mainly because his elderly mother had been stricken down with an incurable illness and he wanted to be there to look after her.

He had enjoyed his time in the Daintree and felt he'd made a huge difference to the children's education.

The day went smoothly as always with everyone enjoying themselves immensely.

Eva and Isobel collected three threepences each for their efforts.

Keith had watched fascinated and kept being reminded by Burton that he would be running next year so he needed to know what to do.

Marion had to ask Burton to take her home early as she wasn't feeling well.

It was unfortunate that the Johnson family wasn't at the picnic when Mr Phil Porter the chairman of the school board presented Mr Craydon with a gold pen for his years as Headmaster of Daintree School.

On arrival at home, Marion went straight to bed.

Burton settled her down and ushered the children outside.

There were a few minutes of whispering before Burton appeared and set off for the milking shed.

He called to the others and then surprised them all by whistling tunes all the way to the barn.

Although it was difficult, Madeline was able to guess the tunes, 'Danny Boy' and 'Green Grow the Rushes, O'.

The mystery to all the others was why was their dad in such a bubbly mood when he'd just put his unwell wife in bed?

Christmas Eve, to the delight of all the children, followed the exact line as last year. Marion insisted on the Nativity scene and reading the story from the bible.

The community lorry came with Father Christmas handing out boiled lollies and the helpers singing Christmas carols.

When they all woke up on Christmas morning they headed for the barn to start milking.

To their surprise, Burton was not with them.

They were all trained well enough to cope without him.

All the talk though centred around Burton's mysterious absence and of course Marion's spells of sickness.

Madeline was the expert in female matters so she theorized, "If it was every morning I would say she was pregnant so get ready for baby seven. However, I don't think it can be pregnancy because her nausea only occurs occasionally and usually in the evening."

Eva was more concerned about her father, "I hope dad hasn't got that optic nerve thing back again. He's had so much bad luck lately surely he can have good luck."

"If mum's caught a flu type thing I don't want it, I hate being sick," added Isobel.

They finished the milking and the separating of the cream. Ginger and Burton moved off with the cans full of cream for the crossing with Brutus pulling the slide. They would deliver the cans by flattie and return with the empties from yesterday.

In the meantime, the other children trudged wearily back to the house.

They walked up the steps and into the lounge room. Isobel was the first through the door and she stopped and exclaimed, "What happened to you dad?"

Burton was standing in the centre of the room covered in black soot. He had it in his reddish hair, all over his clothes and his face made him look like a chimney sweep.

"Been helping Father Christmas," he said all too nonchalantly. "Poor blighter tried to come down the chimney but got stuck. I had to reach up into the chimney to try and pull him out."

By this time all the children were in the room and staring googled eye at the sooty stranger.

"Father Christmas then pulled a huge sack through the chimney and wandered off towards the rooms in the rest of the house. When he returned I noticed the sack was empty."

Without any further clues or prompting the children ran off squealing with delight and anticipation. The girls reached their bedroom and they were delighted to find they each had a red stocking, fringed at the top with white fluffy cotton wool, lying on their beds.

"We've got Christmas presents, real presents," called Isobel. "I don't believe this it is so wonderful."

Each girl had something different and each was over the moon.

They ran back to their father carrying their gifts. Isobel had a rag doll, Eva hugged a golliwog and Madeline had a decorative sewing box.

The noise from the boys was even louder than the girls had made.

Soon they too trooped through the door carrying the present they had found. Ginger had a new pair of black boots, Burt carried a new axe, Keith had a toy rifle and Max dragged a teddy bear behind him.

"Did Father Christmas get stuck when he left?" asked Isobel rushing to the fire place and looking up the chimney. A splattering of soot made her jump back.

"No I had to help clean him up and then I got the ladder so he could climb onto the roof where the reindeers were waiting. He waved me goodbye and said that it was a pleasure giving presents to such well-behaved, polite and hardworking children as the Johnson family."

Ginger had made for the window and was looking out in misbelief. There against the wall of the house was the wooden ladder just as Burton had described. "Gosh," he said, "I've never had a Christmas like this, ever."

Everyone else nodded in agreement.

Isobel was again ahead of the pack when she suddenly said, "What about mum, she's missing out? Come on let's go see her."

They all tip-toed into the bedroom anticipating that Marion was asleep.

To their surprise and delight she was sitting up with a pillow tucked behind her back. "From all the noise and joviality I take it something extraordinary has happened. Who's going to tell me about it?"

As always it was Isobel who was quickest off the mark. "Father Christmas has come and left us all presents on our beds for being good and working hard and he got stuck in the chimney and dad had to pull him out and then lean the ladder against the wall so he could reach the sleigh and reindeers and fly away to the next house," she said all in one breath and as one sentence.

"Isn't that wonderful, I'm so pleased you are all enjoying Christmas this year. We will be having roast chicken, roast ham and vegetables for lunch. This will be followed up with Christmas cake and custard watered down with fresh lemonade," said Marion.

"Sounds delicious mum, thank you so much," said Madeline on behalf of them all.

Everyone nodded in agreement.

"Now before I shoo you all out to play games and have fun in the warm sunshine I have an announcement to make," said Burton. "As you all know, today nearly two thousand years ago, Jesus was born in a manger in Bethlehem. Well in about five months mum is going to go on a holiday for a few weeks."

There were quick nods between Isobel and Eva as they were ahead of the announcement.

Madeline was grinning knowingly.

"When mum comes back home she will be bringing a brand new brother or sister for you all to get to know."

There was a general babble of excitement among them all as they digested this news and the inevitable questions flowed.

"Stop," said Burton, "Off you all go and have fun until your mother calls you for lunch."

Chapter 25

Keith was up early on the 30th of December as it was his fifth birthday.

This would be his last as a free boy as in February he would be sent off to school. He didn't like the idea even though the older girls said it was so much fun learning. The older boys gave him the sports angle and how he could earn threepences and sixpences at the annual sport's day.

All he thought about was being stuck in one room with a crabby teacher and not being outside running amok and doing whatever you fancied.

He could see from the verandah that the milking was in full swing and that would be another expectation next year.

When any of the children started school they were considered old enough to help with the milking and rowing the cream to the Butter Factory.

Keith was beginning to wonder how he could stall this school thing for a few more years, say until he turned 12 and then he would be able to leave. That would mean he wouldn't have to go to school at all.

His thoughts were interrupted by Max who had toddled out and was standing at the top of the steps.

"Wait there Maxy boy," warned Keith, "Or you will tumble down and split your head."

The baby stepped back and walked to Keith and cuddled his leg.

"Birthday today," he said and Keith was pleased to think his baby brother remembered his birthday.

The cake was delicious as always and the family sang the Happy Birthday song with gusto followed by the three hoorays.

Keith would remember this birthday for years to come not because it was celebrated so keenly and loudly by everyone but because it was the start of his purgatory.

The Singer sewing machine had been getting a full run for over a month before New Year's Eve. The girls were flat out making themselves new outfits and Ginger and Burt were trying to kit themselves out with new shirts and long strides. Marion had completed a lovely white dress with a bright red sash for herself and had almost finished a new coat for Burton.

By nightfall, all would be in readiness to attend the New Year's Eve dance that was to be held at the Butter Factory.

For the family, this would be their very first New Year's Eve Dance as the last two that they could have gone to had been washed out by torrential rains.

Marion had been cornered by Maggie the manageress of the Lodge one day while she was in the Daintree Village buying supplies.

"Well, long time no see," said Maggie as she and Marion bumped into each other outside the butcher shop.

"Why, hello, Maggie. How are you?" said Marion politely.

"While I've got your attention are you aware of the up and coming New Year's Eve Dance here in Daintree?" asked Maggie with excitement in her voice.

"Only a few comments, you see we missed the last couple due to the weather," said Marion.

"Don't worry about rain this year because our long-range forecaster has promised a fine New Year's Eve. Now you must come and bring that delightful family of yours. The children have party games beginning at 6 o'clock. Then they will all come over to the Lodge and stay the night. We pop the girls in one room and the boys in the other and the parents collect them the next day. Parents have their dances from eight to late with the special 'Old Lang Syme' at midnight."

"That sounds all very exciting," said Marion, "I'll have to talk it over with Burton. He's a great dancer so I would expect he would love to attend."

Burton was rather impressed by the organization for the dance that Marion outlined to him.

He was pleased to hear that they had been invited

as he had not had a social night out with Marion since they arrived in the Daintree 32 months ago.

So all the excitement and sewing had finally come to a head and the family was dressed to the 'nines' and walking happily towards the crossing.

The sun was high in the sky and wouldn't be setting for another two hours.

They all piled into the flatties with Max being held firmly by Madeline for his safety.

As the jetty came into view Burt, who was rowing the lead flattie, could see the ferry tied up and lots of people moving around between the boat and the Butter Factory.

The boats were rowed onto the sand and Burton jumped out and pulled them higher.

All the others alighted onto the dry sand and began to walk up the slope towards the Butter Factory.

Other children and adults called out greetings and they called back.

The whole district seemed to here all decked out in their finest fashions.

"The treadlies must have been going faster than ours at home," thought Marion.

The Butter Factory had been cleared of all items that weren't bolted down and this gave a large cement floor in which to conduct games and dance. The ceiling was decorated with coloured crepe paper twisted and stuck to opposite walls. It was so colourful and cosy. Around the edge of the floor were lots of seats of varying sizes and shapes.

Maggie came bustling up in a flowing green gown tied at the waist with a black ribbon.

"I'm so glad you could make it Marion. Now all the children need to find a chair and sit down, as all children who are school age or younger have all the fun for the first few hours. Towards the end, we will serve them a supper and then they will be escorted across to the Lodge. I have hired babysitters to take care of them. All the oldies stay for the New Year's Eve Dance that starts at eight o'clock."

Marion pointed to the chairs and told Eva, Isobel, Keith to sit down.

She sat next to them and placed Max on her bulging tummy.

Lots of other mums and their children took up other seats and then Maggie got the fun underway.

For two hours it was full on with game after game, non-stop.

Everyone was encouraged to join in and everyone received a lolly for participating in each game.

Isobel loved the game of 'Poison Parcel' for which she won a small block of Cadbury's chocolate.

Eva was delighted with 'Musical Chairs' because she and Sheryl Walwork competed for the last chair.

It was declared a tie when they both fell over and up ended the chair. They both received a sweet, pink penny stick.

Keith found 'Blindman's Bluff' the game he liked as he pinned the ribbon closest to the donkey's tail and was given a licorice for his skill.

Max won the crawling race as he was the only boy available. He was pleased with his mint leaf lolly and spent nearly an hour sucking on it and trying to pry it off the roof of his mouth.

All in all it was a great evening and was beautifully rounded off when a procession of mums came into the Butter Factory carrying red frankfurts, with tooth picks stuck in them and with tomato sauce squeezed over them, fairy bread, sandwiches with various fillings, cupcakes with different coloured icing, bowls of fruit and bottles of lemonade.

They walked along the chairs offering the savouries first. Each child was allowed to pick one item to eat. A few minutes later the mums walked around with the savouries again.

This was repeated for savouries, sweets and fruit.

The children were asked to form a line and lemonade was distributed in glasses to each of them.

After a few minutes for the supper to settle all of them were marched across to the Lodging House and went to bed.

Now it was time for the parents and grown up children to have fun and dance the night away.

The band members organized themselves near the far wall; one had a piano accordion and the other a set of drums. The drummer kept the beat and made the clashes and bangs to get attention. The accordion player knew all the songs and played with gay abandon. They were a band that made your feet want to move and that's what everyone did until a minute to midnight.

The first dance was the Progressive Barn Dance in which Captain Osborne and his wife were asked to start dancing and when the music ceased they broke apart and selected a new partner each. It didn't take too many stops before the whole crowd was on the dance floor.

"Gentleman, take your partners for the…" came time and again from the Master of Ceremonies, Bryan Poole.

They danced the Quick Step, Pride of Erin, Gypsy Tap, Maxina, Veleta, Boston Two Step and Polka with a few dances repeated.

At a minute to midnight, the drummer did a ta da on his cymbals and the dances stopped and everyone looked expectedly towards Bryan Poole, who in turn was looking at his gold pocket watch.

He had his right hand in the air. At the exact moment that his watch showed midnight he slashed his hand down and everyone cheered and called, "Happy New year."

Burton turned to Marion and gave her a loving kiss on her lips and she blushed.

Ginger, who just happened to be dancing with Madeline, gave her a hug and a peck on her cheek.

She made an, "Ugh," sound and pretended to wipe the kiss off but secretly she was over the moon.

Lots of other partners were kissing and hugging each other.

The band then struck up with, 'Old Lang Syme' and everyone joined in. They didn't all know the words but that didn't matter they were having too much fun.

The next dance was announced as a medley so they were all aware that the dancing side of the festivities was fast coming to a close. They danced the Barn Dance, Fox Trot, Pride of Erin and finished the medley with a Waltz.

Bryan Poole stood up and made all the thank you speeches before wishing everyone a Happy New Year.

He then announced, "Supper will be served shortly. If you can all take a seat the ladies will set up the tables and bring in the food."

The supper was a feast and there was so much food left over the catering mum's organized a paper bag full of goodies for each family to take home.

Burton and Marion were cuddled up in the back of the flattie while Ginger tried to get as close to Madeline as he was able while at the same time keeping the rhythm of the oars.

In the following boat, Eva and Isobel sat chatting excitedly about the evening, while Burt pulled on the oars.

The walk from the crossing was under a full moon. "Let's hope the New Year brings us as much happiness as tonight has," said Burton.

Chapter 26

Rain, rain and more rain, it pelted down day after day.

Each morning everyone would wake up and get dressed in their waterproof clothes and trudge through the slush and mud to the temporary milking stalls.

The cows would be milling around mooing.

As soon as the gate was opened there would be a mad pushing as they crowded forward seeking the dry food in the feeders. It was not a job for the faint-hearted to push and shove them back beyond the gate and then try to let one through at a time.

The girls and Ginger would soon get into full swing milking. They would pour the bucket full of milk into the separator where Burt and Keith spun the handle and watched as the cream spun off into one can and the skim milk into another.

After all the cows had been milked they would all wander home ready for a hearty breakfast.

Burt would stay behind and wait for the launch to come and pick up the cream cans. Then, and only then, would he go home for his meal.

By the 26th of January, the rain gauge at the co-op had registered 53 inches and most of it remained sitting in the paddocks. From the verandah, the whole world looked awash with water flowing swiftly passed the barn, only two hundred yards away.

The next day dawned bright and clear.

"It's my birthday," said Ginger, "So it has to be a fine day. I ordered it last year so come on and let's enjoy the sunshine."

"I thought your birthday was the 5th January," said Madeline.

"Well yes, sort of, but this year I've changed it so we can enjoy the first fine day of the new year," said Ginger. "Being an orphan I never ever knew when my real birthday was anyway."

At lunch time Marion brought out a double layered sponge cake for Ginger's birthday. It had fluffy, cream all over it and eighteen candles flickered brightly.

"Happy birthday George," said Marion and she gave him a cuddle.

"Thanks, mum," he said. Marion smiled. He had started calling her mum because Burton had encouraged him to do so.

They all sang Happy Birthday with gusto and then lined up for a wedge of the delicious cake.

After, they went outside and played games in the slush.

It was fun watching others slip and slide and fall on

their bottoms as they tried to avoid being caught in a game of chasey.

When they had exhausted themselves they went to the verandah to play less energetic games.

All too soon the cry of, "Milking time," echoed through the house.

The sun continued to peep out for a few days before the drizzle and dampness returned.

They all got a fright when the telephone rang one evening and Barry Hayden informed Burton that there was a tropical cyclone forming out in the Coral Sea.

Burton called them all together to tell them the news and answer the myriad of questions that flowed.

He explained that cyclones or violent circling winds crashed into North Queensland every wet season.

The Daintree rarely was battered by these winds but every now and again they would hit the valley.

Barry Hayden had told him the last one was in 1921 and a lot of people on the coast and out in the sea perished.

It was expected that this cyclone would make landfall further south and apart from strong winds, a lot of rain and flooding the valley would be spared.

Burton warned them saying, "We need to be ready and it's a good preparation in case one does hit us hard one day."

Teams were picked and sent out to various areas around the house to batten down anything might take flight in a high wind. All loose things that could be stowed in sheds and under the house were to be put away.

Marion went about making sure there was fresh water in the house, food to last a week, all the lamps were full of kerosene and boxes of matches were in easy reach.

They all went to bed with reluctance and anticipation.

Isobel was awakened by the shrieking of the wind and the rattling of the bedroom window. She lay quietly trying to determine if this was the full cyclone or just the strong wind her father had talked about.

As usual, she let her mind wander and the next thing the roof and ceiling flew off and disappeared into the night. The wind was howling and the rain was pelting down but she was snug in bed watching trees and cows fly over her head. Then the walls started to fall in and peel off and blow away. She looked around the bedroom but her sisters weren't there. Their beds were missing and as she looked back at the sky she could see them flying upside down in their beds. She saw Madeline reach down and grab her shoulder…

"Wake up Isobel," said Madeline as she shook her awake, "You must be dreaming."

Isobel looked around and the room was normal.

She listened and outside it was still. "I thought we all got blown away in the cyclone. It was so scary."

A lamp illuminated the room and Burton was standing in the doorway. "The good news is the cyclone missed us, the bad news is, it's milking time. Up we all get, quick sticks."

Dampness was the order all the way through February but the rain did ease at times.

Madeline was patiently waiting for her sixteenth birthday on 22nd March.

She had asked her mother if she could have a boiled fruit cake smothered in whipped cream. As this was likely to take a long time to make Marion had declined to cook this. She noted the disappointment in Madeline's eyes so she telephoned the café and asked if it was possible to buy a fruit cake.

Annie Cockram, the owner, was only too willing to help.

She ordered one from Port Douglas Bakery and when it arrived Annie asked the launch driver to deliver it to the Johnson farm.

Madeline was so excited when she discovered that she had a birthday cake exactly as she had asked.

"You're a miracle maker mum, how did you do it?"

"My little secret my darling but Happy Birthday and may you have many more."

Unfortunately, it was a mother's wish that would not come true.

Marion was now in full bloom in her pregnancy. She was bulging way out and most of her clothes were no longer fitting.

Madeline and Ginger collaborated and made her two lovely maternity shifts. They were beautifully embroidered with roses and leaves.

On the 24th of March Marion made the announcement that she would be going to Port Douglas by ferry and would be away a while.

She left them all with instructions to cover her jobs and wished them well.

When Burton returned from seeing Marion off in the ferry he told them all that their mother was off on a holiday.

Rain again fell in earnest on the 30th March with 21 inches falling in four days.

Burton was becoming edgy what with his wife away and the constant rain and flooding it was enough to drive a man to distraction.

"Something needs to be done about the communication systems in the valley," he declared. "If no one else wants to lift a finger then I will."

Burton spent the next days, whenever he had a

spare moment, crouched over the kitchen table draw-ing and writing. Anyone who wandered near was politely shooed away.

At last the sun came out and stayed out.

Slowly the water receded back to the creek beds and the cows were moved to the bottom paddock.

Burton took a ride on Gypsy over to see Bill Hayden.

Bill Hayden and Burton took a ride to town to see Ted Hitch and Bryan Poole.

They spent hours in the saw mill office talking, ges-turing and writing.

A few days later signs went up and telephones began ringing. There was to be a meeting of all residents in the Butter Factory on Friday afternoon 3 pm sharp regard-ing roads and bridges into and out of the Daintree.

Burton had stirred up a hornets' nest and he was determined to get something done.

The number of the crowd was promising when Bur-ton appeared at the meeting.

At three o'clock Ted Hitch called them to order and explained the agenda.

He then handed over to Burton to outline what he saw as the problems and the solutions to the commu-nications within the valley.

"We must start up a petition to take to the Mossman Shire asking for a hearing of our communication concerns. This will mean selecting a committee to go to the Shire meeting. Please think hard and long if you want to be involved. It could take you from your jobs for several days."

Burton paused and unrolled a map of the district and stuck this with sticky tape onto the side of the wall.

"I apologize if you can't see this map from where you are seated but you can come forward later and examine it.

"I will happily answer your questions and concerns as will Bill Hayden, Ted Hitch and Bryan Poole.

"Every time we have the wet season or rain the whole valley shuts down. We need to be seeing an all-weather road from Mossman to here. The main sticking point other than money is the Barrett Creek Crossing. Even at high tide, the water is too deep to bring a machine across. A bridge that was 15 feet high joining the steep banks would solve this problem.

"A sealed road all the way from Mossman to the Daintree Village would allow us to move our butter, cream, pigs, cattle and other produce and our families."

"What about the Osbornes?" interrupted Bill Weinert, "Won't this put the ferries out of business?"

"That could possibly happen," agreed Burton, "But like everything else, we must move on or we will be stuck in a time warp forever."

"This is not good. Were the Osborne's invited to the meeting?" asked Bill Weinert.

"Everyone was invited. If the Osbornes aren't here then that should not stop us from pressing on," said Burton.

At this point, Bill Weinert left followed by five others.

"This was not supposed to be a divisive meeting but one where we all found common ground to help us move to a better future for our families and our farms," said Burton.

Ted Hitch stood up and tried to bring common sense to the meeting.

"I believe we should hear Burton out and then take all the information with us and to discuss it around the valley. We can then return later next week and make a decision as to the most sensible action to take."

Everyone in the meeting nodded their agreement to this.

Burton was allowed to continue uninterrupted.

"The next major concern is the junction of the Stewart and Douglas Creek. An all-weather road from the village along the track that borders the Stewart is essential. This road needs extending up over the Bump as well as along the Douglas past the Hayden farm. A bridge over the Stewart just below the Douglas would open these areas.

"Next is an upgrade of the telephone lines right

through the district. Most of us have single lines on poles and trees that easily get broken and we can be cut off for weeks."

"So to summarize," said Ted Hitch, "We need a petition signed by everyone, a committee to meet with the shire, upgrade of roads and bridges and permanent telephone system. Thank you, gentlemen, for your time. Our next meeting will be Friday 3 o'clock."

"I don't think that went all that well," said Burton as the meeting broke up.

"Don't worry yourself too much; many of these fellows need time to digest new ideas and things. Let's see what happens next week. In the interim I think we need to get the Osbornes on side," consoled Ted Hitch.

Burton was not his normal self over the next week. He was withdrawn and in a daydream. Whenever anyone spoke to him they had to repeat the question or be satisfied with an answer that was not remotely to do with their query.

For Burton, it was a week of trying to find a solid argument to commit the Osborne brothers that change was coming and that they were perfectly placed to take advantage of it.

Ted Hitch, Barry Hayden and Burton rowed over to see Captain Chas Osborne, Eric Osborne and Dan Osborne on the evening before they were going to have the second public meeting.

They envisage it being a tough get together as they were asking the men to throw away all they have worked for and start over.

Chas was the natural leader and he was also the one to take careful heed of anything that might be worth listening to.

Unlike most men, he was a good listener and saw the sense in ideas far quicker than his brothers.

The Osborne boys had built up the ferry to move people and produce in and out of the Daintree, they had shares in the Butter Factory and the saw mill and of course, they each owned a dairy farm. So whatever happened in the valley would affect them.

Burton, as the leader of the deputation, put the case to the brothers just as he had at the meeting last week. There were several interjections from Dan and Eric but Chas hushed them and allowed Burton to continue.

At the end of Burton's speech, Chas said, "This plan will hurt us a lot. We have worked long and hard to develop the industries we run. We will need to think long and hard. Maybe I should have let the croc take you when I first met you down at the entrance instead of feeding it a chicken."

That comment deflated Burton as he took it that the arguments that had been put were lost and that the meeting was turning personal.

"I think you should think about how you can take advantage of the changes that are coming, and mark my word it will happen either through our own pushing or from the outside. There's already a demand from the Mossman Sugar Refinery for the Daintree to grow sugar and have a tramway built. Just that change will impact on us all and you fellows more so," said Burton.

Suddenly Chas changed tact, "I must say, Burton, you are one hell of a thinker. Let me ask you what you would do if you were one of the Osbornes?"

"It's not for me to tell you your business but as you asked I would sit down with the other brothers and see how to take advantage of the changes," he said.

"If there were no ferry customers what would we do, if there was a road opened to Mossman how could we take commercial advantage of that, if the sugar industry took off what could we do to be part of it, if the roads to Stewart and Douglas Creeks were all weather what would that mean to us?" suggested Burton.

He stopped talking and looked at his companions, "I think we need to leave you to discuss what we have told you. There's the meeting tomorrow at 3 o'clock, we'd love to have you all on board."

Ted Hitch, Barry Hayden and Burton left the Osbornes sitting in the lounge silently looking at each other.

Chapter 27

The Butter Factory was packed and Burton was rather pleased. He spied a five gallon keg of beer sitting in a corner and thought, "Well done Ted Hitch but I hope that is not the only thing that has attracted everyone to the meeting."

Ted Hitch called for quiet and went over the agenda. He pointed out that there was a petition on the table and anyone who hadn't signed it as yet to do so before leaving.

He then handed over to Burton.

Burton stood and surveyed the faces searching for the Osborne boys but alas they had not shown up.

He began to tell those in attendance that the valley had to change and in doing so it would become more prosperous and the farmers in the valley would benefit immensely.

He was interrupted by the hooves of a fast galloping horse that reined up almost inside the Butter Factory doorway.

Lucas-Hughes dismounted and walked purposely to the front of the crowd.

He turned around and said, "Sorry to barge in Burton but I have been riding hard to be here from Bloomfield."

He turned to the gathering and said, "I want to support Burton and plead with you all to sign the petition and start showing a community spirit by forming parties to clear roads, build bridges, fix the telephone poles and lines. Seek support and money from the Shire. I will offer to find funding for you from my own enterprises, the Butter Factory and the saw mill. All in together we can change the Daintree for the better, and gentlemen your wives and children will love you even more."

To the sounds of laughter, he sat down.

Burton stood looking around at the laughing crowd and thought, "What else can I add to that. Lucas-Hughes sure knows how to draw a crowd."

The meeting should have ceased at this point and everyone invited to a drink or two from the keg but there was another interruption. This time the Osborne brothers walked purposely into the Butter Factory.

Eric and Dan stood at the back while Chas moved forward directing his steely gaze at Burton.

Burton was alarmed at the new entry and was caught between the dying laughter of the crowd and what he saw as a threat to his physical being.

Burton stood nearly six foot and was muscular from all the timber cutting and other outdoor labour. He was, a pacifist and hated fights or fighting. Chas advanced all too quickly and then stopped a yard from Burton and eyeballed him.

The entire room had gone stony silent and all wondered what would happen next.

To their utter surprise, Chas extended an open hand to Burton, who automatically returned the gesture.

Chas shook Burton's hand and said, "You are one hell of a thinker Burton."

Chas Osborne turned to the meeting and said, "My brothers and I have listened to the arguments and ideas put forward and we can see so many opportunities staring at us. We can see a changed Daintree that will flourish into the future. We believe we should send a deputation to the next Shire meeting and take a fully signed petition. I wish to nominate as one of the committee members."

In the early hours of the morning on the 10th April the telephone rang. It shrilled through the house on the three short and one long ring repeated until a member of the Johnson household answered it. This was scary to most of the children who had jumped out of bed. Telephone calls this late meant trouble, accidents and even deaths.

Burton finally lifted the receiver and shakily said, "Burton Johnson speaking."

"Mr Johnson," said the stern female voice on the other end, "You have a baby girl and your wife is fine. Good night."

Burton burst out cheering while he replaced the

receiver and then he grabbed Madeline and began to waltz her around the kitchen table. "Mum's had a baby sister for you all and she's doing fine. Yippee."

That was the end of sleep for the night and the beginning of celebrations.

The only one who didn't stir even as the celebrations got louder was Max. He slept on until Eva remembered him and tiptoed into tell him the good news.

Max rubbed his eyes, sat up and tried to take the news in.

Then he said quietly, "I'm not baby no more."

Most of May was turning out to be delightful. The days were sunny with pleasant breezes blowing but the grass underfoot continued to be soggy.

The double eyed fig parrots swarmed into the native fig trees devouring the little figs that grew in abundance.

The timber cutters had left these trees standing as they were of no commercial value. The farmers on the Johnson block had also decided to leave three of them for shade.

One was near the pigsty, another at the back of the wood heap and a further one over the Hayden crossing on the other side of the Douglas Creek.

The children liked to take picnics under these when the weather was warm.

They would seek out Marion and ask if she would make them a picnic basket and then they would invite Marion and Burton and off they'd go to sit under one of these lovely big trees.

The orchard had been expanded and was growing an assortment of fruits.

Fruit salad and whipped cream were a favourite all year round with the fruits changing with the seasons.

Burt had even introduced watermelon and rock-melon into one corner of the orchard.

So along with figs, mango, pawpaw, bananas, passionfruit and oranges they were kept very happy in fruit.

Marion had been given a recipe for lemonade by Sally Hayden, so that's where all the lemons went.

One day Ginger had ventured into Mossman to watch the pig sales. He had been pleased with the prices they got and while waiting to go back home he had gone for a walk.

Along the road, he saw a man tending to a dozen or more pineapple plants.

Being gregarious he called out a greeting. The elderly man came over for a chin wag and Ginger asked how he managed to grow pineapples.

"Son," said the old fellow, "These are the easiest of all plants as long as you got good soil and live in the tropics. Where are you hailing from?"

"Daintree River, sir," he replied politely.

"Then you can grow pineapples as easy as pie. You take this here pineapple that is ripe and you cut it off leaving leaves at the base. When you cut it up to eat it, leave about an inch of the flesh at the bottom. Plant these in your garden and within months you will have a pineapple growing that will have several off shoots where another pineapple will form. Take a while before they are ready to eat but worthwhile. Here take this one home. If you want more call into the fruit and vegetable shop in town."

Ginger located the shop in town and bought another dozen pineapples.

The children had pineapple and cream for three days and Ginger started the pineapple portion of the orchard.

Easter was another win for Burton.

Marion was still away on her holiday and all reports coming through indicated the new baby was prospering.

Burton insisted on the telling the Easter story of Jesus being nailed to the cross and then rising again as Marion would have wanted.

Everyone went to bed at the normal time of seven thirty and they were all soon in a deep exhausted sleep.

Burton stayed awake and then went into the main bedroom and found a tin of baby powder. He then snuck into the boys' bedroom and placed his bare foot at the entry. He sprinkled powder all around his foot then stepped forward. At each step, he left a clear print surrounded by white powder. He continued to do this until he had tracks to each boy's bed. He placed a chocolate Easter egg under each of their pillows.

He backed out carefully ensuring he didn't mess up the footprints.

Next, he carried out the same idea in the girls' bedroom.

He then went to bed and slept soundly.

At four thirty in the morning, there were excited yells and screams from all over the house.

"The Easter Bunny has been," called Eva, "And he's left a chocolate egg for each of us."

At that point, she stuffed the chocolate in her mouth and that stopped her saying anymore.

"I knew he was true," said Isobel as she began to use her nails to tear off the pretty red wrapping of her chocolate egg.

"Come along you lot it's time to get the milking done." said Burton.

They all strode down the steps and off towards the barn.

Burton hesitated at the top of the steps and called out, "Be a while I need to telephone your mum and sister to make sure they're alright."

Burton turned away and walked back inside but went passed the kitchen where the telephone was.

He instead headed for the main bedroom where he bent down and pulled from underneath a cardboard box. He opened the box and inside were lots of small chocolate Easter eggs.

Burton hid the eggs inside the house and outside. He was going to give the children their very first Easter egg hunt.

The milking was going with its usual efficiency by the time Burton arrived.

Burt was on the separator with Keith, Ginger was milking, Madeline and Isobel were just finishing their last cows and Eva was amusing Max by getting his little hands and squeezing the cows teats. Max squealed with delight whenever a stream of milk shot out into the bucket.

"Come on let's get this all finished and then we'll have breakfast. Burt you can wait until after breakfast to take the cream into the factory,' said Burton.

Burt was rather surprised at his father's direction as it was normally imperative that the cream gets rushed to the Butter Factory as it could easily spoil. He didn't question his father but continued to whirl the handle of the separator.

After breakfast and the washing up, drying and putting away were completed Burton took them all out on to the verandah.

They all knew he was up to his secrets but no one guessed what this one was going to be.

"Now," said Burton, "Today is Easter Sunday and you've all been visited by the Easter Bunny so it's my turn to surprise you. I have hidden a number of chocolate Easter eggs inside and outside of the house. All you have to do is find them and eat them. Remember you also must share one egg with each of the others as your Easter Gift to them. Away you go."

With squeals of delight, they scattered in all directions. Eva and Madeline made for inside the house while Ginger and Burton took off down the steps to hunt in the garden. Isobel ran to the back door and looked near the wood heap. Burton took Keith and Max by their hands and encouraged them to look where he pointed on the verandah.

There were whoops of joy as each child found an egg.

The hunt continued for over half an hour before Burton called a halt.

"Was that enjoyable?" he asked once they had all assembled on the verandah.

"Yes thanks, dad," said Madeline, "I can't wait to tell mum."

"Talking about mum," said Isobel, "When is she coming home, and what's the new baby's name."

Burton tapped his nose as if holding a secret and said, "Don't tell but mum is due home on Thursday and your new sister going to be christened Mary Elizabeth."

"Molly!" blurted out Isobel, "That's the nickname they give girls who are named Mary."

And so Molly it was and Molly it would be forever.

It was June 4th and Max was kneeling up on his chair, and he knew he shouldn't, but it was the only way he could reach to blow out the three candles on his birthday cake. He took a deep breath and blew until his little face went from red to a bluish tinge.

"Stop and breathe," said Marion who was nursing Molly. "You'll never be able to eat your slice if you conk out on us."

Everyone began to sing Happy Birthday and the loud noise caused Molly to start crying. She had been a beautiful sight to them all when mum finally brought her home. She lay all bundled up in a white rug and you could barely see her little screwed up face.

"Isn't she so cute," said Madeline sounding all clucky.

Eva was into the mothering role almost immediately saying, "Can I have a nurse mum?"

Marion carefully held the baby's neck and handed her to Eva.

Molly made sucking noises and Eva said, "Does she need another feed, mum."

"She's certainly a big eater I can tell you that. She also has a strong sucking action. But no she has just had plenty of milk."

Isobel looked down at the baby and noted, "She's

got dad's red hair."

"Yes that's true," agreed Marion, "But it's very fine so I think it will go light brown with a tinge of red as she gets older."

All this baby talk was too much for Burt and Ginger so they nodded at each other suggesting they go and find jobs outside.

"Happy birthday, Maxy boy," said Ginger as he and Burt scurried off.

The birthdays seemed to come at regular intervals as Isobel had her eleventh next. Her special day fell on the 26th June and then Burt celebrated his fifteenth on the 17th July. Eva followed with her thirteenth falling on the 4th August.

The one constant throughout these birthdays was the weather. It was glorious; warm, blue skies and gentle cooling breezes in the afternoons.

Perfect to go outside and play games and have fun.

During the days when there wasn't a birthday, there were outings to the swimming hole or picnics under the wild fig trees. Life couldn't have been better for the Johnson family.

Burton had finally attended the Mossman Shire meeting and heard all sorts of excuses for not helping the Daintree residents with their demands.

In the end, the delegation did get an okay to at least start improving their own conditions.

They were also encouraged to write submissions to the council and this might then result in money being allocated for projects.

At the next community meeting in the Butter Factory, the delegation that had ventured to Mossman outlined what had occurred.

The general feeling was one of disappointment until Burton pointed out that self-help was often a better motivator than outside offers.

It was agreed that working parties would be allocated to three areas. Burton would take charge of the Stewart and Douglas Creek, Chas Osborne would gather the forces for the Daintree River and village and Jas Cobb would muster those around and opposite the Barrett Creek. The leaders were to be in touch with each other so that men could be added to any major job from another area.

The first job Burton put his group on was the Stewart Creek Road.

Up until now, it was virtually the walking track that Marion and the children had traipsed along back in 1926 when they first arrived. Burton wanted it turned into an all-weather road capable of allowing lorries to use it.

Clearing began in earnest on the Stewart Creek Road in September but unfortunately with milking and scores of other jobs to be done the progress was painfully slow.

Life was good for the Johnsons and they were happy with Ginger and the seven children that they now had. They would sit on the verandah and look contentedly across the fields and see the progress they had made in such a short time. Nothing could shatter their bliss, or so they thought.

Chapter 28

Twelve thousand miles away an economic tsunami was about to shatter the lives of millions throughout the world. Would it crush the Johnsons and put an end to their Daintree lives? Only time would tell.

October 1929 saw the epi centre of an economic tsunami rock the New York Stock Exchange. The wave sped across America in one direction and across the Atlantic Ocean in the other. It was so overwhelming that everyone and everything were affected.

The wave continued on through Europe and Asia while the other way it raced across the Pacific Ocean. Nothing was left untouched.

The world slumped into the worst Depression it had ever known. People lost savings, they lost jobs, marriages broke up and families were torn apart. Money was scarce and those on the land found that they couldn't market their produce for a fair price.

Men began to pack swags and take to the roads and bush tracks searching for food and jobs. It was a dark time for all.

The Johnsons continued their daily routines completely oblivious as to what was happening in the outside world.

The first warning sign came when Burt returned from delivering the cream and handed his father £2 10/- which was 5 shillings less than normal.

Burton was quick to ask, "Where's the rest of the money?"

Burt replied, "Mr Poole said to tell you that there is a problem with the butter market and he has to cut the cream price to one shilling."

"That's a lot of money to lose in one hit, I'll have to ask Bryan what the problem is," said Burton.

He didn't have to wait long before the telephone rang. It was Barry Hayden, "Have you heard the news Burton?" he asked.

"About the cut in the price of cream, yes and I'm not happy," said Burton.

"No, worse than that, apparently the New York Stock Exchange has collapsed and we are all going to suffer. The rich are now poorer and they can't keep the industries going, the banks have had a run on their money and are almost broke, produce can't sell because no one has any money to buy food and the employed are being put off. The world's a mess," said Barry Hayden.

Burton was sure he could hear Barry sobbing in between the sentences.

"What's this all mean for us?" asked Burton but the line had gone dead.

Burton gathered the family in the lounge room and tried to explain what had happened.

"It appears that the downward trend of the stock exchange and the economies of the world will be with us for a while. That will mean less money for our cream, eggs and pigs. What we need to do is become totally self-sufficient. That means eating things that we grow or raise and make sure we replenish the supplies as we use them. It will mean no more special days like Guy Fawkes Night, Christmas, Easter, birthdays and so on. Don't look so disappointed I'm hoping this will pass and we'll be back to normal within the year."

Burton took himself off to the main bedroom to do calculations.

He had savings in the Port Douglas Commonwealth Bank so that would see them through. He believed the Australian Government would back the Commonwealth Bank in a crisis like this one.

He figured out that he could come down to six pence a gallon for his cream and break even. After that, the farm was in the hands of God.

Bryan Poole called a meeting to explain how the Butter Factory would function during this unprecedented situation.

He also told them that the price of their cream would fluctuate but the positive for the valley was the fact that it could produce at high levels all year round. This gave them an advantage over areas further south where the dry summers would reduce the output to almost zero. This could jeopardize the factories chances of remaining viable. That would be unlikely to happen in the Daintree.

The dry period had been extended across June and into October and many of the farmers were becoming anxious.

As if their prayers were heard, and answered, there was steady rain on 17th and 18th of October. The official amount was 17 inches and that refreshed everything and had the streams flowing once again.

Guy Fawkes Night came and went and no one said anything.

The School Sport's Day loomed as the end of the school year snuck closer. Isobel and Keith were the athletes and they were getting more and more excited as the big day came near.

At school, there were the challenges between the older boys.

The girls were content to talk about their families and what they might do in the holidays.

On the sand track by the river, Isobel managed a second

in her race and combined with Sheryl Walwork to win the three-legged race.

Keith showed his prowess in sprinting by winning the 'Bubs' race comfortably. He also combined with Burton and Marion to win the rowing race across the Daintree.

Isobel went home happy with her threepence and Keith proudly showed off his sixpence and threepence to the family members who had not attended the races.

Christmas came silently and went silently as did the New Year's Eve dance and the New Year.

Everyone was trying to remain positive and austere.

The Great Depression was not only having an economic impact but a psychological one as well.

The weather didn't help although by now the Johnsons had come to expect January to the end of March would be wet. The flooding was not as bad as previous years and that in itself was a blessing.

Mr Clancy welcomed everyone back to school as the 1930 school year began.

He was in his second year and had gained a lot of confidence in his ability to teach and run a school.

As he grew in confidence he also grew in ambition.

He was determined to show the Inspector that he was promotion material and by the end of the year he would be headmaster of a larger school in a better location.

The star pupil at Daintree School number 1027 was

Isobel Johnson so she had to be nurtured along and made ready for the scholarship at the end of the year.

Her results would be his passport to his promotion.

The other important part of the plan was to ensure the other students were well behaved and well trained.

They chanted their time's tables as they entered the room at every break, they wrote out the spelling words ten times each and if they made an error in their list tests they would write the word 100 times.

Every day they needed to read to their partner out loud from the reader. Whole class reading was essential for improving fluency and accuracy. So each child would be required to stand and read out loud while the others listened or followed. Each year level, of course, would read the material at their age level.

Mr Clancy was a stickler for homework and plenty of sums were sent home on worksheets as well as lists of spelling words to be learned off by heart.

During the third week of school in February, Mr Clancy chanced upon a clever idea that would put him front and centre in the Inspector's eyes.

He knew that Mr Woodside, the senior member of the Queensland Education Department and Inspector of Schools, had pet likes and dislikes.

One of these was poetry and according to the

grapevine, he had a soft spot for 'The Highwayman' by Alfred Noyes.

The important thing was to make sure that the whole class was involved and that sound effects were used in the appropriate places.

Mr Clancy formed a plan that involved Isobel Johnson reciting the poem. Lou Fischer, one of the year 7 boys making the sound effects and the whole class joining in the refrain.

He had until October to get this ready and Isobel was very clever so she should be able to do a fantastic job.

"I have an interesting idea that I would like you all to help me with," Mr Clancy addressed the class. "There is an exciting poem that I want you all to learn so that we can put it on as a play in front of all your parents. We could dress you up as characters, it should be fun. Now the poem is called 'The Highwayman' and it was written by Alfred Noyes. It is about a highwayman who is like an Australian bushranger except lived in England and held up and robbed rich people.

"The highwayman has a girlfriend called Bess, who works in an inn or hotel. One night he visits her but there is another man called Tim who wants the lady's heart and he becomes very jealous. He hears them planning to run away together on the next night. The jealous man alerts the Red Coats who are soldiers that hunt down highwaymen. The soldiers come to the hotel and tie Bess up with a musket or gun pointing at her heart. When the highwayman comes riding to the hotel the next night, Bess warns him in a tragic way. Here let me read you the poem."

And so began the special lessons that were to culminate in Inspector Woodside listening to his favourite poem being recited by the Daintree School students.

Isobel was delighted to be asked to be the narrator while various others were allocated the roles of the highwayman, Tim the ostler, Bess, the inn keeper and redcoats. Those left over were to support Isobel by reciting the refrain.

The wet season seemed to go on forever and the dense cloud cover made the valley appear to be in darkness.

The routines continued unabated from before dawn to past sunset.

The veil of grey finally lifted in mid-March and the overflowing creeks abated, the grass and ground dried out and a semblance of normalcy returned.

Burton had continued to think about ways to keep the farm viable during this Depression that was causing so much angst everywhere.

Chapter 29

One morning, as Burton, was walking to the barn to start milking he, heard grunting and squealing coming from the vegetable patch. He ran towards the noise to find a number of wild pigs trying to crash through the vegetable patch fence. He yelled at them and threw sticks that were lying around. Reluctantly they made off.

Burton turned away to continue on to the barn, when it struck him, "Pork and cheap, at that! We could organize pig traps of vegetables and fruit that would entice the wild pigs to come out of the rainforest to forage. If we had a hide we could shoot them and hey presto, ham for a month."

Ginger and Burt were all ears as Burton explained his idea. "We build say four hides around the farm but near to the forested areas and then lay out food scraps. The pigs come down and we shoot them. All I need to do is teach you both how to use the Lee-Enfield 303 so that whoever is on watch can shoot accurately. Of course, you'll need to learn fast as we can't afford too many practice bullets."

Within a week Burton and the youths had selected four sites where they thought the pigs would appear to eat the scraps from the kitchen.

They dug out a fox hole and covered this with branches to camouflage the shooter's position.

They began shooting lessons as well as safety lessons on how to use a Lee-Enfield 303.

"The rifle belonged to your Uncle Jack and when he returned from the fields of France after the First World War he brought it with him. He gave it to me as a going away present and said that I would need it more than he did. He believed that where I was going sounded mighty dangerous. He threw in 100 rounds of ammunition for good measure."

The shooting practice took place after milking each day.

Burton took the boys to the back of the high paddock and here pinned a target on a tree at the edge of the rainforest.

The target was a drawing of a pig or closer to a piglet as it was small.

He had commandeered Isobel to use her drawing skills and her coloured pencils to make it easier to see.

In her helpful way, she had even printed very neatly Porky as the pig's name.

Ginger proved he had not lost any of the skill he had shown on the wild pig hunt when he shot the weaner.

Burt took longer to learn to use the bolt action to

load the bullets in the chamber.

He found the nine pound weight of the Lee-Enfield to be difficult to hold. Burton encouraged him to rest the huge rifle on a log then push it against his shoulder.

The kick or recoil and the ear-splitting noise as the bullet exploded were things they never got used to.

Burton slid the sights to 40 yards and this was the exact distance they had used when setting up the hides and the sticks where the fruit and vegetable scraps would be laid out.

Burt used up 23 bullets before he finally scored his first 'Porky'.

Burton was satisfied that they were ready to go hunting.

He explained that each would take a day and that they would go directly to the pig hide and not to milking on the day that it was their turn.

Burt was to take the first shift the next morning.

While the rest of the family headed to the barn, Burt grabbed a lantern and the bucket of food scraps and trudged off for the pig hide down near the crossing.

He had the Lee-Enfield slung across his left shoulder and ten bullets in his coat pocket.

As a safety precaution' Burton had insisted that the gun would only be loaded in the hide, it was never to be loaded while being carried and to ensure this was the case the bolt had to be removed and carried in a pocket.

When Burt reached the pig hide he selected a log to lean the rifle on and then proceeded 40 yards further where he found the sticks they had left the day before yesterday.

He took the food scraps out and stuck a rotting rockmelon and a swede onto two of the sticks. This would give the pigs something to see as well as smell. The other pieces from the bucket were scattered around.

He moved off back to the hide to await the pigs.

For a week the three hunters kept up their vigils, swapping from one hide to the next but without even hearing a grunt.

On the eighth night it was Ginger who strode off in the opposite direction to the rest of the family.

As he passed Madeline he whispered, "I'll bring home the bacon this morning just for you."

Madeline slapped him on the shoulder and blushed, saying, "Be careful with that gun."

Ginger did not take long to construct the trap of food stuff and settle back in the hide and made himself comfortable.

It was becoming a waste of time and the only sensible thing to be gained was a couple of hours sleep.

He awoke with a start and fumbled for the gun. He

thought he'd heard the sound of a herd of wild pigs. He wiped his eyes and peered out into the growing light.

Some fifty yards ahead was a movement, in fact, lots of movement. The herd of pigs was advancing quickly on the food scraps.

Shaking like a leaf in excitement and anticipation, Ginger reached into his pocket for a bullet. He quickly placed this into the chamber and slid the bolt forward then down to lock it in position. He looked through the closest sight and then lined this up with the foresight. He could see the biggest pig now directly in the sights.

He knew the power of these guns so even if he didn't get a head hit the bullet would do a lot of damage and the pig would be his.

He squeezed the trigger and heard the ear-splitting noise reverberating around the hills. He heard the scream of a pig and the squeals of the herd as they raced away to the safety of the rainforest.

Ginger left the gun on the log and sprinted hard towards the place where he thought the downed pig was laying.

He searched around but there was nothing.

He had lost the opportunity to go home a hero.

He was furious with himself when he heard a noise at the edge of the tree line. He walked cautiously forward and found a weaner lying on its side and there a few feet ahead was the huge boar that he had fired at.

Talk about going from zero to hero he had brought down two pigs and one was over 200 pound in weight.

The Johnsons and Haydens feasted on pork and ham for the next month.

Burton was so pleased that Ginger had shot the pigs and that this idea had been successful.

He suggested a week layoff to let the pigs settle after their scare before the next round of pig hunting would begin.

Marion was going through difficult times and spent time lying in bed until after the sun had come up. Madeline whispered her belief, "Mum's pregnant again."

Eva decided that Madeline was the expert in these matters but she couldn't believe that her mother and father would have any more children especially considering the socio-economic mess the world was in.

Another mouth to feed would add further pressure on the family and the budget.

Isobel knew that direct action was the only way to get to the bottom of situations so she marched into the main bedroom one morning after breakfast and said, "When's the baby due mum?"

Marion, who was used to her third daughter's directness and confidence, didn't batter an eyelid as she replied, "September my dear. The way I feel at the moment it might be more than one."

Twins," said Isobel and placed her hand over her mouth.

"I will have to go on my holiday in September," said Marion, then added, "I was a twin and I have twin sisters as well so they do run in the family. Of course, your father is from a very small family. He had a sister and a brother whereas my mum had 15 of us."

"Gosh, 15, that's a lot of children to bring up. Who was your twin?" asked Isobel.

"Your Uncle Hersee is my twin but you were too small to remember him. One day we'll all go visit grandmother Mary Jane back at Bray's Creek and I'll introduce you all to my brothers and sisters," said Marion.

Isobel dug deep in her mind as she tried to remember something that her father had mentioned some time ago. It had to do with his brother or sister and dad was going to tell them the story.

"Mum, are dad's sister and brother still alive? Can we go and visit then too?" asked Isobel.

"I know Aunty Ruby is alive but you will need to ask your father about Uncle Keith as he is the keeper of the story."

Satisfied that she had got all the information she needed Isobel ran off searching for the other girls. "Guess what I know?" she boasted to Madeline and Eva.

"What's that?" asked Burt as he walked into the room where the girls were sitting.

"Don't forget me too," said Ginger as he came in after Burt.

"Mum's pregnant and she's going to have the baby in September," confided Isobel.

She didn't tell them about the possibility of twins that was too much to believe.

Chapter 30

April weather proved to be glorious and the family was relieved to feel so much warmth drying the coolness from their bodies.

The mustiness throughout the house slowly dried away.

Chores became more engaging and even challenging.

Molly's first birthday was celebrated on the tenth of April.

Burton had said that it was only fair that the family give her a proper birthday as she had never experienced one before.

Marion baked a chocolate cake and iced it with fluffy, white, whipped cream. She decorated it by placing crushed chocolate as a number one followed by an S and a T. A pink candle was stuck in the centre of the chocolate number one.

Molly was squealing with excitement when Marion brought the cake in and the family sang Happy Birthday to her.

She had great difficulty blowing out the candle until Eva came to her aid.

When the first piece of cake was put in front of

her, Molly squeezed her hand into the cream and put the mess into her mouth. Between swallows, she kept saying, "Ta, ta, nice."

Max's fourth birthday came and went as did Isobel's 12th.

It was disappointing but they all knew how serious the economic situation had become. Burton had emphasized time and again that they had to be very careful about the budget.

Anything that was remotely a luxury was not to be entertained.

July and August were pretty months weatherwise although they did get days of drizzle. Burton was pleased with the rain. This to him would mean replenishing the water supplies and freshening up the grasses.

Birthdays for Burt, who turned 16, and Eva, who was now 14, flashed by.

Burton was especially pleased to see that the number of bees humming around the orchard and the vegetable patch. The ones across the fields were inestimable.

As a lesson, he had taken the family on a picnic to the old fig tree beyond the wood heap. Here he had shown them how the bees came into a flower and walked all over it gathering pollen on their bodies and wings. He explained that they were also using their long thin tongues to sip up the nectar from the plant.

They watched as one bee flew off carrying tiny spots of yellow pollen on itself. It hovered over another flower nearby then flew down on to it. Here it began once again to get pollen and nectar. The pollen from the first flower was soon mixed with the second flower's pollen.

Burton explained, "By mixing the pollens this will result in seeds being made that will then grow into plants. Many plants reproduce like this. Other plants of course, can be grown from tubers like potatoes and bulbs like lilies. Several others you can grow from cuttings but most reproduce from cross-pollination."

"So bees are important dad?" asked Isobel.

"Yes they are very important to the plant world. So we must never kill bees," he concluded.

"Where does honey come from then?" queried Keith.

"Good question, son. Bees take the nectar back to their hive which will be in a tree nearby. Here they deposit the nectar for other bees to use it to feed the Queen Bee. If you get this runny liquid out of the honeycomb before it is used then you can make honey for eating," Burton explained.

The picnic and science lesson was not the highlight of that week. Another incident happened that amazed all the family.

It was a dark, cloudy night and the humidity was touching 95% so they had all wandered out onto the verandah hoping to find a breath of air.

The clouds were scudding across the sky and every now and again a gap would expose the moon.

The moon was in its waxing or waning phase which made it look like an old sailing ship, a windjammer.

Isobel had been helping in the kitchen with cleaning up the dirty dishes so she was late arriving on the verandah.

She stood for a while looking up at the sky and noting the phase of the moon and the movement of the clouds. Suddenly she broke into a recital of 'The Highwayman'.

"The moon was a ghostly galleon tossed upon stormy seas…"

When Isobel had finished all those present remained motionless.

Burton was the first to break the silence, "That was so beautiful the way you recited that poem. You've brought tears to my eyes. How did you ever remember such a long and complicated poem?"

Isobel proudly told them all about the concert that the school would be putting on for the parents later in the year and how Mr Clancy had chosen her for the narrator part.

She also told them how she had practised and practised until she knew the poem off by heart.

"Tonight, when I looked at the moon it really did look like a ghostly ship riding huge waves on the ocean. Now I can see why Mr Noyes, the poet, was so taken that he began the poem with those words."

"Ugh," said Madeline, "I wouldn't shoot myself to warn my boyfriend that he was going to get caught by the Red Coats."

"Yes you would," said Ginger, "If you really loved him." He winked at her.

Eva couldn't stay out so she added, "You haven't got a boyfriend anyway so you don't know how you would react."

"Haven't I?" teased Madeline and she again looked in the direction of Ginger. Ginger turned away and lent on the verandah railing. He could see that this little spat would develop into a fight and he didn't want the girls arguing.

"Well it looks like bed time to me and silence is a great way to get to sleep," interrupted Burton.

They all knew what the message was especially the antagonists.

They all moved quickly and quietly to their beds.

Burton came into the kitchen where Marion was

organizing places for breakfast in the morning.

"You missed special night," he said.

"Please tell me what happened." said Marion.

"I think we have a little romance springing forth between Ginger and Madeline but there is an extra in the mix. Seems Eva has her thoughts on the boy as well. It must be the red hair. It seems to do wonderful things to the girls." He smiled broadly and ran his fingers through his own red hair.

"You could be right about that my Burton, now for the second revelation?"

"Isobel recited a poem about a Highwayman and it was the most beautiful thing I have ever heard. She is one clever girl. Apparently, they are going to put it on as a school play for parents later in the year."

The diversity of flora and fauna in the valley did not intrigue the family until late in 1930.

They certainly knew about crocodiles and the need to be always on the lookout and they knew about the deadly poisonous snakes that slithered around or rested in trees.

They were acutely knowledgeable about the wild pigs that frequented their vegetable patch and the orchard. They saw and heard a number of birds but these never had a name nor were they readily discussed.

The family had heard about the strange cassowary that was supposed to roam all through the rainforest foraging for nuts but no one had seen nor heard one.

What started the family on their nature study path was not the bee lessons nor the sunbirds that nested in the barn but the Musk Kangaroo Rat.

One cool October morning they were walking back from milking when an animal bounded across their path and disappeared into the grass.

"What was that?" asked Eva.

"A kangaroo," said Madeline.

"No it was too small for a kangaroo and anyway it's in the grass so it can't be too big," said Eva.

"What about a tree kangaroo?" said Ginger trying to be helpful. "They are found in the trees throughout the rainforest of North Queensland."

"Aren't they a reddish-brown colour and live in trees where they hop from branch to branch? Why would one be this far from the protection of the thick scrub?" said Burt.

The conversation continued all the way to the house and throughout breakfast.

"I'm off to school," said Isobel. "Come on Keith or we'll be late and you know what that can mean?"

"Yeh," said Keith, "Lines and more lines and then spelling lists. You'd think Clancy would find a less boring way to deal with lateness."

"That's enough of that talk," scolded Marion. "It is Mr Clancy, he is your teacher and you will respect him no matter what. If we hear any more of that kind of talk I will repeat it to your father."

Keith fled from the room, grabbed his school bag and continued down the steps heading for the crossing.

Isobel turned to her mother and said, "Don't worry about Keith mum he rarely gets into trouble. He actually likes school now and I can help him."

As she went to leave and catch up to Keith she said to the others, "I'll search the encyclopaedias at school and see if I can find out what animal nearly bowled us over this morning."

With that she dashed from the house and set out after Keith who was already half way to the flatties.

Isobel searched long and hard in the encyclopaedias that Mr Clancy had near his table. She even asked him if he knew but he showed little interest so she continued her own research.

The strange little animal would continue to crop up in conversations but no one really knew what it was.

Chapter 31

The school inspector, Mr Woodside, arrived on an overcast, drizzling day. He came in a ford model A tourer all splashed with mud. His jacket was soaked and he was not in a good mood.

Mr Clancy met the inspector at the door and was horrified to see the state his clothes were in. "May I suggest, sir, that I take you to the school house where my lovely wife, Myrtle will serve you a nice hot cup of tea and scones. While you are there you can dry off and freshen up."

"That would be very nice and I thank you for your concern," said Mr Woodside.

It was twenty minutes later that Mr Clancy caught sight of Mr Woodside looking drier and happier coming from the school house.

The children had all been primed and double primed as to what they had to do and how they had to do it.

Mr Clancy had his programmes ready for inspection, his daily lesson book open at the day and the students had their subject book open at the page they were proudest of.

The students were all seated and backs were straight

and feet together on the floor.

Isobel had been made to check that the bags were all hanging from the hooks allocated.

Everything was in readiness and Mr Clancy had rehearsed in his own mind how the inspector would congratulate him on running such a fine school and then tell him he was going to nominate him for special promotion.

The inspector was ushered into the room by Mr Clancy and once they reached the teacher's table at the front they turned to face the children.

Everyone stood up on cue and chorused, "Good morning Mr Woodside, good morning Mr Clancy."

Mr Woodside took over and asked a question, "Can a student tell me what three times three is?"

All hands in the room flew up straight and still. Mr Woodside was very impressed. One of the things he believed made a great teacher, as he had been, was that every child in the class could answer every question put to them. He selected one of the students in the middle of the room. "You young man,' said Mr Woodside.

"Nine, sir," was the reply.

Mr Woodside nodded clearly impressed and began to ask more questions, at the same time flicking through children's workbooks. Every now and again he would make a positive comment such as, 'Lovely handwriting,' 'Very neat', 'Well ruled up,' 'Beautiful colouring'.

For every question, he asked he noted all hands

would shoot up and the student he nominated gave the correct answer.

Mr Woodside was now looking through Mr Clancy's evaluation book and the test book that showed the progress of each pupil. While he was busy concentrating Mr Clancy quietly but efficiently organized the children ready to recite the poem 'The Highwayman'.

Mr Woodside looked up and said, "What have we here Mr Clancy? Am I going to hear a poem or maybe a song?"

"A poem Mr Woodside and I'll let my star pupil Miss Isobel Johnson introduce it."

Isobel was standing left front of the class and she stepped forward and in a clear well-modulated voice said, "The Highwayman, by Alfred Noyes."

She continued the recital while Lou Fischer made the sound effects using his tongue on the palate of his mouth.

Every time Isobel got to the part where the highwayman came riding she would wait for Lou to click the tlot- tlot of the horse's hooves on the cobblestones.

When she got to the Redcoats came marching she waited for Lou to stamp his feet as if marching. When the gun went off Lou banged two dusters together.

The whole school joined the last verses making their voices sound like eerie ghosts.

Mr Woodside could hardly contain himself. He clapped and walked to Isobel and took her hand saying, "Perfect, so beautifully recited. The most heart-felt I've ever heard. And you young man," he turned to Lou Fischer, "Where ever did you learn to make those sounds?"

Mr Clancy was proud of himself and he began to get everyone back in their seats.

While the quiet movement continued Mr Woodside went to the table and clicked open the locks on his brown brief case.

He drew out a sheet of paper that had the Queensland Education Department's heading on it. He signed his signature at the bottom with a flourish of his fountain pen and blew on the ink to dry it.

"Now I must take my leave of you all. Thank you, Mr Clancy, for a wonderful three hours and to all the children keep studying hard and being respectful to your teacher and parents."

Mr Woodside moved towards Mr Clancy and proffered the piece of paper to him.

As Mr Clancy reached out two things happened almost simultaneously. First, Mr Clancy caught sight of the writing just below the Queensland Education Departments heading and it read 'Recommended for Special Promotion, Mr Clancy. Second, Mr Woodside turned to face the class and this stopped Mr Clancy from taking the sheet.

Mr Woodside addressed the class again, "One last question I need to ask. I have here a picture of an animal. You should recognize it as there are hundreds in the Daintree Valley. When I've got my answer I will give the picture to Miss Isobel Johnson for her superb rendition of the Highwayman. Now, who can tell me the name of this creature?"

Isobel was excited that she had again received the approbation of the District Inspector and that he was going to give her a special gift, but what met her eye was the little creature on the poster. It was the mystery animal they had seen on the farm the week before last, the one they couldn't find the name for.

All hands had shot up to answer the question. Mr Woodside pointed to a lad at the back of the class. "You look like a lover of animals what is this little fellow called?"

"Please Mr Woodside you can't ask me 'cause I don't know," said the boy clearly embarrassed.

"Why on earth have you got your hand up if you can't answer the question?" demanded Mr Woodside.

"Mr Clancy said we had to all put up our hands when you asked a question. Right hand if you knew the answer and left hand if you didn't. I had my left hand up, sir."

Mr Woodside did not turn around, he walked with heavy, determined steps to the door and opened it and disappeared around the corner.

The class was stunned and it wasn't until they heard Mr Woodside's car careering along the road they let out a collective sigh.

When they were all released at the home bell, Isobel found several pieces of paper in the muddy school yard. It was difficult to tell what was on them due to the mud and the fact that they had been screwed up. She was sure she could make out the letters Mr Clan…

Chapter 32

Isobel came running into the house puffing hard with Keith several steps behind. "We know what the mystery animal is," they both shouted.

"Stop, take a breath, have your afternoon tea and then you can try again," said Marion.

Once settled and munching on a chocolate crackle, Isobel told the family about the Inspector's visit and about her getting the poster.

As she talked she handed the picture around. There were several marsupials in the scene from tree kangaroos in the forest, red and grey kangaroos on the grasses, wallabies close up and the little musk kangaroo rat by itself front left.

"Well, well a Musk kangaroo rat. Now you can look up these creatures in the school encyclopaedias and tell us all about them," encouraged Burton. "Time to get the milking done I'm afraid."

The next day Isobel and Keith arrived at school earlier than expected.

They saw a strange lady writing on the blackboard. She was short and plump with blond hair pulled back and tied in a bun. She wore a black dress, black stockings and black flat shoes. Her posture was erect and she appeared all business like.

A group of senior students was speculating as to who this strange woman could be.

They tried to push one of the group to go and ask her but each refused.

Isobel walked up to them all and said, "I'll go talk to her and ask her where Mr Clancy is."

Isobel entered the classroom and quietly walked towards the woman at the front of the room.

If she knew Isobel was approaching she didn't indicate in any way.

Isobel stood six feet from her and waited.

The scrawling sound of chalk on blackboard continued.

Isobel tried the clearing of the throat trick to attract her attention. Again nothing happened except the chalk scrapping.

"Excuse me miss," said Isobel, "I'm Isobel Johnson may I speak with you?"

The chalk scraping sound stopped and slowly the woman turned and faced Isobel. "You may if you make it quick can't you see I'm very busy trying to get my lessons on the board."

"Sorry miss," said Isobel. "Where's Mr Clancy?"

"Mr Clancy is no longer employed by the Queensland Education Department. We shall not speak of him again. You may tell your inquisitive, gossiping friends that I am Miss Cameron and I am your teacher until the end of the year." The voice was cold and strong.

Isobel said, "Sorry miss, thank you, miss, welcome miss," then fled.

A few days after the August Holidays for Isobel and Keith, Marion announced that she was going on her own holiday.

Everyone knew what that meant.

Burton set off with her on the slide headed for the crossing. Here he carried her to the flattie and rowed it to the jetty.

The ferry was waiting for the final loading to be complete.

Captain Osborne called, "How do folks? Make yourselves comfortable. Cost you £1 10/- Burton, one down one return am I correct?"

"Yes sir, you are," replied Burton.

"This will be the last time you'll travel this way to town. Our new bus arrives tomorrow and a new truck next week. The Osborne Brothers are taking advantage of change in the valley. We'll run to Mossman and back every other day starting Monday with a rest on Sundays."

Burton grinned and felt well satisfied.

Another baby on the way and the Osbornes had taken his advice.

Marion went into labour on the 7th September at the Port Douglas Hospital.

There was consternation among the doctors and staff because the word was out that Port Douglas Hospital was to be closed on the tenth of the month and everything and everybody was to be transferred to the Mossman Hospital.

This was going to be a big move and had to be carefully organized.

The staff had not anticipated a pregnancy right on the deadline.

By the morning of September 10, Marion was in labour. The continuous spasms were wearing her out and the doctors and nurses were at a loss as to what else they could do to move the baby along.

There had been a lot of speculation that Mrs Johnson may be having twins but until the event arrived that would prove or disprove the theory nothing else could be done.

It was agreed by Dr Shoemaker and Matron Binningham that they would stay in Port Douglas until Mrs Johnson had the birth.

In the meantime the Port Douglas Hospital had been

moved and was now part and parcel of Mossman Hospital.

The twins arrived at half past five that afternoon to the relief of Marion. They had slipped out and announced their arrival with a scream each. The final part of the birth was smooth and straight forward. The doctor and matron stayed with Marion and the twins and organized the transfer of themselves and the patients the next morning.

Burton received the telephone call he had anxiously waited for, "Congratulations, Mr Johnson your wife has had healthy twin girls."

"Twins," he whispered and then shouted, "Twins, mum's had twins. They are both girls."

The hospital staff member on the other end of the telephone simply said, "Goodbye." The line went dead.

Burton was over the moon and kept repeating, "That makes nine plus Ginger, the family grows."

He sat down in the kitchen chair as the children all ran in from all directions to give him a hug and start talking about the twins.

Burton said, "I'm sure glad that I made the table top bigger." He looked at the shiny redwood cedar top and ran his brawny arm across it giving it an extra polish.

Marion arrived in the Daintree Village on the eve of Guy Fawkes Night.

She had the twins bundled tight in pink rugs so that you could see the foreheads and closed eyes of both.

She had decided to call one Margherita and the other Phyllis.

The Margherita was in memory of Burton's grandmother who had made the hazardous journey by ship with her husband, Ambrose, from Denmark all those years ago. Phyllis was a name she liked so it was a mother's choice.

Burton was waiting on the jetty and extended an arm to help her off.

He caught the overnight bag that the deckhand threw to him and then gave Marion a squeeze and a light peck on the lips.

"So these are our precious little twins," he said peering at the blankets. "Welcome to our family and welcome to your new home."

Phyllis began to cry and Marion said, "Well past their feed time so let's get under way in the flattie and I'll feed them in private."

All the Johnsons and Ginger were waiting anxiously at the ford when they saw the flattie being rowed towards them.

"Here they come," shouted Eva.

The boys waded out in the shallow water and grabbed the boat. They hauled it into the shore, ran it up onto the sand so Marion could get out on dry land.

"Welcome home mum," said Madeline.

"These are your new sisters. This one is Margherita and this is Phyllis." She pointed at each in turn.

Isobel said, "How do we tell the difference?"

"That will take time because they are identical. I think we'll have to embroider their names on their clothes for the time being."

Eva took Phyllis from her mum's arms and said, "I'll carry this one."

Madeline said, "I bags this one."

Ginger took the overnight bag from the bottom of the flattie and said, "I'll carry this one as it won't cry or cause me any trouble." Everyone laughed at his joke.

Just as the family began climbing the steps of the house they heard a loud bang in the valley. They all turned to see the stars of an exploding sky rocket light the sky.

"Wow, look at that isn't it beautiful," said Eva.

The first was followed by four more in quick succession. "It looks like one of the farms is celebrating Guy Fawkes Night."

"Our time will come my dears. Please be patient that this depressing Depression will soon be over," said Burton.

Chapter 33

The sunny days were a blessing for Marion as the washing from the twins mounted quickly. Add that to the normal wash for the rest of the family it was a big job.

Marion was lucky to have three hardworking and sensible daughters who took on the added responsibility of raising a couple of more sisters.

They put Brutus in the slide and moved all the washing to the crossing. Marion was happy to walk along behind and conserve her energy for the washing and then, of course, to feed the hungry new born.

Once at the ford Marion and the girls soaked the clothes in the waters and spent time on each article squeezing and slapping it onto the rocks. This would clean away the mud, grime and other soiling. They would then work in pairs to rinse out the water. This was done by each holding an end and then rotating the article clockwise and anticlockwise. This would result in the water being squeezed out. The article was then hung on the nearby fence or fallen tree branches.

With the lovely hot days drying was rapid and soon the folded washing was on its way home where the ironing would take place.

The School Sport's Day was not held in 1930 as Miss Cameron did not have the organizational skills of her male predecessors.

This was a disappointment for all but understandable.

Several of the men offered to do the planning and organization for 1931 if they were required.

Miss Cameron was a real live wire when it came to drama. She was always being dramatic and acting out parts of stories, poems and plays.

The cold demeanour she had shown Isobel was actually opposite to her real self. The students had warmed to her as she had to them.

She apologized for the loss of their sports day but was willing to compensate by getting them to put on a play. She read them three of her favourites and allowed them to vote for the one they wanted to perform in front of their parents. Goldilocks and the Three Bears won hands down.

Isobel was selected as the narrator and Keith was Baby Bear.

Marion sewed Isobel a blue pinafore that was so pretty it had the whole valley talking.

Burton went off in search of King Billy and when he found him he managed to get him to sell five animal skins that Marion then sewed into a bear costume.

Miss Cameron was so pleased with the costume she drove her buggy out to the Johnson farm, via the newly cleared Stewart Creek track, to ask Marion if she could make Father Bear and Mother Bear costumes as well.

Marion was happy to oblige but explained how she got the fur and that it was not possible to catch up with King Billy as he had taken his tribe walkabout to the sacred grounds.

Miss Cameron was able to make inquiries around the valley and Chas Osborne found furs in Port Douglas.

So within three days, the furs were delivered and Marion and her helpers were able to finish the other costumes.

The concert night was cloudy and humid.

The Johnson family was not the first to arrive in their flatties. There were several other row boats pulled up on the sand.

Burton carried Max while Eva carried the baby Molly. The twins were in carry baskets with Marion looking after Rita and Madeline in charge of Phyllis.

Miss Cameron welcomed everyone and the show began. A few missed lines and a couple of costume malfunctions later the show was over.

The audience clapped and called for an encore.

Miss Cameron stood up and made a speech thanking the students for their consistent studying and the wonderful concert they had performed.

She presented prizes for each year level and then announced the Student of 1930 as, "Miss Isobel Johnson".

Isobel clambered to her feet and came forward. She looked radiant in her blue pinafore and her long plaits. She accepted the book prize and the sixpence. Miss Cameron wrapped an arm around her and said, "There's one more surprise for you and your family. This afternoon I received confirmation that you are the recipient of a Queensland Education Department's Scholarship."

Marion clapped so loudly that it woke up the sleeping Molly, Burton had a look of pride and bewilderment and the others broke out in applause.

As was the norm in the Daintree Valley social events were concluded with a supper. Mountains of food found their way onto the student desks and hot cups of tea were served from the teacher's table. All the rubbish was placed in the bins around the room.

The trip home in the flatties was a fascinating contrast.

The children were babbling with excitement about Goldilocks and the Three Bears and the parts played by Keith and Isobel.

The family was proud of Isobel for being the first ever Johnson to win a State Scholarship.

In the lead boat, Burton rowed determinedly towards home.

The lantern out front illuminated enough water ahead for him to navigate.

He was deep in thought over Isobel and what winning a scholarship meant.

Marion had sensed his mood and sat quietly waiting for him to say what was going through his mind.

She was pleased with Isobel but afraid that it would not be possible to let her go away to school.

Like Burton, her sense of family and closeness made her envelope her babies with loving hands and she was not prepared to let anyone of them out of her protection.

She also knew that deep down Burton had an even fiercer need to look after his children and not let anything happen to them.

The milking had been done by the sleepy group and they all trudged back home for breakfast.

Burton hushed them all and said, "I need to talk to you all in the lounge before you go off and catch up on the sleep you missed last night."

They all knew if Burton was calling a family meeting it generally meant family crisis. They all searched for a reason for the meeting. There had been nothing too disastrous in the past week so what could it involve?

Burton cleared his throat and addressed them all. "Your mother and I love you all very much and we feel we need to keep you all close so that we can protect you from the evils of the world. We were so proud of Isobel last night and she will be able to hold onto the memories of being presented with a scholarship forever. However, we cannot allow her to go off to boarding school."

Isobel felt a tear welling in her right eye. She looked from her father to her mother and knew they had talked long and thought hard about their decision.

She was caught between feeling so proud and wanting to continue her meteoric rise in her education, to not wanting to leave the warmth and happiness she found living in the Valley.

Isobel stood up and came across to her father. She gave him a hug and said, "I understand dad and I will do whatever you wish for me."

Burton had not finished.

He wiped away the tear that had run down his cheek and said, "Isobel's loyalty to us as her parents is so strong and I thank her for that. You must also understand that we must stay together to run the farm. We need each of you to pull your weight to make this a successful enterprise. I intend at a later stage to buy land here for our own farms."

Everyone looked at each other and was nodding approval.

"Now there's another matter that I think you are ready to hear and I'm ready to tell you. I have a morbid fear of losing family and no matter what I try to do about it I just keep being haunted by past experiences."

Marion looked at Burton and silently urged him to continue. Getting his fears out in the open may help him overcome them in the future.

"Your Great Grandfather, Ambrose, who was the first

Aussie Johnson had two sons. Your Grandfather Fritz and another boy called Ambrose Junior. The boys grew up together with their older sister, Bertha, in Daylesford in Victoria. This was a gold mining town and Great Grandfather Ambrose was a mining surveyor.

"The boys would wander the town enjoying their freedom and playing games, talking to the miners especially on Wombat Hill. You will recall Wombat Hill was where Great Grandad planted the tree and lit the bonfires."

They family was listening intently and each nodded.

"One Sunday morning 30th June 1867, four boys were playing together on the other side of the valley to where Fritz and Ambrose Junior lived. They saw four wild goats eating on a nearby hillock so they decided to go hunting. One of the group declined and went home but the others wandered off.

"The three boys were only little being six, five and four and a half. They were in shorts and shirts. By evening they had not returned and their worried parents set out to look for them. Others they met joined in but nothing was found. Unfortunately, it got too dark to continue to look so they reported the missing children to the police.

"During the night the wind picked up and a misty soaking rain began. The temperature dropped to almost freezing.

"By the next day, Great Grandfather Ambrose and lots of the town folk and miners had heard about the boys and offered to search.

"All through the day, people looked but again nothing was found. Great Grandfather Ambrose went home to his family and told them the news. He was saddened by the event and wanted his boys to learn a lesson. He told them of the importance of family and staying together, of loving each other and telling people where they are going.

"The next morning the weather was worse with rain and bitterly cold winds. The town population met at the Town Hall and made up search parties and designated areas for each group to search.

"Great Grandfather Ambrose offered £10 for each boy as a reward for anyone who found the boys dead or alive in the hope that this incentive would keep everyone searching. Others joined in and altogether £60 was raised.

"By nightfall, the weary searchers had found nothing. Even a black tracker who had been able to follow the boys' movements for over three miles could not determine the final part of their journey. They had disappeared.

"Great Grandfather Ambrose was exhausted and miserable in not being able to give the boys back to their parents. He continued to look even when others stopped and had returned to their gold mining. His searches proved fruitless.

"It was three months later the boys were found. They had perished.

"A dog brought a boot home to its master. The master had trouble getting the boot out of the dog's mouth but when he did he saw a foot inside. It was a child's tiny foot.

"The police were called and they came with a small search party. The dog was encouraged to find the other boot and ran off towards a forested area. Here it sniffed and scratched around. The searchers looked every-where in the vicinity and one man found the skeletons of the other boys in the hollow of a tree.

"The third and oldest boy's body was scattered around. They were laid to rest in the Daylesford Cemetery and a huge monument was erected from public donations.

"The three lost children had a profound impact on your Great Grandfather and he became very protective of his family and that was passed onto your Grandfather and then to me.

"To add to Great Grandfather Ambrose's fragile emotional state worse things were to come.

"In June 1869 Ambrose Junior came home and complained of a sore throat. He was sent to bed with a honey and lemon drink. Next morning he said he was feeling worse and was having trouble breathing. His mother, your Great Grandmother Margherita felt his forehead and knew from the hotness that he was very ill. She sent for the doctor.

"The doctor's diagnosis shocked the family and your Great Grandfather was overcome with grief.

"Ambrose Junior had diphtheria and that was incurable."

Burton stopped talking and wiped his eyes. His audience had not moved and each had a glistening in their eyes. They waited for Burton to continue.

"Your Great Uncle Ambrose Junior lingered in agony for two weeks before he passed away. It was the worst fortnight of their lives.

"After the funeral at the Daylesford Cemetery, Great Grandfather Ambrose was so overcome with sadness that he sold up, packed up and headed to northern New South Wales. He could not afford to lose another member of his family.

"Your Grandfather Fritz was also affected by losing his brother. Not so long ago he lost his son and my brother Keith.

"I was deeply affected too with Keith's passing. We were close and he was my baby brother and indestructible. I wasn't there to help him when he suffered four excruciating days dying from blood poisoning after scratching a pimple on his neck.

"Keith was a very clever man and was destined for greatness until he was taken in such an unexpected manner.

"It seems we are fated in odd ways. I cannot afford to lose any of you. Now you may understand better how I feel and why I make the decisions I do.

"So please understand Isobel when I say no, you won't be going away to school."

Isobel was devastated by the stories she had just heard and now knew why her father was so protective.

Secretly she was pleased that she was staying home. It was so full of fun and her family meant the world to her. She could read and continue her story writing.

Chapter 34

After listening to Burton's story the family had remained sad through Christmas and to Keith's seventh birthday. Things didn't feel quite the same although there was a feeling of closeness among them all.

Marion decided someone had to shake the family out of their morose feeling.

After breakfast, she called the girls to her bedroom one at a time and got them to select their dress for the New Year's Eve Dance. They presented these and she asked for instructions to jazz them up as pretty as can be. Most asked for a different coloured ribbon to tie around the waist and embroidery.

Marion told the girls to get ready for the dance and then she went to seek out the boys with the same message.

Ginger was over the moon because dancing enabled him to have an excuse for getting up close and personal with the girls. He was keen on any girls for that matter, although he had always had a special spot for Madeline. She was yet to show any signs of reciprocation.

Burt rushed off to polish his shoes and select a tie to

match his light blue shirt.

Burton reluctantly agreed with Marion it was time to throw off the morbidity yoke and have fun.

It was a spick and span group that went tripping off to the New Year's Eve dance.

The children would get first go followed by the adults.

'Old Lang Syme' was sung to mark the precise time 1930 became 1931.

The next morning the family was full of chatter as they competed for anyone's ear to tell them what they did and what they saw others doing. There was a lot of ribbing towards Ginger and Madeline as they seemed to save every dance for each other. Eva was being unusually naughty with snide remarks as she had been rejected by Ginger five times when she asked him to dance.

January was humid and wet.

The perspiration ran in rivulets down every part of their bodies as soon as they exerted themselves. It was easier to find a place where they could catch a draft and lay still.

Of course, there was the call of 'Milking time' but other than that the days were just too energy sucking.

February snuck up and then Max was given the news

he wasn't happy to receive. "School starts Monday, Max," said his mother.

"But mum I'm only five. You have to be six to go to infants."

"You are correct with your ages but Miss Cameron needs an extra student to keep the school open so we have decided to send you along. It will be of great benefit to you and of course to the district. Anyway, I don't see you having a problem as you have the lovely Miss Cameron teaching you and you like her don't you?"

"She's alright," said Max but secretly he thought she was really nice.

Keith was attending school so he found himself with a new role as he would be looking after his little brother, teach him all the tricks and protect him from the dangers.

Miss Cameron had taken a shine to Keith and as much as he refused to admit it, 1930 had been one of the most exciting years of his short life. Now he hoped that the coming year, even with a younger sibling in tow, would be as wonderful.

It was Keith who started the biggest project the Valley would ever know. It was quite accidental but turned learning for the 20 students into so much fun. Adults joined in and it even got outside into the big wide world.

On most school days Keith would be accompanied by Max and one of his older siblings as they would row the cream to the Butter Factory.

One day Max had complained of a sore throat and was left in bed. Keith was late and had been left behind as Burt had to deliver the cream before it spoiled in the heat.

Keith's first thought was to go hide in the bush and skip school. This he decided would get him a whipping from his father so he launched the flattie and rowed off.

As he was about to leave the Stewart Creek and row into the main river he eyed a bright blue object floating just ahead. He shipped the oars and leaned as far out of the boat as possible. As the object swept past he saw that it was a feather. He lunged to grab it and fell out of the boat.

He was almost in mid-stream, over three hundred yards from the jetty, the flattie was floating away and he was soaking wet.

He knew it was futile to call out as he was too far from anyone.

The river was on the ebb and was taking him towards the jetty so he turned on his back and floated.

He was only tiny but this manoeuvre saved his energy and his life.

There were three people on the jetty and they noticed the empty flattie floating past. One dived in and retrieved it and the others frantically looked about to see where the rower could be.

"There, it's a kid," shouted one of the men.

The man who had retrieved the flattie rowed towards Keith and they finally came close to each other.

Keith was hauled aboard. He was grateful to his saviour and thanked him.

He was already late for school so he set out at the double.

Miss Cameron saw him coming and met him outside.

He explained that he'd been tipped out of the boat but had not suffered any ill effects.

As he sat down at his desk he opened his right hand and in it was the bright blue feather.

"What's that?" asked Miss Cameron.

"A feather Miss, but I don't know what bird it came from."

Miss Cameron took the feather and held it up in the air. The light streaming in from one of the high windows caught the colour and it was the prettiest azure.

"Does anyone know what bird this feather may have come from?" asked Miss Cameron.

There were a number of answers given but no one was certain. So Miss Cameron gave them all a challenge. They had to take a piece of drawing paper and sketch and colour in a feather. This was to be done at home for parents to offer their opinions.

This started the most frenetic and longest lesson known to the community of Daintree.

It all began slowly and built up pace as all good things tend to do.

Keith came running into the kitchen where everyone was getting ready to do the afternoon milking. "I've got me a feather and Miss said to take it home and see if mum and dad knew what bird it was from."

His enthusiasm was clear to all as he thrust the bright blue feather at his father. Burton took the proffered object and turned it over and over. "I've seen lots of the birds with this colour down by the creek. They do a lot of diving into the water. Seem to be after the minnows."

"Sounds like a kingfisher," said Ginger and Madeline nodded in agreement.

"We don't have any books to look it up so I suppose we could try a guess seeing as we think it is a kingfisher and it's blue. Pretty Blue Kingfisher, try that one on Miss Cameron."

Several children offered ideas the next morning at school during 'News Telling'. Keith offered his dad's thoughts and Miss Cameron was pleased. Other ideas included Blue Swallow and Bright Blue Duck.

The problem as Miss Cameron pointed out was that they didn't have a sighting of the bird and this was important.

So she sent them all home with a lead pencil, three sheets of art paper and a box of coloured pencils.

Their task was to find any bird and carefully sketch it. She would then use the school encyclopaedias to identify each one.

The next day five sketches were presented of three different birds but Miss Cameron couldn't find any in the encyclopaedias.

"When I was studying at College the lecturer introduced us to an organization that looks after and studied birds. It was named after a naturalist called Gould. The organization was called the Gould League Club. All you had to do was join and you received badges and stickers. What do you think of the idea that we all join? Then we could make drawings of the birds and a description and send these into get a proper identification."

The class was enthusiastic and soon had their parents keen to be part of the outdoor activities and the Gould League Club.

A fortnight later all the badges and stickers arrived along with a membership certificate. Miss Cameron got them all to stand up and recite the Gould League Pledge.

'We promise to protect all birds and never to collect their eggs'.

There were furtive glances between the senior boys who had made it a part of their fun to track down birds and find their nests. It was only the most cunning who was able to find such well-camouflaged nests and then collect the eggs.

At recess time three of the senior boys met in a huddle to discuss the change that was being contemplated. "If we promise not to hurt birds and not collect their eggs does that mean we have to keep that promise?" asked Charley Hughes the eldest of the trio.

"Nah. You can break a promise if you want to. No harm in that. Anyway we've been hunting down birds' eggs forever so why stop now?" said Graham Ingham.

"You are both wrong about this," said Henry Andrews. "I've been thinking about what miss said and she's right. If we keep taking the eggs then there will be no chicks and that means no birds and no eggs. So we need to stop and obey the promise."

"Did you just make any sense at all Henry? Sounds like the chicken and the egg question to me," said Charley.

While they were in deep discussion Olga Claus had approached and heard the last part of the conversation. "I'm glad you boys can see the sense in protecting the birds. As the senior students we have an obligation to set an example to the other kids," she said.

The three boys were taken back by Olga's interpretation of their conversation but all were not going to get in her bad books. Olga was the blue-eyed blond beauty of the school and all the boys were just starting to see her as a future girlfriend.

Graham broke the silence that had ensured, "You're right Olga we must be the ones to step up and take this Gould League idea seriously. Don't you all agree fellows?" He turned to the others and they nodded.

Miss Cameron was pleased to hear that the seniors had taken on the Gould League Club and were ready to carry out the promise.

The birthdays of the Johnson children continued on their annual rotation. Madeline turned 18 on March 22nd and celebrated with scones, mango jam and cream. The austerity programme remained in place and if the economy didn't pick up this would be the case for years to come.

Madeline who was not one to complain had said, "I'll be an old grandmother before I can have a proper birthday celebration."

In April little, bouncy, giggly Molly had her second birthday and Isobel turned into a teenager.

Isobel had taken time to come to grips with her dilemma of being a scholarship winner and not continuing onto high school.

On the one hand, she saw her future as a writer slip from her grasp and on the other, Isobel was glad she didn't have to give up her wonderful life with her family in the valley.

Burton had tried to add extra fun into Easter that arrived towards the end of April. He maintained his stance on keeping things simple and not spending too much.

He cut up lots of pieces of coloured paper and rolled them to look like eggs. He then hid these in and around the house.

He explained to the eager hunters that they had to find the eggs one at a time and bring these back to him.

He would keep a running total for each and the winner would get a block of Cadbury's chocolate. This person then was to give each of the family one piece of chocolate and then they could eat the rest.

Chocolate was a rare treat in the Daintree and for the Johnsons so the hunt was prepped and the incentive made for frenetic hunting.

At one stage Keith came running into the kitchen, where Burton had stationed himself to do the count, and said, "We shouldn't be collecting eggs as we promised as members of the Gould League not to."

"It's alright my son," said Burton, "I'm pretty sure chook eggs and Easter eggs are exempt."

Chapter 35

The Gould League Club at school was starting to occupy everyone's lives and learning. The ideas had filtered in but now, every day, students arrived with captivating news of bird sightings.

Miss Cameron decided that the way to deal with the information was to get the children to bring in their sketches and the ones identifiable were glued to large pieces of butcher's paper that were stuck to one of the classroom walls.

Those that could not be identified were posted off to the Gould League Club Headquarters in Brisbane. To help with identifying the bird the student who had seen the bird had to add notes as to the environment they were observed in.

It took a fortnight for the post to get through and back although, if there was a flood, then the time could not be estimated.

The first birds to come to the class notice were those that foraged on the rainforest floor. Here these birds dug for insects and other creatures and laid their eggs in nests in mounds made of leaf and other material that fell from the forest.

Nearly all the children could identify the ground

dwellers; The Australian Bush Turkey with its bright red neck and black plumage. Their fan-like tail and yellow wattles were talking points among the class.

The Orange Footed Scrub Fowl was seen and drawn by over half the class. The steel blue of the neck and chest was a difficult colour to put on paper but the brown on the back proved easier. The orange feet were distinguishing features and because of the feet colouring everyone could see how it got its name.

The Red-necked Crake was found wading in the shallow waters of the creeks and river. They had reddish brown head, neck and breast. Most of the rest of the bird was a greyish- brown.

The Bush Hen had dark colours of grey and brown and foraged in dense vegetation near water.

The Emerald Ground Dove was easily seen because it fed on the wild figs and other fruits found on the ground. The beautiful emerald green wings and grey body made them easy to identify.

All of these birds adorned the wall of the classroom in various shapes and sizes and all drawn by one child or another.

Miss Cameron was interested to find out from her class why these birds were the ones that they had seen so easily.

Rosemary Hughes, the brother of Charles, suggested, "These are the only ones that are found in the Daintree, Miss."

"Intelligent thought Rose but no that is not so. In fact, there are over 430 different types of birds in the Daintree."

The class gasped at this extraordinary number. "We won't possibly find them all but we need to try different methods to see if we can find some of the others, any ideas?"

"They must live in the thick scrub, miss and that's why we haven't seen them," said George Williams one of the year 4 students.

"That is quite so and that should give us a few hints as to how we can find them. We need to use another sense in our bird watching. That means we must not only use our eyes to see the birds but we must use our ears to hear their calls."

"What about if we build a cubby in the scrub and spy on them?" asked Keith.

"That's a really good idea Keith and that's called a hide. You hide away and watch. As a word of caution though, you must always talk to your parents before you do anything. That is important in this case as it is dangerous to climb trees and to wander into the rainforest," said Miss Cameron.

Little Max had been quietly growing up at home. It was his fifth birthday on 4th of June.

Marion spared the money and made only fairy bread as a treat. Max was rather pleased with the idea as he loved all the colours of the 100s and 1000s that were plastered all over his pieces of bread.

He was also pleased to be able to count his five candles and to blow them all out in one breath.

Max was pleased to hear Eva say, "Happy Birthday Max."

He had been at school now for half a year. He couldn't get used to sitting and listening to a teacher drone on about nothing. It wasn't his idea of heaven. He wanted nothing better than the run of the farm and all the mischief that might allow him to get into.

June proved to be a glorious month for the valley community. It was warm and sunny each day with mild to warm temperatures.

The farm activity was at its most productive and loads of animals were being transported down the river to Port Douglas in the ferry which had not entirely been retired. From here they were taken by lorry to the sales yards in Mossman.

Prices continued at rock bottom but this didn't stop the sales taking place.

Each breeder had to cast off part of their old stock to make way for younger animals. Overstocking was the worst possible outcome for any farmer.

Work on the roads and bridges continued to be done

by the volunteer groups that had been established.

Unfortunately, there was little time available for the men to come together so the progress was slow.

The Barrett Creek Bridge was only part finished but it was becoming evident that the Osbornes were starting to use the road to Mossman to carry produce. There would come a time when this would be seen as the only efficient transport system.

Burt and Ginger had been busy discussing the future and one day went to talk to Burton. "Dad can we chew your ear for a moment?" asked Burt.

"Sure son, what's on your mind?" asked Burton.

"Ginger is 20 and I turn 17 tomorrow which means we are both old enough to get our car and truck licences is that right?"

"Yes I believe so but having a licence for anything out here is not much point," said Burton.

"When did you get your licence?" asked Ginger.

"When I was 17 your uncles bought an old ford together and we all learned to drive around the farm and then into town. We used to take girls to the dances," said Burton.

"So 17 is the right age for a licence. Ginger and I thought that if we went and got our licences we could drive vehicles in the valley for other people and then we could go into the trucking business ourselves. What do you think?"

"Good to see you both looking to the future and showing a bit of enterprise. The only thing I can say is don't think too big or you may be disappointed. There's never going to be much work for trucking around here and anyhow the Osbornes have it all sewn up."

Bird hides popped up everywhere. Every farm had at least one and many had more. The Daintree fathers were as enthusiastic about bird watching as their offspring.

The amount of time children and fathers spent in these hides became a point of contention among the woman folk

At one of their meetings at the Hayden farm Mrs Clauss even ventured to suggest that the men were a little too smitten by Miss Cameron and maybe she was more the motivation than helping their children's education.

As the days past the classroom wall began to be covered with an ever increasing number of birds.

This time they were found in the mid canopy areas of the rainforest.

All in all there were 36 birds that the children identified and drew.

As an added lesson Miss Cameron got the children to write the bird's names in alphabetical order. Henry Andrews won the prize for most accurate and neatest. His list was placed near the drawings for all to see.

Next to each bird's name Miss Cameron added a

description. She sent the information off to the Gould League in Brisbane and included a note, "These are the birds and descriptions that the students of Daintree have found."

Barred Cuckoo-Shrike mostly grey feathers with the bands of light grey and white. It has pale yellow eyes.

Black-faced Monarch has a black and grey head and wings with orange under the breast.

Black Butcher Bird very black feathers all over with a sharp pointed beak of black tip and white.

Black Bittern dark brown and black with yellow patches on the neck and breast.

Buff Breasted Paradise Kingfisher has brilliant blue wings, orange breast and beak, a long white feather down the tail and orange legs.

Double-eyed Fig Parrot mostly green although darker on top. Red cheeks and forehead with blue around eyes. A very small parrot.

Fairy Gerygone grey on top and lemon yellow on the breast and white patches on the throat.

Gould's Bronze Cuckoo bronze on top, grey breast that is banded white.

Great-billed Heron mostly grey with a long neck and wades in water.

Grey Whistler very small bird that is plain grey brown colour.

Grey Fantail mostly grey with white throat and tail feathers. The tail is like a fan.

Large-billed Gerygone is pale brown top and white underneath.

Large-billed Scrub Wren a small bird mostly brown with grey. Flits everywhere.

Leaden Flycatcher has a shiny grey top and white breast.

Little Bronzed Cuckoo has a bronze back and a white breast that is banded with grey.

Little Kingfisher has pretty bright blue on the wings and head, white breast with orange under the wings.

Little Strike Thrush is mostly brown with light orange on its breast.

Lovely Fairy Wren has a brilliant blue crown, blue cheeks and blue stripe across the neck. Black and browns fill in the other feathers and the tail,

Macleay's Honeyeater is a patchy brown and grey with a black cap and orange around the eyes.

Mangrove Robin has very dark top and a white breast and neck.

Metallic Starling is mostly black, green and purple and looks like metal. It has a chunky bill and red eyes.

Northern Fantail is mostly grey with a yellow breast, white throat and a long fan tail.

Pale-vented Bush Hen is dark grey with a dark olive top and grey face. It walks in the water.

Pale Yellow Robin is little with grey top, yellow breast and orange to forehead.

Papuan Frogmouth looks like an owl and a grey and

brown broken piece of a branch.

Pied Imperial Pigeon is mostly white with black on wing tips and black bands on the tail. It has a yellow beak and grey legs.

Pied Monarch is black and white with a collar that is white.

Rufous Fan-tail has a red and brown fan tail, grey brown head with white throat and a dappled breast.

Spotted Catbird has green wings, black cheeks and green and white tips on the breast and throat.

Woompoo Pigeon has a purple chest and throat, yellow on the lower belly, lots of green on the underneath and a light grey head.

Varied Triller has a black back with white markings on the wings and breast. The breast also has grey bars.

Victoria's Riflebird is mostly shiny black with blue parts.

Yellow-breasted Boatbill is black on its head, back and tail, lots of yellow on the under part of the breast and tail. It has a yellow stripe on its head.

The most beautiful bird voted by the children was the Azure Kingfisher with its striking bright blue back and orange breast.

The Gould League Club of Queensland sent out a representative to congratulate Miss Cameron and the students on their efforts. The school was presented with a trophy and Certificate thanking them for their willingness to identify birds in the Daintree and to leave a legacy for future generations.

The School Holidays brought to a tidy conclusion the bird identification activities and the bird project stopped.

Chapter 36

Eva turned 15 and continued to grow into a motherly type. She loved to take care of her four youngest siblings and was always fussing around them. Marion was more than happy to encourage this as she was finding it hard work keeping up with the growing brood.

Ginger and Burt had left for a few days holiday in Mossman.

They had intended to hitch hike in and return by the Osborne bus.

During the time they were in Mossman they learned how to drive and then applied for their licences.

Everything went to plan and it was relatively easy to obtain a licence as there were so few people interested in driving. Most were still trapped in the horse and buggy days and these new-fangled machines were too complicated and noisy to be of any use. Besides there was an economic down turn so any capital expenditure such as on a car was out of the question.

The boys returned by bus and because they were the only ones aboard talked Eric Osborne into letting them drive. They produced their new licences and convinced

Eric that they knew what they were talking about.

Burt was first and after crunching the gears while moving from first to second drove faultlessly for over 12 mile. He pulled off the road and switched with Ginger.

Ginger, was not only competent, but had the confidence to take on anything. He drove at a steady 30 mph for over 20 mile. He reluctantly gave up the driver's seat to Eric.

When Ginger and Burt arrived back at the farm they were full of stories of how they were taught to drive, how they got their licences and drove the bus home.

George then ordered everyone outside and took them to the big old fig tree near the wood heap.

He asked the older ones to line up and then sat the younger ones in front.

"From now on we can have lots of photographs of the Johnsons in the Daintree," he announced and produced a Box Brownie camera.

"Always wanted one of these," he said. "If I had one on my travels I could have shown you who I was talking about when I mention people on my journey from England."

The family was all ready for their very first Daintree photograph. The sun was low in the sky as they all smiled happily. George focussed the camera and they all heard the click of the shutter. "It will take a week or more to get back the photographs," he said. "I've got to take 12 on the reel and then it takes three weeks to get them developed."

George was besotted with his camera and it wasn't too long before he was off to the Daintree Post Office with his first reel of film.

The Postmaster was happy to show him how to place it in the special envelope and address it to the photographer in Cairns. Then he had to wait to see what he had captured.

After all the bird sightings and the energy that went into this activity it was rather a quiet time in September and October.

This quiet was broken for Isobel, Keith and Max one late afternoon.

They had been sent to check on the fencing on the top side paddock and were nearing the end of their chore when they all stopped dead in their tracks.

From somewhere in the rainforest they could hear a tom tom noise as though someone was beating a drum. They looked at each other and Keith ventured, "It could be the aborigines with King Billy."

"No, I don't think so," said Isobel who was being held by a frightened Max. "It's coming closer so I think we should run back home."

At that precise moment a large black bird walked

out of the rainforest about 20 yards away from them.

"Look at that," said Keith. "It looks like one of those cassowary birds we saw in the books."

"And look what's coming out behind it. Two, no three, no four little chicks."

The three children ceased being frightened and had forgotten the lessons about how dangerous the cassowary could be. They were transfixed by a sight that they had never seen before and would probably never see again.

The male cassowary was jet black all over except for his bright blue neck and red wattle. A large, grey, horny helmet protruded from his head and he had legs like those of a dinosaur. The three large pointed toes looked menacing.

The four chicks were wandering behind pecking and scratching, totally oblivious to the children ahead. They were striped in brown and white and looked nothing like their father.

The old man cassowary stopped and looked at the three children. It made a deep rumbling sound and the chicks all ran to him. They ducked down, bending their legs and necks. The protective male made the tom tom noise that the three children had heard earlier.

"I think we are being told to go," said Isobel.

She gripped Max's tiny hand and began to edge away.

"Come on Keith through the fence and run," she said.

They ran into the kitchen and flopped on the floor out of breath.

"Whatever is the matter?" asked Marion. "You look like a ghost is after you."

"Cassowary that's what was after us," said Isobel. "It was huge and scary. It had four chicks and kept making a drumming sound. We ran as fast as we could."

The weather continued to be fine throughout the final months of 1931.

Miss Cameron had organized a group of fathers to make all the arrangements for the end of year sport's day. The five men led by Olga Claus's father had all the lanes marked and the flatties in position when the day dawned for the big contest.

Keith was brimming with confidence that he would win his races and the shiny sixpence for being the year champion.

He had not counted on Miss Cameron changing the rules.

She had made certificates that were presented to winners with their names neatly written in the centre.

Although disappointed Keith was proud to show off his certificates and to carefully put them into his bottom drawer for safe keeping.

Miss Cameron had explained her decision before giving out the certificates, blaming the Great Depression on the lack of funds available to everyone. The parents all agreed with her decision.

The community tried to make up for the solemn mood that had prevailed in the valley during 1931 by hosting a special Christmas Party in the Butter Factory.

Although no presents were given out there were games, dancing and mountains of food for everyone who attended. Father Christmas arrived on the back of the lorry and the helpers all sang the Christmas carols with added gusto.

Burton and Marion added to the gaiety back home by placing a small handmade present at the end of each of the children's bed.

The excitement in the morning could be heard all over the house.

Molly ran into Burton and Marion and said, "Father Christmas came down the chimee and look what he left me." She held up a little knitted doll then gave it a hug.

Keith's eighth birthday was celebrated with games and laughter. He said what everyone else was thinking, "I sure hope this depression thing goes away so we can get back to birthday cakes."

The weather soon closed in and the rain came. New Year's Eve was spent quietly on the verandah watching the creeks fill to brimming.

When they all woke up on New Year's Day, 1932, the water was creeping towards the barn.

The cows had been moved to higher ground where they would be safe during the wet season.

The makeshift milking shed was put back into use and the launch began its daily pickup of the cream.

Keith was hoping that the rain would continue forever so he didn't have to go back to school.

School began in early February. Max and Keith were the only Johnsons to attend.

Max had already had a year of education and the problem facing Miss Cameron was whether to leave him in the infants' class or progress him into the next year level. His results from last year showed him to be a capable Arithmetic student but he struggled with Reading and Writing.

Miss Cameron decided to advance Max and to offer him tutoring in his weaker subjects at lunch breaks. Max was very pleased with these arrangements, as was his mother and father.

In February there was a new excitement throughout the valley.

One of the farmers had bought a bull from the Mossman saleyards. He was a huge, dusty brown animal that was unsettled throughout the trip by Osborne's lorry.

By the time they reached the Daintree Village he was throwing his head and horns around trying to break out.

In their wisdom the lorry driver and mate decided to off load the bull in the village common and give it freedom to settle down. The bull jumped from the truck as the gate was swung open, landed on its nose as its front legs buckled, regained its balance and charged off towards the township.

It demolished the fence, ran through town and disappeared into the forest area along the Stewart Creek.

For several days it menaced anyone who took the road by charging out of the trees and bellowing loudly.

A meeting of several farmers decreed that it had to be put down so they formed a hunting party. Later on it transpired that the grandfather of the bull had also been a rogue and had actually mauled a farmer's labourer to death.

The Johnson family had been forbidden to use the Stewart Road during the days of the wild bull so it was back to flatties to deliver the cream to the Butter Factory and the boys to school.

Flash floods were always a menace and it became imperative to look to the mountains during each day to see if there was cloud over them.

Thick, dark clouds or huge thunderheads were a

sure sign of rain over the highlands. Often these would presage rain and flash flooding.

It would be too late to hear the sound of crashing, tumbling trees and the rushing of water if you were in the creek bed. A flash flood would move at remarkable speed and take everything with it.

Once trapped in the raging waters there was no chance of survival.

The children were taught never to stay long in the creek beds and to always look to the mountains to determine if it had been raining there. They were also taught to err on the side of caution.

During the Great Depression many thousands of men took to the roads and railways in search of employment

They were also lacking in local knowledge and this caused the demise of one poor man in the Stewart Creek in March 1932.

Isobel and Eva had been sent to the low paddock to find cows that had wandered off.

As they approached the crossing they could see a tent on the sand and the smell of a fire.

A swaggie was camped but they couldn't see any sign of him.

They found the cows and shooed them to the barn.

At lunch they told the family that they had seen the swaggie's camp.

Burton looked concerned and said, "I sure hope he understands that we get flash floods at this time of the year and the clouds over the mountains have been building all morning. I'll take a ride down and warn him."

Later in the afternoon Burton rode up to the barn where everyone was busy with the milking. "Can't find your swaggie," he said to Isobel and Eva but I left him a note. Only problem is he may be illiterate."

"What's illiterate mean dad?" asked Keith.

"It means he hasn't learned to read. That's why you have to go to school so you learn to read and write and do the sums."

During the night there was a flash flood.

Burton heard it crunching and crashing its way down the Stewart Creek. It was faint at first but he recognized it instantly and said to Marion, "It's a flash flood coming down the Stewart, I sure hope the swaggie got my message."

The roaring continued in intensity and swept past.

Burton and Marion snuggled up in bed knowing they were safe and that the family were all asleep.

The next morning after breakfast Burton suggested they take a stroll down to the creek to check out if the flash flood had caused any damage.

Often the floods would rip out hundreds of yards

of fencing which allowed the cows to wander into the rainforest and get lost.

When they all reached the crossing the evidence of the flood was everywhere. The grass was laid flat, branches of trees were entangled along the bank, the fence was broken with several posts ripped out, and evidence of erosion was along both banks.

The girls walked onto the remains of the sandbar that once was over 30 yards wide. It was now barely five yards as the sand had been scoured out and pushed down stream into the main river.

"This is where the swaggie had his tent," said Eva.

She bent down and found a piece of china. It looked like the handle of a cup that was decorated in blue on a white background.

"Look here's more," said Madeline from five yards downstream.

For the next hour the girls hunted for remnants of the swaggie's camp.

The men in the meanwhile had repaired the fence and sent Burt up to the high paddock to count the herd.

"Let's go home," called Burton.

"One photo we need before we all go home," said Ginger and he lifted the little camera. The family crowded around and then sat on the bank of the creek and smiled.

As they traipsed along the track towards the house

Isobel said, "I hope the swaggie is alright and that the china and cutlery we found are pieces he left behind."

Burton looked glum but didn't reply. His thoughts were indeed, darker.

Chapter 37

Molly had her third birthday just before Easter and then Burton went on a journey he would never forget.

King Billy arrived at the wood heap and chopped the wood as he had done often before.

As Burton was paying him in goods the kindly aborigine said, "You are a true friend of my people Burton Johnson. I asked myself how could I repay you then it came to me. We would like to take you to our ceremonial grounds and invite you to be one of the tribe. Will you come?"

Burton was taken back by such a suggestion.

He had never known anyone to be given such a privilege and he felt sure that it was not an invitation made lightly.

He agreed readily and made off to get provisions to what would be a fortnight away from the family.

He explained to them all what he was doing and that he would be away for a time and they were to do all their chores and look after each other.

Burton returned after an absence of ten days.

He had been high in the mountains but would not

talk about his adventures and experiences. He was a changed man and held his head high and had an air of confidence about himself.

Marion knew better than to ask any questions but she did note that there were odd looking scars that ran down Burton's chest. She had seen the same ones on King Billy's chest and remembered being told they were evidence of initiation into the aboriginal tribe.

June, July and August were beautiful months with warmth and moisture combining to make the grasses grow, birds to sings and the butterflies to swarm in their thousands.

The birthdays of Max, Isobel, Burt and Eva went quietly by.

The price of cream was at an all-time low and at the same time the unemployment in Australia reached 30%. The valley struggled to make ends meet but it wasn't in the dire straits that the rest of the country was in. Burton remained optimistic, "It can't go on forever, eventually we'll see a change in our fortunes."

The wild pigs continued to be a source of meat for the community. The hunting parties kept up a steady supply of pork to everyone.

In October a near fatal incident left the whole family shaken.

As was the practice the cream was taken by flattie by the boys on their way to school. It was left on the jetty and the empties collected in the afternoon.

One day it was decided that Burt would row into the village with Keith and Max.

Molly was determined to go as well and put on a performance to the point where Burt said, "She'll be alright with me."

The four set off with Hercules towing the slide upon which was loaded the cream. Molly had insisted she be on the slide as well.

The boys all walked along near the gigantic horse.

At the crossing the cream was loaded in the flattie along with the children.

Burt whacked Hercules on the rump and said, "Home, boy, home." The horse trotted off up the track.

Burt pushed the flattie into the deeper water and clambered in. He placed the oars in the rowlocks and rowed.

The trip was an easy one as long as the boat was kept in the centre of the creek.

Unbeknown to Burt a tree had fallen over during the night and part of a branch was beneath the water and reaching out into the middle of the creek.

As the tide was going out it was easy rowing and the boat was moving swiftly along.

They were within 80 yards of where the Stewart flowed into the main river when disaster struck.

The bow of the flattie hit the submerged branch and it came to a sudden stop.

The four cream cans shifted forward taking Molly overboard. Burt saw his little sister hit the water and his survival instincts kicked in. He threw himself after her and managed to grab her flailing hand.

When he looked up the flattie tipped sideways spilling Keith out. The boat righted itself and went spinning towards the river with Max standing in the middle screaming.

Keith reached the mangroves that grew alongside and managed to squeeze his way in and out of the tangled roots until he found solid ground.

He didn't see what had happened to the others as everything happened too fast.

He called out to each in turn but didn't hear a reply.

He kept hearing his father's voice over and over in his head. "If you ever get into trouble I will help you."

To Keith the only thing to do was to run home and get dad to help.

He struggled through the undergrowth and eventually came into clearing.

He could make out the Hayden farm house so he knew that he had to run along the creek to find his father.

He ran with a determination that he didn't believe

he had. His brothers' and little sister's lives depended on him.

Marion was sitting on the verandah with the twins playing at her feet when Keith emerged from the tree line down by the Douglas Creek.

"What on earth is going on?" she said aloud and the twins looked up.

Marion called out to Madeline who came running onto the verandah followed by Eva and Isobel.

The urgency in their mother's voice alarmed them all. "Something's wrong," she said and handed Rita to Eva and Phyllis to Isobel. "Madeline run to Keith and help him along. I'll get Hercules and ride down to you. Your father has just gone to the Hayden's house so I need to catch him. Go."

Madeline took to the steps two at a time; Marion rushed out the back door heading for the stables.

Hercules had come home as ordered and the girls had taken off the slide and fed him. He was standing motionless in the yard hoping for a pulling job.

Marion grabbed his mane and flung herself onto his back. Although a fine horsewoman she had miscalculated and tumbled back down. Her age was showing as was her lack of riding practice.

Marion moved the huge horse along until he came to the post they used to get the children to mount the horses. Burton had built with steps so that it was simply a matter of stepping up, throwing a leg over the horse and the child mounted.

Marion held the mane in a fierce grip and urged Hercules into a trot.

He could sense that Marion wanted him to move faster so he settled into a canter. Marion bobbed up and down as she sort the rhythm that would make the ride smoother.

Ahead she could see that Madeline had caught up to Keith and was helping him along. Marion called to Hercules to whoa and he stopped just in time.

"Mum the others have been thrown into the Stewart Creek just before the outlet to the river. Keith doesn't know what happened to them," called Madeline.

Marion turned the horse and galloped at speed towards the Hayden farm. She had to get to Burton and raise the alarm. Their precious children were in danger and every second would count.

Burton and Barry were on the verandah when Barry jumped up and said, "Who is that going hell for leather?" and he pointed to the track from the Johnson farm.

"It's Marion riding Hercules, bareback which means there's an emergency." said Burton. He ran down the steps to where Gypsy was tethered.

Barry ran through the house calling, "I'll get my horse and catch up."

Burton mounted Gypsy and spurred her away

towards the approaching horse and rider.

Marion was relieved to see Burton galloping towards her and pulled Hercules up. "The children have been dumped in the creek just before you get to the river. Burt, Max and Molly are missing. Keith ran all the way home to alert us."

"Oh no not again, I can't lose anymore," said Burton and he urged Gypsy into a gallop heading cross country towards the junction of the Stewart and Douglas Creeks.

Barry Hayden caught up to Marion and heard her story. He galloped after Burton after calling back, "Go onto Sally and ring for help."

Marion's hand flew to her mouth and she began to sob. "Telephone, oh how foolish. Why didn't I use the telephone instead of dashing off in a panic."

She pushed on to meet Sally Hayden.

Sally took over and telephoned the telephonist who set in place a rescue party.

Burton reached the area he was led to believe his children had come to grief.

He began shouting names and listening for replies.

Nothing.

He began to move down stream calling.

Nothing.

Barry Hayden reined up alongside.

"The children could be anywhere between here and the river," said Burton.

"I'll ford the creek and come down the other side," said Barry.

Burton heard the launch as it raced along the river and knew that a search party was coming from that direction. He heard it slow up as it reached the mouth of the Stewart Creek.

Several minutes later he heard voices calling. He yelled back the names of the missing children and heard the strong male voices calling these into the bush.

Gypsy shied and nearly threw Burton and when he steadied the horse he realized he was looking at Burt who had stumbled from the scrub right in front of him.

Burt was a mess but was holding Molly in his arms.

Burton jumped from his horse and grabbed his two children.

"Sorry dad," was all Burt could whisper before he collapsed. Burton eased him to the ground and took Molly from his arms.

"We've got one here," called a voice from the direction of the river. "He's frightened but seems okay."

"I've got the others," called back Burton.

There was a loud tooooot from the launch to indicate that the search was over and everyone could return home.

Burt was helped onto Gypsy by his father. Burton

had taken the girl from Burt and now hugged her into his chest and led the horse towards home.

As the trio came out into the clearing they could see horses and lorries making their way to the Johnson house.

The launch was on the sand at the crossing.

Everyone had gathered at the Johnsons to make sure the emergency had ended well and that the full story could be heard.

"The difficult thing in this environment is to know what is happening. You can be a yard or less from another person and not know they are there," said Chas Osborne.

He was one of 23 men who sat around on the verandah at the Johnson house. They were the ones who had down tools and rushed to help a fellow farmer in trouble.

The story had been slowly pieced together and Burton had thanked them all for their quick response and favourable outcome.

The Johnson family was back as a whole and all were safe.

Keith was happiest of all because he was the hero of the day and he managed to miss out on a day of school.

It would take him months to stop feeling the pain of the stinging nettle that he had brushed past on his desperate race to get help. He did wear the scratches and welts as badges of honour and his stories became more and more embellished at each new telling.

Max had stayed in the boat which had then become entangled in the mangroves. The men in the launch found him and had to swim to get the flattie back out. He enjoyed the launch trip up the Stewart and the big hug from his mother.

Chapter 38

Several days after the near tragedy of falling out of the boat the family was surprised to see Burton riding Gypsy up from the crossing with two other horses in tow. He reined in at the hitching post below the verandah and looked up to see the whole family looking down in expectation. "No more flatties for the little ones and quicker journeys for all. I've bought these extra horses so we can all ride where ever we are going."

Marion had the equestrian knowledge and she was pleased to see the new horses. She would teach the younger ones so that they could ride to school.

"The grey with the dappled black on its hind is a mare and looks very gentle. The sorrel is only young and a bit frisky but seems to have a nice temperament."

"What are they called?" asked Isobel, always the first to seek out clarification in any new situation.

"Well, the owners I bought them from told me it was for us to name them and train them so that they would ease into our family. I'm leaving it up to you all to come up with names. Remember that one is a boy and the other a girl," said Burton.

Everyone spoke at once and names shot around the verandah at a rapid pace.

Marion asked for quiet and then asked each child to nominate the name they would call the mare. She then had Isobel write these on a sheet of paper. "Now we shall take a vote on the grey mare's name. One vote only as you hear the names that Isobel reads out," explained Marion.

The mare became known as Queen Bee and even neighed loudly when Marion made the announcement. This caused a great deal of laughter.

The gelding was a bit trickier as two names received the same number of votes. Marion declared that she would have the final vote so he became Prince rather than Neddy.

As Burton led the horses away towards the stables he called back, "Merry Christmas to you all as these are your presents."

Max, Keith and Molly were soon put in the saddles by Marion who taught them all to be sensible and reliable riders.

It wasn't long before the boys were allowed to ride to school and even carry the cans of cream tied to the saddles.

For Max and Keith going to school became a lot easier although there was an absolute rule that now had to be obeyed. Burton spoke to all the family about riding across the creek. He said, "Always follow the horse's lead as it has far greater senses than we do. If it baulks, shies or turns away then do not go on especially into water. It is likely the horse has sensed a snake or a crocodile. If it happens at the crossing you will go upstream and cross near the Francis farm. That is a rule I expect you all to obey."

Guy Fawkes Night was one to forget as the Great Depression continued unabated and finding money to blow up was not on anyone's mind. Although the family missed out on one explosive incident they were in the thick of another.

Ginger had been readily accepted into the family and felt more like a Johnson than a Whittaker. His flaming red hair wasn't easy to miss although Burton and some of the others had similar colours. He had become a reliable youth who fitted into the family. He was easy to converse with and joined in all the activities that the others enjoyed.

He was, however, a point of interest for the older Johnson girls.

They had never fully accepted him as a brother mainly because he was handsome and engaging and had a worldly view. Madeline and Eva spent a lot of time being jealous of each other while Isobel was fascinated by the tall, ginger headed youth but didn't quite know why.

All came to a head one evening when Keith came into the kitchen and said, "Guess what I saw? Madeline and Ginger were kissing in the barn."

Eva's hand rushed to her mouth but not blurting out, "How could she…?"

Isobel was not happy with the news.

The others all sat quietly waiting for Burton or Marion to hit the roof. The silence continued as they all waited the arrival of the couple and the explosion that they could see coming.

Madeline and Ginger walked in and stopped. "What's wrong?" asked Madeline concerned about the silence.

Ginger pushed passed and sat in his place at the dinner table.

"Ginger," said Burton, "Are you and Madeline attracted to each other from a girl and boy point of view?"

Madeline blushed and turned her head away; Ginger opened his mouth and closed it again.

"Well?" asked Burton louder than necessary.

"I saw you kissing," ventured Keith.

Madeline could see that the only way to end the speculation was to be truthful. "Yes, dad we love each other."

Pandemonium broke out with whistles, cheering, jeering until Burton called a halt. "We need to talk. Come along Marion."

What was said between the four was never disclosed but Madeline and Ginger were seen walking everywhere hand in hand.

Marion kept a stern eye on the couple to ensure there was no further 'hanky-panky' as she called it.

The school sports were held on the sandbar and both Max and Keith excelled. They were the proud recipients of certificates for winning races and being Year Champions.

Christmas was a quiet affair in the Johnson house although Marion did make sure they heard the story of Christ's birth.

Keith celebrated his ninth birthday by being on his most cooperative behaviour. This was somewhat contrary to what Burton and Marion were observing. Burton had said, "That Keith is headed for a fall with the way he is thinking. Everything he does is full of mischief and daring. I just hope we can avert a major problem and turn his thinking around."

"You are right my dear," said Marion. "The behaviour is one thing but the way he's got Max following his every footstep is my biggest worry. Max has such a lovely nature it would be a shame to see him slip into bad habits and lose his cuteness."

New Year's Eve was spent in the Butter Factory with the rest of the community enjoying the fun, games, dancing and supper that was provided by the more energetic and civil minded of the Daintree folk.

The wet season was late coming although they all knew that when it arrived it would be constant wet and miserable for at least three months.

Ginger began a new project in late February based on the new horses and his love of craft.

He designed and sewed hessian horses. These were stuffed with grasses or straw and handed out to the twins and Molly. The rest of the family were amazed by how lifelike they looked with black buttons for eyes, brown felt for hoofs and hair for the manes and tail. He had taken each strand of hair individually and sewn them on.

He cut up leather from old shoes and shaped this into saddles with shoelaces as reins. They stood over a foot high and a foot and a half long. Ginger dyed the hessian to make one brown and the other two black.

Marion was so taken by the cleverness that she took one along to the weekly club that Sally Hayden was holding. The other ladies were equally as impressed and wanted to invite Ginger to their next meeting.

Ginger declined the offer as he was too shy to sit with a group of mature ladies but he did suggest that Madeline should go as she had been his helping hand and could easily show the process.

In March an engagement party revitalized the family and began a daylong celebration.

Madeline and Ginger had taken to long moonlit night strolls when the weather permitted.

One evening they came into the kitchen, holding hands and giggling.

The rest of their siblings had already headed for bed and were in an exhausted sleep from the day's activity.

Marion looked up from the stove where she was preparing a large pot of scrambled eggs for the next day's breakfast.

Madeline sat down and pulled Ginger onto the next chair and said, "You ask them, Ginger, go on."

"Ask us what?" said Burton and the seriousness in his voice made Ginger hesitate. "Well son, speak up or has the cat got your tongue?" asked Burton.

"Now, now Burton give the boy a fair go," said Marion.

Ginger looked up and looked sheepishly at Burton and stuttered, "May I, I, I em marry Madeline?"

Madeline poked him in the ribs and hissed, "Permission!"

Ginger tried again, "Uh, I mean may I have your permission and blessing to marry your daughter?"

Burton looked at Ginger then to Marion who had a twinkle in her eye. He looked back at Madeline and could see the love she had for this redheaded youth that he was always proud to call son. "Yes you certainly may but I do expect it to be a long engagement."

Madeline hugged Ginger and rushed to her father and then her mother. "Thank you ever so much. We will do you both proud and that's a promise, lots of little red-headed grandchildren."

Marion looked into her daughter's blue eyes and expected to see them sparkling but was momentarily shocked to see them glass over. When she looked again the sparkle was back and Madeline was sitting on Ginger's knee.

The next morning the official announcement was made by Burton at the breakfast table.

As Isobel said, "Worst kept secret ever, dad and the way this pair have been carrying on ever since they got up to go milking. We all knew something was afoot."

Keith was the next casualty that required an emergency trip to the Mossman Hospital.

He was showing off and had been dared by one of the older boys at school to climb to the top of a conifer. He took the challenge and set about climbing up and found the going easy.

Max had called to stop and come to down but Keith's bravado went from strength to strength.

Eventually, he was 60 feet up at the top swaying precariously but not caring for his safety. Even when a gust of wind swept through it didn't stop his skylarking.

Finally, he'd had enough fun and began to descend.

He was chuffed that he's not only climbed the tree but had been a dare devil as well.

Keith was only 16 feet from the ground and making ready to celebrate when his foot slipped.

As he wasn't expecting any problems he lost his balance and his grip and fell. He bounced off several branches and careered into the ground right shoulder first.

Max, who was standing near heard a snapping noise and thought it was one of the smaller branches breaking off.

Keith cried out in agony and knew it was his arm that had made the sound. The pain shot up through his arm and into his head.

"You alright?" asked Max going to Keith's aid.

"No, I think I've broken my arm. Go get help."

As the school was the closest building Max made for this and brought Miss Cameron scurrying back. She confirmed the worst and put Keith's arm in a sling before helping him back to the school house. From there she set about an emergency plan to get Keith to the Mossman Hospital and Burton informed.

Keith came home a few days later with a plaster covering his right forearm and a sling to keep the break immobile.

He was a hero to his mates but Burton and Marion were not so pleased.

They used Keith's demise as a lesson for all. They were all told not to go climbing trees and definitely not to be pressured by your peer group.

All the birthdays through April, June, July and August were held in lovely warm weather.

Molly turned 4 and was a babbling little girl who wanted to help everyone. She was always glowing and asking questions.

Max turned seven and was popular with all his siblings. Marion was always comparing him to her own brothers what with his black wavy hair and dark complexion. She reminded him so much of her brother Rueben although she prayed he would never have his fate. Rueben had been killed in the First World War at Pozieres in France.

Isobel turned 15 and kept the spirit that had been with her throughout her primary school life. She loved to read and write and use her imagination to make up the most enthralling and weirdest of stories.

Burt became a fully qualified lorry driver when he turned 19 and thought about setting up a transport firm.

He didn't think there would be enough jobs in the Daintree but he reckoned he could do business from Mossman as far south as Cairns and north into

Cooktown. To the west, he could take in Mareeba and Atherton and beyond.

All he needed was the money and a partner.

Ginger seemed too pre-occupied with his love life so he would have to keep searching.

Eva turned 17 and continued to be her mother's reflection. She was always so homely and motherly to all the children but especially the three little girls. Marion would never have coped without her constant help in the kitchen and around the house. On top of this, she did not neglect the other chores like milking, mending, sewing, washing and ironing.

Chapter 39

In September Madeline and Ginger decided that their engagement had lasted long enough and they married. It was a community affair with everyone in the valley coming from near and afar.

Madeline was beyond excitement as Marion fussed around adjusting the beautiful lace wedding gown.

Marion had been hard at sewing for weeks on the Singer sewing machine and had received more than enough advice from her daughter and the women of the club.

The day dawned gloriously and Madeline was excused from the milking as she had so much to do personally before walking down the aisle to the love of her life.

Eva and Isobel finished their milking chores and after a small breakfast they rushed off to be fitted into their gowns as they were the Maidens of Honour.

Molly waited impatiently for the adults to be ready before excitedly being told it was her turn to put on the white dress made especially for her by Sally Hayden.

Burton had taken the boys and Ginger off to the lodge in town for the night as he was a stickler for tradition.

The bride and groom were not to see each other on the day of the wedding until they met at the altar.

Marion was likewise determined that the marriage would be a church one or at least as close as she could make it.

She had arranged for the Mossman Anglican priest, Father Hegarty, to officiate. Marion had paid his fare on the ferry from Port Douglas and put him up in the lodge. He would accompany the males when they came in the Osborne lorry with other guests.

By one thirty the house had been transformed into a quasi-church. The lounge room was to be the chapel with rows of chairs separated by an aisle and a table with a white cloth acted as the altar.

The whole room was decorated with floral arrangements made from the orchids and ferns found in the rainforest. Pretty pink and blue ribbons were tied in bows on the arms of the chairs along the aisle.

The lorry arrived along with cars, horses, buggies and people.

Almost the entire community was there.

Burton had Ginger and Burt dropped off at the barn.

Here he had Eva organize a borrowed spring cart to be harnessed to Gypsy so that at the exact moment he could signal the boys to trot up to the house where

Keith would tether the horse and Ginger and his best man, Burt, would make their way up the steps and into the lounge room.

A few seconds later Madeline would follow Molly out of the boys' bedroom, which had been converted into a temporary dressing room for ladies, out the back door and around to the steps and into the room where the crowd was anxiously waiting.

Molly waited at the front door to get her signal to advance. She had a small wicker basket crooked in her left arm that was full of petals from numerous plants found around the farm. Molly walked with measured steps reaching into the basket to withdraw a handful of petals and scatter them on the floor.

Molly looked up and saw Ginger looking resplendent in a navy blue suit, white shirt, polished black shoes, tie of contrasting blue stripes and his flaming red hair. She could have burst from pride but was concentrating hard so as to not trip or forget to throw out another handful of petals.

As Molly neared the altar Marion reached out and guided her to the seat next to her.

There was a gasp from the crowd as Madeline appeared looking like a princess disguised as an angel. She held her head high and moved as if floating on air, towards her beloved. She clasped her father's arm with her right arm and held a bouquet of orchids in her left. A lace veil cascaded from her head down to her shoulders.

Ginger nudged his best man Burt and grinned from ear to ear.

Burton who was escorting Madeline was looking every inch a city slicker. No longer in farm clothes with wind swept hair and grime over his hands and face. He had been transformed into the bride's father all in a light brown double-breasted suit, white shirt, yellow tie and black shoes.

He towered over Madeline and as they walked he kept nervously patting her arm that was entwined in his.

Behind Madeline were the Ladies in Waiting, Eva and Isobel. Both wore dresses and carried lovely bouquets of flowers made from orchids found in the rainforest.

Father Hegarty waited for the bride to reach the altar and watched as Burton gave her away to Ginger. He then began a short but moving ceremony.

At the point where he asked if any man or woman should see fit to object to the couple marrying only Eva showed signs of fidgeting.

Burt as best man produced the wedding ring without any hitch and Ginger slipped it easily on the tiny finger of Madeline and noted how beautifully it fitted next to the small diamond engagement ring.

Finally, the priest declared Madeline and George to be husband and wife. George kissed Madeline with a tender and most endearing kiss and felt her warmth flow back through him.

After signing the Marriage Certificate everyone followed Madeline and Ginger out onto the verandah.

Here Ginger had arranged for Keith to take wedding photos. He had placed the Brownie on a makeshift tripod and all the boy had to do was press the shutter. He had practised the day before for several shots until Ginger was confident that he could accomplish the task.

"Smile," yelled Keith and he pushed the shutter. An audible click told Ginger the photograph had been taken.

With a few more changes of position, several other photographs were taken of the wedding party before the crowd followed Marion back inside for afternoon tea.

Afternoon tea was a banquet as Marion and the girls had spared nothing in what they had cooked and the amount was enormous.

As Marion said, "Depression or no Depression, my girl will get all she deserves on her wedding day, no horses spared."

At an appointed time in the afternoon, Madeline and Ginger snuck away to the bathroom where they changed into their going away clothes.

They reappeared and climbed into the buggy with Chas Osborne acting as the driver.

They were setting off on the first leg of their honeymoon which would take them to Cairns for three days and then over the ranges to settle in Atherton.

They were leaving the valley although they would return on visits.

Marion said a teary farewell and told them to take care whereas Burton hugged his daughter and told Ginger, "You look after that girl of ours I want no harm to come to her."

Marion had had a long and delightful day. Everything had gone like clockwork and she nestled down beside Burton ready for a well-earned rest. "Thank you, my wonderful husband," she said and cuddled him tightly.

Marion felt a twinge in her midriff and smiled. "Number ten was alive and moving. She hadn't told anyone yet although the older girls may have guessed but were staying quiet.

Marion had had a dream run ever since missing her period back in May. Thankfully she had not experienced the morning sickness and nausea that usually followed during the day. All was developing so easily and Marion was headed for a Christmas birth. "Imagine having a baby on the Saviour's Birthday, that would be special," she thought.

A few weeks later Ginger picked up the photographs from the Atherton Post Office.

He was so excited to see how they turned out he opened them.

He was shocked and unnerved to see the first

photograph which was of everyone who attended.

It was as exactly as he recalled with all the community standing behind him and Madeline. Above Madeline's laced veil was an aura. Not large but distinct enough to make Ginger uneasy.

"Must be that the camera is broken," he muttered. He looked at the next and the next and each one showed the same aura sitting above Madeline. Three photographs did not have Madeline in and these were perfect. The light imperfection was not evident.

"How can that be?" wondered Ginger.

Knowing that Madeline was superstitious and would possibly read something sinister into the auras Ginger tore all the imperfect photographs into tiny fragments and then deposited them in a nearby bin.

He would have to tell Madeline a 'little white lie' but it did not augur well.

Chapter 40

The students were busy with their story writing on a warm Friday afternoon when they were disturbed by a loud knock on the classroom door.

Miss Cameron looked up from behind her desk and then smiled. "Hello there Mr Osborne, please come in." The huge frame of the amicable Chas Osborne sauntered into the room. "Beg your pardon miss but I would like to ask you all if you would like to come to a picnic at the entrance on Friday?"

The children all burst out into cheers and it took all Miss Cameron's skill to regain order. "I shall get them all to copy an invitation from the board so that the parents all know what you have proposed. From my point of view, it sounds like a jolly good idea, A bit of community spirit is just the thing we need."

The community rallied around Chas Osborne's idea and hordes turned up at the jetty where the ferries *Daintree* and *Echo* were moored.

The Osborne brothers had not yet been able to part with the boats even though several offers to buy had been put forward.

Everyone was carrying a basket of sorts filled to

brimming with goodies and a travel rug.

The journey downstream was full of fun and laughter as people caught up with each other and the children played games.

The ferries, with the larger *Daintree* leading made a wide sweep out into the ocean and then lined up with the end of Snapper Island. About half way to the island they made a further adjustment and headed for shore.

The crowds on each ferry were pointing excitedly at the sweeping yellow sands of the beach.

The boats anchored and the lighters were lowered and one by one the people were transferred to the beach.

It was a warm day with blue sky in every direction. The fun and games continued unabated until Eva said, "I'm hungry let's eat." So they all agreed with the idea and out came the food and drinks.

After a lazy hour, it was swimming time as the temperature had continued to climb and it was quite hot.

The day seemed to come to an end all too quickly but it was cut short by the hooting of the *Daintree's* fog horn.

It wasn't long after the community picnic that Marion announced that she would be going on holiday. There were nudges between Eva and Isobel. Burton grinned broadly. Marion packed her overnight bag and caught the Osborne bus headed for Mossman.

Miss Cameron was fidgety and nervous and had been ever since the students had sat at their desks. It was most unlike her as she always appeared confident and in charge.

By recess time the older students had become concerned so much so that they took a vote and Beverley Carson one of the senior students was elected to ask Miss Cameron what was bothering her. "Excuse me miss," said Bev, "I don't mean to pry but you are not your old self today. Is something bothering you?"

Miss Cameron looked over her glasses and grimaced, "Very perceptive of you my dear. I have had news which I am dreading to pass on to you all but for me it is wonderful."

"I'm confused miss," said Beverley Carson. "You are happy with the news but sad that the news will upset us?"

"That's it precisely."

"Well, I suppose the only way to deal with this is to tell us and let us be pleased for you."

"Yes you are right and it will bring everything out rather than me feeling miserable."

At that point, Miss Cameron rang the bell and when everyone was seated she said, "I have good and bad news for you all. Please let me finish before you put up your hands to ask questions. I will be leaving the valley at the end of the year as I have been notified of a transfer to Mareeba. This is good news as my elderly parents live in Mareeba and they need my help in their dotage. The bad news is I will be leaving the most wonderful group of students I have ever met. So I'm pulled between staying and going but alas I have little choice but to go."

The look on the students' faces told the story and the solemness for the rest of the day attested to their sadness.

Everyone in the valley was saddened to hear the news of Miss Cameron's transfer and they rallied around to ensure the rest of the year would be memorable for her.

The Sport's Day was organized by the father's committee and was a huge success.

Keith and Max received certificates for winning their races and being champions of their year level.

A special send-off afternoon tea was held for Miss Cameron where she made a teary thank you speech and left everyone with wet eyes. The community presented her with a gold fountain pen which pleased her no end.

On the final day of school, the students kept up an incessant amount of "thank yous" and giving of hand-made presents.

The big question on everyone's lips was, "Who would be the new teacher and what would she be like?"

No one ventured to suggest it would be a man.

Christmas was quiet with Marion carrying out the traditional celebration.

The lorry came around and the Johnson family happily joined in the carol singing. Father Christmas gave out little stickers with Christmas messages on them.

Eva and Isobel tried to keep everyone happy on Christmas day by cooking one of the turkeys that the family was now breeding. They added roast potatoes, pumpkin, sweet potatoes and cabbage. Everything came from the farm so the cost was minimal. For sweets, they ate fruit salad of diced mango and diced watermelon and this was smothered in cream.

The telephone rang three days after Christmas and Burton answered it. "A girl, right and Marion? She's fine and the baby's a ball of energy. Thank you, matron."

He put down the receiver and turned to the family who had all stopped eating breakfast. "Your mum has had a baby girl and all is well."

"Baby name?" asked Rita.

Phyllis was more concerned with her position in the family than names, "I'm no more baby?"

"Now we will have to celebrate all these birthdays and Christmas and New Year together or we will be forever partying," said Isobel.

"That's not fair," said Keith who had been waiting

excitedly for his tenth birthday that was due in two days' time.

"You won't miss out boy but I agree with Isobel, next year we will need to rationalize the celebrations across Christmas and New Year," said Burton.

The New Year Party in the Butter Factory was organized and ready to roll when the rain pelted down.

The creeks flowed, swelled and flooded as the valley copped ten inches in an afternoon.

The telephones began ringing to let everyone know that the New Year's Eve Party was cancelled.

Isobel was so looking forward to New Year's Eve Party because she had an interest in Tommy MacGregor and it would have been the perfect opportunity to get close and personal.

"I think they need to have a New Year Party in July when it's sunny and dry," Isobel said. "It seems that January first in the Daintree Valley has a 90% chance of being a washout."

Burt was also miffed by the cancellation. The Francis family had moved into a farm further up the Stewart Creek and Connie had caught his eye.

He had been driving the lorry for the Osbornes as they were being snowed under with orders to move animals around so they had taken on an extra driver.

Burt had been sent to the Francis farm to pick up a

few head of cattle and pigs. They were destined for the Mossman Sales Yards.

When he arrived he was met by Mr Francis who told him to wait in the house until they could get the cattle from out of the rainforest. They had crashed through the fences and gone AWOL.

Burt offered to help but the old fellow would have nothing of this. He kept saying, "You go in the house and the wife and girl will entertain you and give you morning tea."

Burt was mystified by the reluctance to accept the help but was pleased to be going to see Connie. She was unusually pretty with a high forehead and long dark trusses that reached to her waist. Connie was slim with a ready infectious giggle and always seemed happy and no amount of teasing would faze her.

As Burt entered the kitchen he was greeted by Mrs Francis who pointed to the tea and scones on the table and said, "They're yours, eat them up now."

A few seconds later Connie entered the room and sat coyly in the chair opposite Burt. "Hello," she ventured, "I'm Connie Francis and you must be Burton Johnson."

"Burt," he corrected her through a mouthful.

Mrs Francis said, "Do you want a scone, Connie?"

"No thanks mum," she said.

It didn't take Burt long to polish off the morning tea. He was too embarrassed to take the second helping offered as his mother had always said it was bad manners to eat other people out of house and home.

Connie sat opposite him looking intensely at him but he kept his eyes averted.

She was the confident one and was in charge of her destiny.

He was unable to converse with her and his tough exterior didn't tell the turmoil inside.

Suddenly Connie jumped up and said, "Come on Burt I'll show you the new piglets we've got."

He sheepishly said thanks to Mrs Francis and walked after the girl.

She was well ahead and pretending to be an aeroplane by holding both arms outstretched. An engine noise came from her mouth and at the same time she ducked and weaved.

Burt had to run to catch up.

"Do you talk?" Connie asked him as he reached her.

"Of course I do, it's just that I don't know you or your parents so it's hard to know what to say."

"I talk incessantly so my pa says. He reckons I could talk the hide off an elephant."

They both laughed and the iciness between them was broken. The relationship was destined for great things.

Chapter 41

On the 22nd January Marion arrived home after taking the Osborne's bus from Mossman. Chas was driving and in his helpful way he insisted on taking Marion along the Stewart Creek Road and home.

In her arms Marion cuddled her tenth and final baby, little Marjorie to be forever called Marge. She was a happy child, readily hungry and went to sleep when put down.

Life for Marion soon returned to normal and the help of Eva and Isobel with the baby was appreciated.

Life for the Johnson family settled into a routine although the incessant rain left everyone glum.

"Should be used to this by now," said Burton, "This is our eighth wet season since we arrived and they've all been pretty much a carbon copy of each other."

Burton was to be proved wrong in his prediction for the weather of 1934.

But before that was to happen Keith and Max were to meet their new teacher.

They arrived at school on the first day rather late. It was a constant problem the boys faced. They had to be up at four thirty, make their beds, dress for work, get the cows in, help with milking, separate the cream, have breakfast, feed the horses and brush them, check the horseshoes, have a wash, get dressed for school, saddle the horses, pick up the cream cans and ride into the Butter Factory.

During the wet season the ford was often awash so they had to go upstream to the Francis's crossing which added more miles to the trip. So being late was excusable when any reasonable thinking person took in all the things the boys had to do.

As they dismounted from the horses a loud, male voice called to them, "What are you two up to? School commenced ten minutes ago. I will not have unpunctual students at my school. Get inside this instance."

Keith and Max had met the new teacher who they were to find out went by the name of Mr Severly. He was a hard task master and a very strict disciplinarian. The boys were quick to learn to do as they were told and to be punctual.

Mr Severly went by the motto 'Children should be seen but not heard'. He wasn't tall but was energetic almost running between places or activities. He was always dressed in a suit and tie and looked immaculate. He never favoured anyone and if there was discipline to be handed out he would wield the cane with gusto.

The students all came to fear him and after the

delightful Miss Cameron they all felt they had been sent the devil incarnate.

Max tried to be on his best behaviour and offered to help out in any capacity he could. He rarely got any acknowledgement for his kindness.

At home things were the opposite as Max found that everyone delighted in his company. He was becoming a clever story teller although had a long way to go to catch up to Isobel.

Marion was so taken by the way that Max was growing up that she confided in Burton one day, "Max reminds me of my brother Frank. They are certainly both Stewarts with their black, wavy hair and dark complexions. The real likeness though comes in their natures. They are both kind, considerate and gentle. Mary Jane, my mother, saw Frank as a future priest and guided him in that direction. He is training in Melbourne at the Seminary. I think Max has this same disposition and he could be gently guided in the same direction. What do you think, Burton?"

"You know your children better than me my love. All I need are willing and strong hands to do the chores around the farm," replied Burton.

The wet season had been depressing with most activities outdoors being put on hold except the necessities like milking. The weather had been unkind and the rain was a constant reminder that the family lived in the tropics.

Ginger and Madeline made the trip from the Atherton to visit. Madeline had pleaded with Ginger to make the trip as she missed her family. Unfortunately, her timing was to be disastrous.

The tropics are where cyclones form and take on a power that can be awesome.

As February came to a close the waters in the Coral Sea a few hundred miles south of the equator began to heat up. Days of above 72-degree temperatures caused massive evaporation and this coupled with the convection caused by the heating resulted in thunderstorms. The moisture from the sea was sucked up thousands of feet into the air, where it was cooled and fell as droplets. As the heating intensified so did the winds and the force of the updrafts.

A destructive cyclone came to life and began its drunken sailor wander around the Pacific Ocean. As it moved slowly it continued to intensify and make for the North Queensland coast.

The tiny community of Daintree was isolated and any news that filtered through was many days old. The telephone system had improved but was unreliable. By the time the first farmer was alerted to the danger that was approaching the swirling mass of clouds was approaching landfall just north of Port Douglas. The

Daintree was in the cyclone's direct and deadly path.

The shipping that plied in these waters had observed the build-up of cloud and the increase in wind intensity and had all rushed for shelter on the leeward side of Snapper Island.

March 4th, 1934 dawned and everything in the tiny settlement of the Daintree seemed as normal.

The milking was finished in the dark and the Johnson family was enjoying a well-earned rest when the telephone rang.

At the same time Ginger walked into the kitchen and said, "Don't like the build-up of cloud away to the east. Could be a storm brewing."

Burton had reached the telephone and placed the receiver to his ear. After a long pause he said, "Thanks for the warning any suggestions as to how we ride this out?"

After nearly five minutes an ashen faced Burton placed the receiver in its cradle and sat down.

He looked at his family and quietly said, "Cyclone. That was Chas Osborne. There is a very intense cyclone headed this way. It could be one of the worst to hit Queensland. Chas is taking the ferry *Daintree* downstream to shelter in the Barrett Creek. She's loaded with a cargo of logs and is sitting low in the water. He is concerned that the tidal surge that is coming will be higher than we have ever experienced."

He stopped talking and seemed to be deep in thought. No-one moved as they were all desperately waiting to hear what they had to do to survive the approaching storm.

Although they had heard of cyclones and the damage they could wreak they had so far been spared a direct hit. This time it appeared there was going to be nowhere safe they could hide.

Burton sprung from his chair and began to issue orders. He was back in charge and armed with the information passed on by Chas Osborne he set about organizing the house in readiness for the strong winds that were expected within six hours.

"The safest place I believe will be the lounge room so Ginger and Burt you get all the pillows and mattresses and put them in that room. Marion and Madeline organize the supplies that we might need for the at least three days. Include water and lighting. Eva and Isobel take the cows to high ground and release the horses they will have to fend for themselves. Keith, Max, Molly and the twins can go outside and find any loose things and store them under the house or in the sheds. I don't want anything to be blown around as they can become missiles."

The urgency and anxiety showed in Burton's normally placid voice and everyone obeyed his commands. Within an hour they had all the instructions covered and had returned to the lounge room.

The lounge room was by now a jumble of furniture, pillows, mattresses, water containers and boxes of foodstuff.

"I'm scared," said Rita as she clung to her mother's dress.

"I'm sure we are all feeling anxious because it is fear of the unknown but we will be alright, God is looking over us," said Marion.

"I want the girls to stay with mum and set up the furniture up so we've got spaces to crawl under to keep safe. Put a mattress on top of the table and others on the floor. Keep everything pushed up to the inner wall away from the window," said Burton. "Burt, Ginger, Keith and Max can come with me and we'll nail planks onto the windows to lessen the chances of the glass breaking. We'll also try to tie down the roof with fencing wire."

He moved off with the boys eagerly following.

The younger boys ran off to the wood pile and hauled back a couple of planks at a time.

Burt ran for the blacksmith lean-to and hurried back with hammers and boxes of three inch nails.

Ginger rounded up fence posts and a spade and began to dig.

Burton found rolled up fencing wire and readied to throw these over the roof and tie them to the posts that Ginger was frantically trying to erect.

The day had started with a high humidity and light breeze from the north.

Burton paused in what he was doing and noticed the wind was increasing and was swinging to the north-east.

He took his hat from his head and wiped his sweating brow with the back of his hand. A smear of mud followed across his forehead. The red in his hair caught the sun and flared. "The clouds to the east are building rapidly and are turning dark grey. I think we are in for one hell of a bad night. Come on men put your backs into the jobs we are running out of time."

They all sat in silence in the lounge room listening to the wind howl through all the crevasses that it could find.

Each member of the family had found their safe spot whether it was under the redwood topped kitchen table, the up-turned lounge chairs or with their backs to the wall surrounded by mattresses and pillows. Marion had Marge asleep on her lap, Eva was cuddling the twins with one either side of her, Molly was sitting between Burt and Ginger, Madeline had sidled up to Ginger and had her arm lovingly around his shoulders, Keith and Max had found shelter under the upturned lounge chairs and were shaking from anticipation of being blown away or blasted to smithereens.

Burton paced up and around and went out to the back door to check on the cyclones advance. He came back time and again with a report each more dire than the previous.

Marion was becoming annoyed and said so, "Burton will you please stop you are putting fear into all our hearts."

"Sorry love," he said and sat down.

It was difficult to see what was happening outside although they could see between the planks that were nailed to the window.

What they could hear was the increasing wind and strange noises as the house and its surroundings began to take the strain of the intense wind gusts.

The thunder rolled over the valley and the first large drops of rain pattered onto the corrugated roof. Flashes of lightning illuminated the room as darkness began to descend upon the land. There was the distinct smell of ozone in the air.

As the minutes dragged on the wind began to strike and over the whistling another noise was heard. The corrugated iron on the roof was coming loose and flapping. As the wind pushed the galvanized roofing nails out of their positions the roofing iron flapped louder, then, a pinging noise herald the nails pulling out and hitting the roof some distance away. The corrugated iron was clattering at an ever increasing rate and Burton was fearful that the whole roof would lift and be flung into the creek.

Each member of the family had found another to

comfort them and now they were all clinging tightly and praying that the storm would pass.

Burton clambered to his feet and set off to the back door once again.

He was hit by a wet blast of wind as he opened the kitchen door leading to the back. The rain was being driven parallel to the floor through the gaping hole that was once the door leading outside.

He struggled along until he could see the damage that was being wreaked on the farm.

As he turned to go back to the relative safety of the lounge room there was a tremendous cracking noise.

He turned to see the huge fig tree that was in the yard past the thunderbox come crashing down. It had been caught in a vortex and with winds slashing from different directions the roots that had kept the tree upright for over a hundred years were wrenched outward. The tree fell with a loud crash.

As he watched in awe Burton noted that one of the branches had formed an arc with the stem and he could see a cave like structure beckoning.

He dismissed the thought and ran.

"Burton you're soaking wet whatever is happening?" asked Marion as her wet husband arrived back from another of his wanderings.

"I think we're going to lose the roof unless this calms," he said.

Almost as he spoke everything went still and quiet. The younger ones jumped out of their hiding places and began to cheer.

"Not so fast," said Burton in a loud voice. "This is the eye of the cyclone. It will come back stronger than before so get back into your places and hold on."

Burton turned to Burt and Ginger and said, "We need to do a quick reconnaissance to check if we can stay here and ride this out. Let's go. We've only got a few minutes so run."

From the reports that the three bought back it was obvious that the house was disintegrating and wouldn't hold up much longer.

The back end had taken the brunt of the winds and been speared with branches, fence posts and planks. The asbestos was shattered and gaping holes gouged out. The roof was missing and the back door was hanging by one hinge.

The front fared better but with the shift in winds that was about to happen then it would take a more severe battering.

"There's nothing left here so we need to find shelter elsewhere," said Burton.

"The old fig tree out back has crashed down and there's a cave like area underneath. We are making for there. Burt and Ginger grab as many mattresses as you can carry and get going. The rest take a hand of your brother or sister and run. We need to ride this out for another few hours. Go, go, go," he urged.

Chapter 42

The eye of the cyclone was moving all the time and the first that this registered with the family was when they heard the forest begin to crackle and fall.

They had all made it to the tree trunk and pushed as far as they could under the protection. The mattresses and pillows would give comfort until the rain soaked through.

The first noise that presaged the return of the cyclonic winds was far away along the upper reaches of the Stewart Creek.

One ancient redwood that had been left by the timber cutters as it was rotting inside came crashing down.

The forces of nature played against the old tree with hundred miles an hour winds gyrating through the canopy, soaking rain loosening the soil, the 35-degree slope that it was growing on and gravity all served to bring about its demise. As the tree fell it began a domino effect and with the wind in full blast other trees began to fall.

The family heard the sound far off and then increasing louder and louder, closer and closer as a whole swathe of the forest was laid flat.

The noise abruptly stopped and the whining of the wind took over.

From their new vantage point, they watched as the winds destroyed their house leaving it roofless and shattered.

Every flash of lightning would hang in the sky and illuminate the valley.

The huge trunk of the fig tree provided them shelter and protected them from the flying debris.

The soaking rain eventually seeped in and they became saturated and uncomfortable.

The wind howled for another four hours as they all prayed with their mother for forgiveness and safety.

Somewhere in the torment, they slept from sheer exhaustion.

When they awoke the sun was above the horizon and the sky was clear.

They emerged, wet, shivering and in trepidation.

Their eyes took time to adjust to the devastation that they could see before them. The house was barely recognizable and away to the Stewart Creek they could see hundreds of trees had been flattened and their leaves stripped from them.

They had no shelter and no means of communication.

They were on their own and there was urgent cleaning-up to be done.

Burton took charge.

It took over a week for the family to get the house

and property back to a semblance of what it used to look like.

As the days came and went the community got together and toiled as one helping each other.

After five days of deprivation and a lot of hard toiling, outside rescue teams began to arrive and progress quickened. These men, mostly from the Red Cross and the shire, brought food, water, shelters, clothing and mattresses all necessities that had been destroyed by the cyclone.

They formed into crews and rebuilt all the houses and shops.

They also brought news not only from outside but from the cross-pollination within the community.

The major news was the near miss suffered by Chas Osborne as he tried to run for Barrett's Creek in the ferry *Daintree*. He had almost reached safety when the incoming tidal surge caught the boat. Over twenty feet high the wave picked the ferry up and turned it sideways.

It began to list badly and Chas Osborne and his crew mate readied to abandon the stricken ship. The logs in the hold were so heavy that they kept the vessel from rolling. At the last second, Chas Osborne turned the *Daintree* back bow first and the wave rushed on. Chas Osborne relieved and tired was able to limp the boat into the shelter and here he rode out the fury of the cyclone.

There were other stories of near misses and luck but no one in the valley had died or been severely hurt.

The school had been knocked off its stumps and it took a lot of manoeuvring to get it upright and ready to take pupils.

The children were given a longer holiday and the parents made sure they all pitched in with the building and cleaning up.

On the other hand, the shipping that had run for Snapper Island had been hit hard and the loss of life ran to 74. It was one of the worst disasters to hit Queensland and left a bad taste in everyone's mouth.

Marion became increasingly worried that Burton would see all the death and destruction as ill-omens and want to pull out of the Daintree.

She watched him as he toiled from dawn to dusk on his own property and others.

He seemed to be in a morose state of mind and Marion recalled that day all those years ago when he had been brought home from the Tyalgum Hotel.

He was suffering from trauma and had lost his memory. He did not take too well to tragedy.

After a fortnight the Daintree community was back on

its feet and the Butter Factory was in full production.

Marion began to detect a change in Burton's mood so happily kept her own thoughts to herself. Maybe Burton had grown stronger mentally since moving from New South Wales.

Molly turned five on the tenth April. She was growing into a happy but mischievous child. She was too young to join the milking and the heavy lifting that was part of many chores but loved to play tricks on everyone.

After the trauma of the cyclone and the fear of impending doom, many of the older Johnsons were not ready for Molly and her happy-go-lucky manner. Her favourite trick was to tell one of the boys that one of the girls needed help. Of course, when the boy scampered to play the white knight he would get told that he wasn't sent for.

Another of her tricks was to knock on someone's door and then run away and hide. When a family member opened the door and found no one there Molly would burst out giggling.

The jokes became so bad that Marion decided to step in and call a halt to Molly's shenanigans.

"You will be off to school in nine months my girl and I'm sure Mr Severly will not tolerate this behaviour. I think you need to start practising your best behaviour from now."

Max had been trying to tell Molly that Mr Severly

was a crabby old bloke and that she would get the cuts if she didn't start showing grown up manners and sense.

Max was also taking the roll of mentor for his other little sisters.

Phyllis would hang on his every word but Rita found him boring and often told him to go away and find a chore to do.

Marge was too little to care but giggled and smiled whenever Max began to tickle her or blow raspberries on her tummy.

Max was on Marion's radar as a candidate to be a man of the flock. She would be ever so proud of herself if one of her children followed the good Lord and do His earthly duties for Him.

Max was unaware of Marion's ambitions for him.

He had his fill from school and the farm chores. One of these chores nearly caused him to die an agonizing death.

Max was nearly eight years old and one of his jobs was to fetch the cows and drive them to the wooden shed used as the milking barn.

One evening he found the cows had wandered through the shallows of the creek and were contentedly grazing.

He grabbed a long stick of lawyer grass and ran off yelling at the cows that got the message and begun to move. The wiser ones knew it was milking time and ran across the creek and up the banks.

A stubborn cow was shooed along and Max soon found himself running hard. He was headed towards the highest bank and the cow was almost at the top.

He scrambled up the steep, slippery bank with his broad-brimmed hat bouncing on his head. As his eyesight reached the level of the bank he was confronted by a huge taipan, one of the deadliest snakes in the world.

He froze and stood eye to eye with the monster.

Chapter 43

His instinct told him to drop, roll and run. As he let his legs collapse beneath him the snake struck. He felt the strike hit the top of his hat which flew off.

As he slammed into the lower part of the bank he rolled away, jumped to his feet and ran terrified after the distant cattle.

He told the others at dinner time and Marion was aghast. "You could have been bitten and the venom would have killed you in minutes. This is a lesson for you all to keep a proper lookout when you are wandering around. Max, you must not run blindly after the cows, drive them slowly and keep a sharp look out. The good Lord must have been looking after you. Maybe he has a special job for you here on earth."

Burton smiled to himself as he noted the clever way Marion had introduced her youngest son to the possibility of being a messenger for God.

Max lived to see and celebrate his eighth birthday although it was a quiet affair.

The Depression waged on and the cyclone had caused so much destruction around the farm that a lot of money was spent on fixing the roof of the house, the barn and fences.

Isobel turned 16 on the 26th June and was blossoming into a lovely lady. She would dress up and even Burton was smitten by his daughter's beauty.

"She'll make a great catch for a lucky bloke one day," he said. "I only hope she picks one that will care for her and love her. We need a few more Gingers around as he has proved to be an absolute gentleman and a loving husband to Madeline. They have done well since settling in Atherton. Their future is rosy and prosperous."

He smiled to himself as he pictured his eldest child at her wedding all those days ago.

Burt was closing in on his 20th birthday and was more and more mesmerized by the beauty of Connie Francis. It was more than just a like he felt he was falling for her. Whenever they saw each other she would give him an exuberant wave and call his name. He wasn't always keen for the public recognition especially if his mates were around. They would delight in teasing him after and making him feel foolish.

As they days went on he became more and more comfortable with their growing relationship.

One afternoon he was standing in the rainforest daydreaming pleasant thoughts of Connie when one of the older men shouted out, "Johnson are you concentrating over there? You'll have a tree on top of you shortly."

Burt had been employed to clear ten acres of rain-forest and truck the logs into the saw mill.

He was labouring in a team of five and they had been at the site for several days.

He was a sort after logger, as he knew how to wield an axe and to fall the trees in the right direction.

He was handy in the saw pit using the heavy cross-cut saw.

He shook himself back to reality and began to cut into the huge oak he was falling.

Away to his right, he could hear another axe man in full flight.

He was concentrating hard and sweating freely from the exertion when he heard a call of 'Timber'.

He knew this word well as it signaled that an axe man had finished cutting and that the tree was falling under the pull of gravity.

Shortly the sound of breaking branches and the whack as the trunk smacked into the ground would be heard.

Burt awoke slowly and looked through the blurriness. He was in a room that was painted all white and there were people fussing around.

A strong light was shone into his right eye and he flinched.

"Welcome back Master Johnson," said a kindly

male voice. "You're in the Mossman Hospital and I'm Doctor Shoemaker. It seems that one of your wood chopping mates landed their tree on top of you. Luckily I think you will survive. You may need a day or so to get over your concussion. After that, we'll let you go home for a few weeks of rest."

Burt heard the last words and felt the drowsiness come over him and he must have slept.

He awoke and saw that his father was lounging on a chair near him and snoring. He reached out to get a glass of water that was on the table nearby, misjudged and sent the water all over Burton.

"What the…?" he said as he came abruptly out of his deep sleep

"Sorry, dad spilled the water. Can you get me another I'm so thirsty?"

Burton looked at Burt and said, "Good to hear your voice, we've been so worried about you. We thought we had another Uncle Jack on our hands. I'm beginning to wonder if I'm headed down the same path as the one that fated me back in Bray's Creek. With friends and relations dying, being badly hurt and traumatic experiences dogging me. I won't be able to stand it if it brews up again."

He handed Burt the glass of water he had poured and slumped into the chair. Burt could see his father was deeply troubled.

"I'm alright," he said trying desperately to sound cheery.

Burt went home from the hospital with his father as company.

They rode in the Osborne bus all the way to the village and rode home on the horses with Max and Keith. The younger boys rode piggy-back with Max clinging to Burt and Keith happily hugging his father.

Marion and all the girls were pleased to see them riding through the pasture towards the house.

Burton was becoming more and more optimistic about the communication system in the valley.

Ever since he had stirred them all up and got them into parties little achievements had occurred.

The Stewart Creek Road was now passable by lorry, the bridge over the Stewart near the Douglas Creek had been finished high and almost dry in all weather, the Barrett Creek Bridge was open and taking all the Mossman to Daintree traffic and the telephone system was slowly expanding and being modernized.

The Mossman Shire had come to the party slowly with an engineer, labourers, heavy equipment and then money.

Much of the heavy equipment became useless during the high floods and the boggy conditions.

Nevertheless, the progress was throwing all the farmers more and more towards using machination to deal with their farming needs.

Burton was a progressive thinker and soon joined the thinking of the others. He was more inclined to suggest that farmers would be better off sharing the farming equipment. This would lower costs and stop the plants from being left idle for long periods. He was able to convince Barry Hayden and William Francis to his thinking.

One of the vehicles that he couldn't share but desperately realized he needed was a car.

He had to fit himself, Marion and eight children in the automobile so he needed one that would fit this bill.

He took Marion and Marge into Mossman one fine day.

They travelled in on a one way ticket on the bus.

Burton found the garage where they displayed a lovely, brand new car in the window. It was a Model Ford A Tourer and had a tray at the back. Burton looked it over and thought how he would get everyone of his brood in the car so they were safe and comfortable.

Marion was excited to believe that the family would have a motor car. Now she could feel important being motored here and there. They could even make more trips to see Madeline and Ginger in Atherton. Burton purchased the car and went off to the bank to withdraw the £785 for it.

The garage owner backed the car out and drove it around the front. He gave the keys to Burton and showed him the main parts of the car. He didn't ask about a licence and let Burton drive off along the road headed for the Daintree.

Marion was thrilled with the wind in her face and the car lapping up the miles.

It seemed like minutes rather than hours before they sloshed over the crossing and chugged towards the house.

Everybody came from all directions when they heard the car.

Once they realized that it was their father driving a new car they knew it was theirs.

Burton pulled up and said, "This is our new car. Once I've got it fixed up we can all go for rides wherever you want. Give me a day or more."

Marion got out, holding Marge who had been lulled asleep by the motion of the car.

Burton drove the car to the barn and parked near the opening of the blacksmith workshop.

A few days went by and Burton spent a great deal of time hammering and sawing.

No one was allowed in the blacksmith lean-to for that period.

Finally, the car appeared and Burton proudly drove it to the house.

He assembled everyone and told them they were going to visit the Hayden's house for afternoon tea.

He opened the door for Marion who slid into the new black seats and then lined all the children up according to height.

He marched them to the back of the car and lowered the tail gate.

From where each was standing they could see on either side of the tray a wooden seat arrangement. It hung snuggly over the sides of the car.

Eva and Isobel were asked to pick up a twin and to sit on opposite sides facing toward each other, next followed Molly, Max, Keith and finally Burt. There were four to each side and they all felt comfortable.

"Hang on tight and if there's a problem at any time bang on the back window so I can stop," instructed Burton.

It was a fine but blustery ride over to the Hayden's farm.

Sally and Barry stood on the verandah and waved to them all as they chugged their way along the track.

The Johnson family was mobile and with the exception

of floods and boggy ground made the most of their new freedom.

Eva turned 18 and was as homely as always. She kept an eye out for a boy to go with but so far no one seemed to fit her expectations. Marion was not overly concerned as she herself was 26 when she met, courted and married her beloved Burton.

The clear azure skies continued unabated and everyone was elated to be in such a tranquil environment.

The cream price remained low although it was a constant source of income. The dairy farmers further south were not faring as well as their pastures dried for part of the year and milking became unviable.

There were long-range picnics for the family as the new car gave them wings to fly wherever they wished to go.

They went everywhere together and even went over the Bump to Atherton to visit Madeline and Ginger.

Madeline had become a home body and Ginger had the little farmlet he had purchased zinging along. He grew all his own vegetables, had an orchard and a few cows for milk and cream.

They had an idyllic lifestyle.

Ginger had continued with his interest in craft and often sold his creations at the local street market.

He had also been talked into learning and playing

golf. At least once a week he would collect his clubs, throw them on his shoulder, kiss Madeline and go off for a round of golf with a couple of mates.

Guy Fawkes Night was fast approaching with all the children at school buzzing with excitement.

Mr Severly was not impressed and gave many a long sermon about the dangers of firecrackers and explosives.

He castigated Guy Fawkes as an evil man intent on his murderous ways to get what he wanted.

Burton just shook his head sadly and told Max and Keith that they would miss out again as the family finances were not strong enough to support the activity.

He did agree to let the boys build a bonfire down near the creek and to add a Guy to the top as long as they did the work themselves and did not neglect their chores.

So the family spent an evening on the banks of the Douglas Creek under a canopy of brilliant starlight waiting for the mass of branches and leaves to be ignited by Max and Keith.

On top of the bonfire, there was Guy Fawkes or at least a scarecrow character representing the master bomb maker.

The sky was lit as the bonfire was torched and flared. They all cheered as the flames licked up to the figure at the top.

Mr Severly was proving to be a difficult teacher to please.

He had all the activities ready each day and a time table of subjects and lessons written on the board in copperplate printing.

He greeted them all at the beginning of the day and then sat at his desk staring down anyone who dared to look up from their slates or reading books.

Whenever a student completed a lesson they had to tiptoe to the table where it was marked and had a written comment placed on it before the student returned to their desk. It was day after day of maddening silence. The soul of the classroom was missing.

Sport's Day was held on the sandbar of the river as in previous years thanks to the dedication of the committee of fathers. It lacked the exuberance of previous carnivals but nevertheless was fun and a break from the classroom routine.

Max and Keith excelled and were presented with their three penny and six penny-pieces. The committee had determined that there had to be an incentive to get the children to understand competition and to reward the winners in a meaningful way.

The end of the school year didn't come quick enough for the students especially Keith who so often had 'REDO' on his worksheets.

Christmas was a happy occasion and everyone

joined in the carol singing when the lorry arrived with Father Christmas on board.

He told them that next year he would bring them all a boiled lolly and if they kept the chimney clean he would bring them all a present.

Burton looked at Marion and they grimaced.

Chapter 44

The quadruple whammy of parties was in sight so Burton gathered the family to explain how they would celebrate Christmas, Marge's birthday, Keith's birthday and New Year's Day. These events all fell over a six day period and they would not be able to afford to have them one after the other.

Burton explained that they would have one big party on the 29th December.

It was a party to remember considering the austerity that the family had been practising for the past four years. Marion made a chocolate cake with cream icing for Keith, a vanilla cake with pink icing for Marge, pork sausage rolls and fairy bread to mark Christmas and New Year. Her reasoning on the sausage rolls was that they looked like wrapped presents and the fairy bread represented the colourful New Year she hoped they would have.

Marion should have tried black sprinkles as they would have been more appropriate.

The New Year's Eve dance was held in the Butter Factory and almost the entire community attended. It was held in such fun that it was as if they were marking the end of the Depression and the beginning of a new era.

No one was psychic but if they were they would not have been anywhere as exuberant.

The children had their games and supper before retiring exhausted but happy.

The adults danced to their hearts' content until midnight when they all stopped and sang a lusty 'Old Lang Syme'.

As they helped themselves to supper they were unaware of a movement on the far side of the river.

The water was moving in V-shaped waves as a 16-foot crocodile swam cautiously along.

It flicked its massive tail from side to side to propel itself and kept its eyes just above the surface. It was on the lookout for any dangers and any food to fill its gurgling stomach.

The crocodile was a young male that had fallen into the trap of trying to muscle in on an old bull's territory.

It had swum into the mouth of the Daintree River a day ago and had challenged the old bull crocodile to a duel to the death.

The old fellow had stayed lazing on the mud bank appearing as though it was acquiescing to the younger crocodile. The youngster had been emboldened by the posture of the older crocodile so to show its superiority it had charged and bellowed.

The old crocodile remained motionless except for one eye that flickered open.

The young crocodile pulled up short, bewildered by the seemingly gutless antics of the old bull.

It backed away readying for a full charge.

As it moved forward and gathered speed it became aware that the old crocodile had turned its head to one side a sure sign that it would open its mouth ready to lash its massive jaws on to a prey.

It was too late to pull out of the charge and as the crocodile smashed into the body of the old bull it felt a strong vice like grip covering its midriff.

It lashed around desperately trying to break free. All the time the old crocodile increased the pressure from its massive jaws. With a final desperate twist, the young crocodile pulled to make its getaway.

The old crocodile gave a parting bite and severed the front leg of its rival. The old bull ripped the leg off and swallowed it whole. It settled back in the mud, gave a bellow to let his brood know he was the boss and closed its eyes.

The young crocodile swam limply away, badly wounded.

It would need to find a quiet, safe refuge where it could mend and recuperate.

It swam up stream keeping to the edge of the mangroves and staying clear of any likely enemy.

As the crocodile rounded the bend it heard the loud music and saw the bright lights coming from the Butter Factory.

It changed direction to cross to the other side away from the danger. The young bull kept swaying its tail as it made its way along.

Once past the noise, it moved back to the other side of the river and soon came upon an entry from its left.

This was a deep stream and was flowing fast.

The young crocodile lifted its snout and sniffed. It could make out a number of smells but the one that it liked was cattle. The smell seemed to be from upstream of this new tributary so the crocodile turned and made its way along the waterway.

After nearly half an hour the bull came to a shallow rocky area and painfully pulled itself over to deeper water.

The stump of the severed leg was painful and bleeding.

It had to find refuge and fast as it couldn't bear to use the leg to get over rocky terrain anymore.

The crocodile slid into the still deeper water then found its way blocked by boulders and a waterfall.

The crocodile dived down and found a cavern with a rocky shelf above water level. This would be ideal and the smell of cattle was even stronger here.

At the moment it just needed to rest and mend.

The New Year's Eve Party came to an end and everyone made their way back home.

Marion had kept Marge with her and she and

Burton were happy to dance together with Marge giggling and laughing between them.

Marge especially loved it when the couple was doing the waltz and spinning around and around. It left her with a giddy feeling.

Burton gathered the older Johnsons and they clambered into the back of the car and settled into their allotted places.

Burton picked up Max, Molly and the twins Rita and Phyllis at the lodge and then drove the car home along the Stewart Creek Road.

They splashed across the ford not knowing what now lurked beneath the still, murky waters.

"Looks so peaceful across the water with the moon reflection, doesn't it?" said Marion.

"Very romantic I must say," said Burton. "Maybe we can all come for a swim tomorrow or the next if this perfect weather holds," said Marion.

Luckily the weather took a turn for the worst. The wet season arrived the next afternoon and the miserable days would last well into February.

The crocodile slept for weeks on the rock ledge safe and comfortable.

When it emerged the stump of the front leg was healed and it quickly learned to adjust.

The tail was the means of propulsion and direction changes and that was unharmed. It found plenty of barramundi in the creek to feed on and it could hear the lowing of cattle nearby so this was an ideal place to stay.

A number of different types of geese and ducks landed on the still waters and these were easily captured and eaten.

Max and Keith commenced the new school year clinging to the hope that Mr Severly had departed one way or the other.

Max went for 'departed to another school' but Keith was more severe with 'departed to be with the good Lord.'

Max had hushed Keith and told him that if their mother caught him using the Lord's name in vain he would get a hiding. Keith kept further thoughts of where Mr Severly should go to himself.

Molly also began school and had become excited with the prospect. Isobel had been teaching her all sorts of things and she was picking up the hints readily.

Molly had to ride piggy-back with Keith until she could ride well enough on her own.

When this happened Burton promised she could ride Gypsy to school.

Max's destiny took a turn for the worst one bright and sunny day.

He and Keith cantered off on the horses to school.

Molly had woken up with a sore throat and a racking cough so she was allowed to stay at home.

The boys had the cream cans attached to the saddles and were nearing the ford when Queen Bee stopped and refused to go forward no matter how much urging Keith tried.

Prince whinnied and began to back away. Max had a torrid time trying to get him to settle. "Whoa, steady boy. Whatever is the matter?"

Queen Bee shied to one side and took Keith away from the water. Keith managed to control the horse and called back to Max, "We'll go around as a snake or lizard has spooked the horses. Dad said that they will know if there's danger way before us. No chances so we go around."

Prince was looking towards the water, head down and his nostrils kept flaring.

Max knew that Keith was making sense so he turned the horse's head and set off after Queen Bee.

They urged the horses up the embankment that skirted the billabong.

The sound of geese honking from over his left shoulder made Max look back.

"Look at that," he called to Keith.

They reined the horses and from their vantage point had a beautiful view of the expanse of water and a flock of black and white magpie geese coming into land.

"Isn't nature wonderful?" said Keith philosophically.

The geese were coming in low, necks outstretched, wings gliding and webbed feet straight. They glided in readying for a perfect landing.

The boys watched in fascination.

Suddenly there was an explosion in the centre of the billabong and a gigantic crocodile launched itself into the path of the incoming geese. The crocodile opened its massive jaws and seemed to hover in the air.

The boys sat transfixed.

Chapter 45

Several magpie geese saw the danger and tried to swerve.

The crocodile had selected one that was on a direct course to where its jaws would clamp shut around it. Black and white feathers flew in all directions and the crocodile's massive body whacked back into the water.

Wave after wave rippled across the water and then all was still as if nothing had happened.

"Jesus Christ," said Keith. "Did you see that?"

"Stop using the Lord's name you'll get a thrashing for that. It was a crocodile!" said Max.

"Let's get out of here and don't tell anyone what we saw they won't believe us." Keith urged his horse forward and Queen Bee responded.

Max followed trying to catch up, he had more to say but Keith was galloping away from him.

He caught up to Keith as they arrived at the Butter Factory.

"Keith we have to tell an adult what we saw in the watering hole. It could eat a person or a cow or anything," said Max.

"Shut your mouth and promise never to open it

again if you are going to mention that crocodile. Got it?" said Keith venomously.

All day Max couldn't concentrate and was reprimanded by Mr Severly over and over.

The flash backs kept coming and going and changed into more dangerous thoughts as the day wore on.

By home time he was bursting with the need to tell.

As they neared the farm house Keith tried again to warn him of the consequences of trying to make anyone believe what they had seen. "Don't you dare tell Max or you'll end up in trouble. They won't believe you and they'll call you a liar."

Max decided that Keith was probably right so he had afternoon tea and started his chores. He managed to get them all done even though the flash backs wouldn't go away.

By dinner time he was agitated and exhausted, Keith kept giving him dagger looks and even at one time drew his pointer finger across his neck as a further warning.

Marion was not one to miss mood changes nor interplay between her children.

After they had all eaten she excused each one and then asked Max and Keith to stay and do the dishes.

When the room was clear of the others and only Marion and the boys remained Marion broached the subject of her concern. "Whatever is going on between you?"

"Nothing mum," said Keith all too quickly.

"And you Max do you think there's nothing going on even though Keith here is giving you withering looks and threatening to cut your throat?"

Keith was shocked to know that all his underhandedness had not got past his mother.

"When your father comes in I shall ask him to join in. If you wish to explain what this is all about before he arrives I will leave out the threat as it will surely result in you getting a thrashing. So who will go first?"

"I will," said Max and Keith shot him another 'don't you dare' look.

"We saw a crocodile in the billabong at the ford this morning and we are too scared to tell anyone in case you won't believe us."

Marion's hand went to her mouth and she gasped and her pupils in her brown eyes narrowed. "A crocodile," she said slowly. "Did you tell Mr Severly?"

"No mum we thought no one would believe us."

"And Keith you saw this crocodile?"

"No mum I didn't see anything," said Keith.

Marion walked out and they heard her calling to Eva.

"Eva love will you fetch your father urgently he's down at the blacksmith workshop."

The boys heard Eva run out of the house and clamber down the steps.

Marion returned to the kitchen with a stern, worried look. Her forehead had more wrinkles across it than they could ever remember seeing.

Silence prevailed in the kitchen as they all waited for Burton to appear.

Keith was busily going over his story in his head and hoping his mother would remember her promise not to tell his father about her threat.

Max was pleased with himself as he had rid himself of the burden he had carried all day. Now the crocodile would be dealt with and he would be a hero.

Burton burst into the kitchen asking, "What's happened is anyone hurt?"

"I'm sorry my dear," said Marion, "I didn't mean to cause you so much angst but the story Max is telling me needs quick and drastic action. He says he saw a crocodile in the billabong this morning."

"And it jumped out of the water and ate a magpie goose. Crunched it all up in one swallow," added Max helping with the story.

"A crocodile are you sure? We rarely get crocodiles this far up the river. You're not making this up?"

Keith smiled as if to say 'told you so they won't believe you'.

"Keith what's your take on this crocodile story. Did you see it?"

Keith puffed out his chest and gathered all his

confidence, "No dad. Max is mistaken. We didn't see nothing."

"Anything," corrected Marion.

"So you didn't see this crocodile but your little brother claims he did?" said Burton. "Max tell me the whole story."

So Max told everything he could recall from the horse's reactions and then all the way to school.

Keith was becoming frustrated and moved from leg to leg countering his tiredness.

Burton turned to him and asked for his version and he told it as a normal ride into school.

Burton turned on Max and with measured words said, "If you are lying you will get a hiding. Did you or did you not see a crocodile?"

Max couldn't believe that the situation had swung against him and now instead of being a hero he was being accused of being the villain. He tried to regain respect by saying, "Keith saw it as plain as I did. He was so shocked he yelled out Jesus Christ!"

Burton hit him across the face.

Max spun to one side and his face felt like a branding iron had been slammed into it. He was now cast in the villain role and no amount of truth was going to change that.

He began to sob.

Burton ignored the blubbering Max and turned on Keith, "Did you use the Lord's name in vain? You all know where your mother stands on blaspheming."

"No dad I didn't Max is making things up as he goes," said Keith.

Max was holding his stinging face but he couldn't believe that Keith was now calling him a liar.

He knew he was done for and that his father would now call him a liar and unchristian.

"Max you have lied blasphemed and tried to blame your brother for something he did not do. This I will not accept nor tolerate. Go to my room, pray for forgiveness and await your punishment."

Chapter 46

Max dragged himself out of the kitchen.

He turned back and gave an imploring look to his mother hoping against hope that she would save him but Marion just shook her head.

Burton dismissed Keith and took several deep breaths. "Whatever has gotten into the boy?" he asked Marion and then he saw tears well into her eyes. All her hopes for Max were about to be dashed.

Max waited, trembling, in the bedroom. He had sat on the double bed and prayed asking for forgiveness but not understanding how he could be forgiven for telling the truth.

Burton walked into the room and said, "Pants down and lean over the bed."

He held a cane of lawyer grass in his right hand and looked bewildered.

"You will get three cuts, one for lying, one blaspheming and the last for blaming your brother for using blasphemy."

Max waited as his father rolled up the sleeves of his shirt and picked up the cane.

Burton had used this punishment sparingly on his children and this had kept them all safe and well mannered. He had never expected to use a cane on one of the younger ones but he could not have them running amok.

Max waited and then heard the whistling sound as the cane cut through the air.

Whack.

He felt the sting as the cane slammed into his loose skin of his bottom. He bit his lip to stop from crying out. Tears welled in his eyes but he sucked hard to prevent them from flowing down his face.

A large red welt erupted on his bottom and it felt like it was on fire. Now he knew how the cows felt when they were being branded.

Another whistling sound and the inevitable whack brought him back to reality.

The second cut was as vicious as the first and he heard a voice scream out. It took a few seconds to understand that it had come from his mouth.

Another red welt erupted next to and parallel to the first.

Max was gasping for breath hoping that his father would see the agony he was in and relent on the third stroke.

No such luck as he heard the third whistling and felt the skin break.

The final hit had landed across the other welts and where they met the skin was ripped and blood seeped out of the wounds.

Burton was aghast at what he was seeing but was too proud to do anything more than to say, "Now behave yourself," and he walked out the door.

Max was cut, bruised and battered and slowly pulled his pants up to try to regain his dignity.

He walked gingerly from the room feeling the scars pull as he moved.

He painfully made it to his bed and flopped face down and buried his head in the pillow.

He wept and moaned until he lulled himself to sleep.

When he awoke the sky was just lightening and he saw a figure sitting next to him. It was Ginger, all concerned and ready to help him.

"You poor little tyke," he said. "I've got water and Solyptol to bath your bottom. Let me haul your daks down and get started you'll feel better for it."

It took a long time for Max to heal physically but it would take decades before he would heal mentally.

Burton and Marion carried on as if nothing had happened.

They were the guardians and what they dealt out went with the job.

King Billy arrived at the front door of the house a few weeks later. Marion heard the knock and was surprised to see who it was.

"King Billy this is unusual for you to knock on the door. Do you want Burton, he's at the barn?"

"Yes Mrs Johnson it is your man I seek and it is urgent. I will take myself to him."

With those words, King Billy went down the steps and made his way to the barn.

Burton was pleased to see the aboriginal warrior and greeted him warmly.

"I need you to get your powerful gun and others to kill the crocodile that is in the billabong," said King Billy.

Burton opened his mouth and closed it thrice before he managed to blurt out, "Crocodile?"

"Yeh he's a big one and by the look of the signs, he has been there quite a long time. Strange one he's only got three legs."

Burton went up to the house with King Billy tagging along.

He made three telephone calls and then went into the bedroom and emerged with the Lee-Enfield 303 over his shoulder. He reached up to the first aid cupboard and found the bolt. He touched his trouser pockets to make sure the bullets were there and satisfied he set off to the crossing.

King Billy was chatting and telling Burton that he'd

move his people away from the sandbar before going to ask for help.

As they neared the camp one warrior broke away and came towards the Burton and King Billy.

"This is Smiley he's the premier tracker in Queensland. What else you found down there Smiley?" asked King Billy.

"I'll show Mr Johnson but he better get his rifle ready 'cause he's big mean one."

Burton stopped Smiley and said, "Let's wait for Barry Hayden and Bill Francis. They're on their way so it won't be too long of a wait."

Almost before he'd finished speaking he could see Bill Francis riding towards them from upstream.

Barry Hayden appeared in his car shortly away to the south.

When all five men were assembled and King Billy had filled them in they advanced together towards the billabong.

"If we keep on the ford where it's shallow we'll get a good look if this thing wants to launch itself," said Burton.

Smiley was moving around slightly ahead pointing excitedly to evidence of where the crocodile had walked or dragged its tail. He showed the men its kill, both animals and birds.

"Any sign of cattle being taken?" asked Bill Francis.

"No sir I think it's not keen on anything big because

he's missing a front leg so it won't be able to pull back all that well," said Smiley.

They hunted around and around but nothing appeared.

King Billy decided he would move his people downstream away from the danger and leave it up to the farmers to set traps and warn others.

Meanwhile, deep under the rocks at the far end of the billabong where the water cascaded gently the crocodile slept peacefully. It felt safe and contented. Its stump was almost healed and soon it would regain all its strength.

Burton, Bill and Barry placed snares on each side of the waterhole.

As a lure, they killed a sow and placed half a carcass in each snare.

If the crocodile was tempted it would push itself through the gap the men had made and try to take the meat that was a yard further on. Just before its snout touched the morsel it would feel a loop of eight gauge wire tighten across its neck. In desperation to get to the meat and escape whatever was across its neck, it would lash out. This movement would tighten the wire and the more it struggled the tighter the wire would become.

Burton went home with his tail between his legs.

Max had been telling the truth all along. What was to happen now? Burton couldn't lose face and he certainly couldn't take back the hiding he had given the child.

Marion could see the anguish and torment on his face as he related the crocodile hunt to them all.

She waited until bed time before cuddling him and saying, "What's done is done so let's just leave it and move along."

For little Max, that message would never give him any comfort. He had been proven right all along but no one was apologizing to him.

The crocodile fell for the trap and Bill Francis finished it off with his Winchester 45.

Many weeks later King Billy returned and was given the skin to make clothes items out of.

He was pleased that he could once again roam free and camp on the sandbar without any danger.

Molly celebrated her sixth birthday and was happy being the centre of attention. She was allowed to select the games that were to be played and everyone else including Burt had to join in.

Molly was enjoying school even though Max and Keith kept grizzling and grumping about Mr Severly. She excelled at reading and was developing a neat handwriting style. She was looking forward to the athletics at the end of the year.

Max had his ninth birthday on the fourth of June. He disappeared and worried the life out of everyone who went looking for him.

He was up before the others and decided he didn't want anyone enjoying his birthday by having fun.

No one, except Ginger, had offered any sympathy so why would he let them prance around and sing Happy Birthday if they didn't mean it.

A few days earlier he had been in the top paddock when he discovered one of the old hides that Burton, Ginger and Burt had built to shoot feral pigs. He pulled out the leaves, sticks and grass and found a deep hollow.

After an hour's digging, he had the hole deeper and then pulled a lot of branches from the nearby rainforest to cover the top. He pulled up sod from nearby and packed this on top. He left a small opening so he could crawl inside. No one would ever know the underground cubby was there.

Max had an ideal place to escape to and he decided he would disappear for the day on his birthday.

The whole district was alerted to Max's disappearance and by one o'clock there were men on horses, men in cars and men on foot roaming the countryside.

There was speculation about kidnapping, running away and being abducted.

As the sun set in the west Max crawled from his burrow and wandered back home.

Marion was overwhelmed to have him back safe and sound and hugged and kissed him.

Burton was angry but had to hide his negative feeling and patted Max on the back and said, "Glad to see you home safe and well, son." He owed the boy too much to take it out on him like he would have normally done.

Burt, Ginger and Keith spent the next few days trying to get the story out of Max but he remained mum. He'd found a way to be the centre of attention without getting a hiding.

Isobel turned 17 and was pretty than ever as she matured.

Marion was always telling Burton that she would be the catch of all the Johnson girls, quick witted, intelligent and pretty.

Burt turned 21 and was given a civic reception in the Butter Factory.

This had become a tradition in the valley. Any girl or boy who attained the age of 21 was hailed by the community as a man or woman and afforded all the courtesies that went with this. It was almost like a New Year Eve party except it was held in the afternoon.

Children and adults danced the time away, speeches were made and Burt got to blow out 21 candles that blazed on top of a monster chocolate cake. He was given a key beautifully crafted by Burton with 21 painted neatly in gold paint on the outside.

He made his wish looking directly at Connie Francis but when asked what it was he went all coy, blushed and refused to reveal the secret.

Keith decided he knew what the secret must have been when he caught Burt and Connie kissing near the saw mill later that evening.

On the fourth of August, Eva turned 19 and she continued to be Marion's helper and showed this by doing everything on the farm that needed to be done. All the while Eva kept up a happy disposition.

Mr Severly had not mellowed. The punctuality question arose once again in October.

Chapter 47

Max, Keith and Molly had a bad run that lasted across a fortnight.

The first problem day was a Tuesday when the trio arrived a few minutes late.

Mr Severly chatted Molly and gave the boys a hundred lines each, 'I must not be late to school'.

On Friday they had another slip up when Molly lost a shoe and by the time she convinced Keith she wasn't fibbing the shoe was a hundred yards behind and lost in the bushes. It took more time than they had to go back, search and find the shoe.

"Late again I see," said Mr Severly before any of them could dismount.

He wouldn't accept any excuses so he demanded Molly writes 20 lines and gave each boy one cut across the hand. It stung and left them with a lingering numbness.

They agreed not to tell their parents for fear of another thrashing at home.

On Wednesday following they were again late this time because Prince decided he wanted the day off.

The boys spent too long in trying every trick they could think of to get the horse to allow them to put on the bridle. He ran away and refused to come, he tossed his head to stop the bridle being put over it and he kicked up his hind legs making everyone scatter.

Burton came to the rescue but by then lateness was unavoidable.

Mr Severly dished out the cane to the boys and more lines to Molly.

"I'm getting tired of being belted," said Keith. "It's not our fault we're late and yet we get a hiding. If he hits me again I'm going to get the canes from his desk and I'm going to chop them up."

"You don't mean that do you?" asked Molly.

"Probably not but that's what I feel like doing," said Keith.

The subject was dropped and they mounted the horses and galloped for home.

The embryo of the idea stuck in Max's head and it slowly festered.

On Friday they had another late day caused by a sudden downpour.

Normally when it rained in the drier seasons the children would ride on and get to school damp.

When it poured there was no other option but to seek shelter. By the time they reached the school the first lesson was almost finished.

Mr Severly watched them enter and said nothing. He watched them take their seats. Still, he didn't comment.

He waited for recess to come and by then Keith and Max had come to the delightful conclusion he had realized the torrential rain had caused their lateness so they were excused.

The bell rang and Mr Severly nodded and the students stood and began to exit.

Suddenly Mr Severly called out, "Johnson, Johnson and Johnson stay where you are!"

He waited for the classroom to clear and then said, "Late again. I don't think you will ever learn punctuality."

"But sir the rain was…"

"Quiet boy you will speak only when given permission. Hand out." The boys copped one on each hand and Molly set to and wrote out fifty lines.

At lunch time Mr Severly went across to the school house where his petite, long-haired, blond wife served him lunch.

He made full use of the hour break.

Max with his fingers numb made up his mind to put his daring plan into action.

He snuck into the classroom and grabbed the four lawyer canes the Mr Severly used as his 'finger ticklers' and shoved them up his jumper and down his shorts. A small section protruded from his jumper so he clamped his hand over this.

He snuck outside and ran for the woodshed which was down the back of the school near the toilets.

He opened the door and closed it.

He was sure no one had seen him.

He propped logs against the door to stop anyone barging in.

He laid the canes across a log and retrieved the axe from the corner and felt exhilarated as he chopped each into pieces. He picked up the bits and threw them behind the pile of logs, removed the propped logs from the door and sauntered nonchalantly across the playground.

Mr Severly didn't twig right away that the canes were missing.

Max went home a happy boy although deep down he felt he wouldn't get away with the crime.

When Mr Severly found out all hell would break out.

Max couldn't play the hero yet because no one knew what he'd done. He would savour his thoughts until that day came.

Mr Severly discovered the canes missing the next day and went on a witch hunt. He demanded to know who would dare steal his canes or anything for that matter from his table. He stared down each of the senior boys and the middle year ones. No one was forthcoming.

Keith glanced at Max and wondered but his brother had said nothing about being involved. The only slight proof was that Keith had mooted the idea a week back.

Mr Severly left a chilling warning, "When I find the culprit he will wish he'd never been born."

The missing cane saga fizzled out and school returned to normal.

It would be a long time before it would come back on the agenda.

Guy Fox Night was celebrated as good news filtered through the community.

They received news that thrilled them all. The price of cream had been put up by one penny. That would make a difference to their bottom line and give them a bigger payout.

It would appear that the Great Depression was starting to lift and hopefully the world would return to normal.

All the boys plus Burton built a bonfire and made a Guy Fawkes. The guy had penny bombs for fingers, Catherine Wheels for buttons, sparklers for eyes, more penny bombs for fingers and sky rockets for hair.

The night was celebrated by the Johnson family and

their guests were the Francis family.

It was a balmy warm night and the sounds and lights lit up the sky.

Burt and Connie stood near each other and then as the bonfire died away they slipped off together.

Everyone else walked back to the house and enjoyed the supper that Marion and the girls had prepared.

If anyone missed the furtive couple they didn't say so.

Bill and Winnie Francis were more than happy to find Connie waiting by the car ready for the trip home.

Molly was getting excited by the approaching sport's day and kept telling everyone. "I can't wait it will be so much fun."

As it turned out it was not only lots of fun but all three of the Johnson children returned home with three penny and six penny coins. Burton made a point of telling them to put money into their Commonwealth Bank tins for that rainy day.

The end of school for 1935 was a huge relief for Max.

He had survived the cane cutting episode although it took only until the next day for new ones to appear on the desk once Mr Severly had realized the old ones were missing.

He now hoped beyond hope that the crabby old teacher would seek a transfer and leave the valley.

Keith was finished with school as he would turn 12

on the 30th December so he had no such thoughts. He could only think about freedom and running amok rather than being tied down by mundane routine.

Molly was trying to believe that school was good because it taught her to read and write and do sums.

She wasn't happy with writing lines but it was better than getting the cuts like the boys.

Christmas was celebrated both traditionally and in a modern fashion.

Burton returned to his character as Father Christmas and the children and grown-ups all found presents with their names on them under the decorated tree.

There was many oohs and ahhs as each present was opened.

The December 29th celebration to mark Keith and Marge's birthdays and New Year was a success with lots of fun, frolic and games.

The New Year Eve Dance was cancelled as the heavens opened and the valley was inundated with over eleven inches in one day. The wet season set in and everything was damp and mouldy.

There was a bright spot even though the rain was pelting down outside.

The family was at breakfast when the telephone

rang. They had their own line so they knew to pick up straight away. Marion was first to the telephone and lifted the receiver.

"Madeline how nice to hear your voice dear," said Marion. "That is wonderful news wait until I tell all the others."

She placed her hand over the mouthpiece and said, "I'm going to be a grandmother and you will be aunties and uncles. Madeline is going to have a baby."

"Let me speak to her," said Burton and Marion reluctantly handed over the telephone.

The conversation was animated and full of praise and good wishes.

It ended and Burton replaced the receiver and beaming said, "She is so happy and you should be very proud of your sister."

The good news spread quickly across the valley with everyone offering Burton and Marion their congratulations.

The bad news was just beginning to develop on top of the distant mountains. Storm clouds could be seen, white and fluffy and they seemed harmless.

As the day wore on the updrafts created by the burning sun began to drag the water droplets thousands of feet into the sky. As they picked up more moisture they became too heavy and fell under gravity back towards the earth.

Again they were captured by new updrafts and the process began again. The moisture laden clouds towered thousands of feet into the sky.

"Look at those cumulonimbus clouds over the mountains," said Barry Hayden. "They're real dinkum thunderheads and there is going to be plenty of rain. I think we need to move the cattle to high ground in case a flash flood hits us."

Burton, who was visiting the Hayden's farmhouse nodded his head and took the advice. He knew that Barry Hayden was rarely wrong with his predictions and anyway it was better to err on the side of caution.

Chapter 48

No one heard the thunderous roar from up the Douglas Creek as a massive wall of water came crashing along the valley. It pushed ahead of itself an entanglement of roots, logs, branches, leaves, grass, fence posts, wire, animal carcasses, soil and rocks. Anything in its path was smashed and dragged down the creek.

Flash floods were sudden and deadly dangerous.

The Johnson family slept on in their exhausted sleep and it wasn't until morning that they got an inkling of the flood and the power of destruction and grief it left behind.

Burton was standing on the verandah eating his toast and vegemite when Burt approached.

"I think we need to go and check the fence along the Douglas. Something seems amiss and I can't place it."

Burt looked across the pasture in the direction his father was pointing. The light was gloomy and to see that far was difficult but if there was something odd then he knew his father's instincts would catch it.

They took off at a brisk pace and soon saw the

flattened grass and the debris that was snarled in the trees and the fence.

"Looks like we had that flash flood Barry warned us about," said Burton.

"The fence has been torn out from here to the far corner that's nearly 100 yards," observed Burt.

"We'd best find the wire and posts and see what we can salvage and then put up a temporary barrier. You start searching and I'll run back to the barn and get the tools," said Burton.

Burt watched his father hurry away and then ventured into the tangled mess that littered the valley.

He soon found a strand of the fencing wire and pulled it out bit by bit.

He to rolling the wire to make it easier to carry later.

He met resistance and could see the wire had been wound around a log and he would need to cut this with a pair of pliers.

As he looked for a foothold to balance on he noticed an odd shape further along the log. It was wedged in the fork of the branch and covered with leaves and grass.

He was shocked as his first impression was a body.

He closed his eyes thinking he was seeing things but when he opened them he could clearly see a little leg and toes.

"Oh, Mary mother of Jesus," he said and he clambered towards the inert body. He reached down and removed the debris that covered the upper body and saw that it was a small aboriginal child.

He gently lifted the body and was shocked to feel that it was cold and stiff. He had heard people talk of rigor mortis and now he knew what that meant.

He turned to see where his father was and saw Burton 50 yards away coming towards him.

He had a shovel and a mattock over one shoulder and a roll of wire over the other.

Burt yelled, "Dad come quickly I've found the body of a little child."

Burton dropped the tools and wire and ran.

He reached Burt and looked at the muddy, still, child that was cradled so gently in his arms.

"She'll be one of King Billy's mob. Poor little baby must have been caught in the flood. Her tribe will be searching for her and must be out of their minds with worry. We need to take her into town and try to find King Billy."

The men walked sadly towards the barn.

They laid the body in the tray of the car and Burt sat beside it.

Burton drove the car to the house where he set in motion his plan to deal with the death of the little baby girl.

Eva was sent to find a clean white sheet and she helped Burt wrapped the body carefully.

Marion was left telephoning the village to get the telephonist to relay an all point bulletin to find King Billy and tell him the shocking news.

She also telephoned the Mossman Police Station to report a death and ask for an officer to attend.

Burton and Burt arrived in the village and went to the Butter Factory where Bryan Poole helped them place the body in the cool room.

It took until the next day for the other pieces of the puzzle to fall into place.

Constable Hewson arrived and wrote out a Death Certificate and then had to wait for identity.

King Billy had been located at the top of the Douglas Creek and he arrived by launch with one of his women.

He greeted Burton and they went into the Butter Factory cool room where the body was stored.

The sheet was unwrapped so that the little girl's face was exposed. King Billy nodded his recognition and turned to the aboriginal woman who waited by the door. She cautiously approached, looked down and then fell to the ground and wailed from grief.

"It was her girl who had gone missing in the night when the flood came," said King Billy.

Burton replaced the sheet to cover the face of the child. Burton and King Billy lifted the child's mother and carried her outside where they left her in the warmth crying and wailing for the soul of her lost child.

King Billy returned to the cool room and lifted the body and carried it to the launch.

"We will take our own to the burial grounds and release her spirit. Thank you, Burton, for returning her to us."

Constable Hewson approached and asked King Billy for the child's name.

The aboriginal warrior took the pen and paper from the policeman and wrote neatly the child's name then said, "We do not speak her name."

Burton and Burt returned home but were poor company as the sad thoughts of the death kept creeping into their heads.

It was a sad time for all the family.

One evening Burton looked at Marion and said, "Everything is falling in again just like it did back in Bray's Creek. I don't think I can manage to cope with too much more."

"My poor darling I'm sure things will brighten up. We've had a wonderful time out here in the Daintree. Let's pray that it will continue."

Madeline and Ginger brightened things up in early March.

The wet weather had abated and the valley had five days of beautiful warm weather.

The humidity stayed high but this wasn't a concern as the warmth and dryness were what everyone craved.

Early one morning Ginger and Madeline's car pulled up outside the house and everybody charged out to greet the happy couple.

Madeline's pregnancy wasn't showing but she spent hours telling her mother and her sisters all about her visits to the doctor.She told them about the changes that were happening to her body.

Ginger entertained the boys with his stories of Atherton life and his golfing prowess.

The couple left an hour before sunset and chugged off into the distance.

Marion looked at Burton and said, "I'm worried for Madeline she talked so much about the doctor's concern for her health and the baby's. She is having trouble with her kidneys. The doctor wants her to stay in hospital for her fifth month on."

"Madeline will be right Marion after all, she's a Johnson with the tough blood of the Stewarts. A bit of Scot mixed with Dane you have to be invincible."

Max and Molly were the only ones going to school in 1936 and they tried to keep a low profile.

Max had escaped so far. No one had been caught for chopping up of the canes although that was about to take a new twist.

Mr Severly appeared to have forgotten the episode probably because he was pleased to see the back of his senior students who had made his life unbearable especially Keith Johnson.

One cold morning Mr Severly found he needed to cut more wood for the fire that he liked to have blazing in the corner of the classroom.

He went into the shed, rolled logs outside and began chopping.

He returned to the shed several times for more logs and was building up quite a pile of firewood.

He decided he had enough and returned to the shed to put the axe away. As he placed the axe his eyes caught strange pieces of kindling at the back. He reached down and saw the pieces of the lawyer cane.

"Ah, so that's what happened. One of them chopped up my canes. Heaven help him if he's still attending my school."

During the rest of the day, Mr Severly kept up a constant tirade about the chopped canes. He accused all the boys and waggled the short sticks under each student's face. No one owned up and they all seemed innocent.

Mr Severly must have decided that it was an ex-student who was the culprit because he never raised the matter again much to Max's relief.

The news from Madeline was full of happiness but in among her telephone conversations, Marion read a different picture. She seemed to be spending a lot of time with the doctor and having tests done.

"I'll never forgive myself if anything happens to our precious Madeline," said Burton after Marion had conveyed her thoughts on the situation.

Mr Severly continued in his strict and stern way much to the chagrin of one of his new students.

Billy Bunker was 12 and he and his itinerant father wandered from town to town looking for employment.

They had arrived in the valley where Billy thought he would be safe and not have to attend school.

Billy's father discovered there was a school and dragged him along to be enrolled.

His father found Billy a difficult boy and that if he dropped him off at a school he would get relief from the boy's stupid escapades.

Billy was anti-authority but soon learned that he could protest without getting involved or found out. All he had to do was get inside another student's head and plant a seed and then keep watering the seed until it grew into a mighty beanstalk just like Jack did.

He could do this with more than one person and often had three or four exploits going at once.

Max, on the other hand, loved to be included in such mischief.

He had begun to hate the world and everybody in it.

No one cared about him so why would he care about others?

He took up a dare at the drop of a hat.

He relished a challenge, where someone got hurt or embarrassed.

Billy cottoned onto Max within hours of his enrolment. It was 'birds of a feather get together'.

One day at the far fence of the school Billy was sharing cigarettes with a couple of the senior boys. Max saw them and wandered over. He had tried these ugly, smoky and smelling things once and hated them so that wasn't the attraction. He needed others so that he didn't feel so lonely and anyway Billy was always good for a nasty idea.

As normal Billy was in a foul mood and this time Mr Severly was in his sights. "Old bugger needs a lesson. I feel like blowing him to smithereens," said Billy.

"Sounds like you need Guy Fawkes he tried to blow up the English Parliament with gelignite," said Max.

"I haven't got the gelignite so that's no good," said Billy.

"I've got a couple of penny bombs if they would do the job?" said Max.

"Hm, let me think on that one Maxy boy and I'll get back to you."

The next day at school Billy sidled up to Max during

recess and said, "I think I've got an idea to ruffle Severly's feathers."

He stopped talking and smiled wickedly. "We lob a penny bomb through the window while he is preparing lessons in the morning. Should frighten him enough."

"Too hard and the windows are too high to open," said Max.

"Well, smarty pants you think of a better idea."

Max looked up and a twinkle registered in his right eye. He was up for a challenge.

He had a dozen ideas floating around but all seemed too remote and complicated.

He was wandering around the house deep in thought when he kicked his toe on a piece of pipe. He looked down and cursed under his breath.

The toe was cut and began to bleed but he wasn't all that worried as a brilliant thought was coursing through his mind. It started small but soon blossomed into a full plan.

He bent down and picked up the pipe. It was used as an overflow from the kitchen sink.

It should have been attached to the pipe that came down from the sink by a U-bend but the plumber had forgotten to finish the job.

Max turned it over and over and his smile stretched across his face. It was two and a half feet long and three inches in diameter.

It was perfect.

The next day Max added the penny bombs, a ball of binder twine, a pocket knife, a three foot stick, the pipe and a box of matches to Prince's saddlebag.

No one saw him.

At school, he took the saddle off the horse and put it over the hitching rail with all the others.

He turned the horse out to graze and then helped Molly with her saddle and Queen Bee.

He wandered over to Billy.

He commenced to tell him what his plan was but then stopped short. He only needed one witness, anymore and he could be dobbed on. The beauty of his chopping up the canes was that no one else knew and so he was the keeper of the secret.

This next plan would be the same. He couldn't afford to trust any of the others. They might guess he was the perpetrator but they would never know for certain.

"What were you saying Maxy boy?" asked Billy.

"Never mind I'll tell you another day. It's not important."

Mr Severly was a man of habit and it was the toilet habit that Max had decided to exploit.

Every recess Mr Severly would wander to the school house toilet and there he would sit out the whole half hour.

Precisely on the dot of eleven o'clock he would wipe the evidence away, hitch up his trousers and tuck the newspaper under his arm. He would leave the little house, wash his hands at the sink on the verandah outside the class room and then begin the lessons.

Max peered through the classroom door and saw that Mr Severly was going through his early morning routines.

This would give him enough time to set up and then at recess the fireworks would begin.

He sprinted to the saddle, took out the pipe and ran for the school house toilet.

The door faced towards the school so the back was out of sight to anyone on the school grounds.

He was pretty sure Mrs Severly didn't awake until near recess so she wasn't going to be looking out the window.

Max pulled the pipe and stick from under his jumper and swung the dunny trap door up out of the way. It was hinged on the top and needed propping like lots of other doors at the back of toilets.

The pungent odour from the pan hit his nostrils and he flinched.

He brushed the gagging feeling aside and pushed the stick into the soft, slushy soil. It would keep the door ajar and help keep the pipe in place.

He grabbed the handle of the pan and hauled on it.

It was heavy and slowly slid halfway out.

He had to check the depth to the top of the paper, liquid and muck so that he could keep the pipe end at least four inches above.

He pushed the pan back and tied the pipe onto the upright stick so that it left enough room for the penny bomb to stick in the putrid mess of the pan and be able to explode outwards as well as upwards.

All was in readiness with the pan, pipe and door so he walked casually away.

At recess, Mr Severly didn't disappoint Max as he picked up the newspaper and walked off towards the toilet as he had done a hundred times before.

Max waited patiently and then scampered to the back of the toilet.

He took out the penny bomb and matches and carefully shielded the flame before he lit the wick.

All the while Mr Severly sat comfortably doing his business and reading the paper. He was totally oblivious to what was happening behind him and what was about to happen.

Max heard the tell-tale sound of fizz as the wick ignited. He dropped the penny bomb, wick up down the pipe and ran.

The penny bomb moved quickly under gravity and slid gently into the muck in the pan. It settled over half its length into the putrid mess.

Mr Severly caught a whiff of burning and looked around.

His thought went to stupid boys playing with matches and smoking then…

The penny bomb exploded. Bits of smoking paper flew out and up followed by a substantial amount of brown, putrid muck.

It hit Mr Severly's unprotected bare bottom and catapulted him forward.

He let out a scream of terror and tried to regain his balance and at the same time, he attempted to fling open the door and run.

Everything became mixed up and his legs and arms became entangled. He tripped and crashed to the ground.

Children came running from all the corners of the playground and gasped at the sight of Mr Severly sprawled on the ground with his bottom exposed to all.

Mrs Severly came running from the house and amongst her protestations of the foul smell that was coming from Mr Severly she helped him across to the house.

Max had made directly for the back of the toilet and had removed all the evidence.

Mr Severly was physically unharmed although his dignity was somewhat shattered.

He spent countless nights having flash backs and pondering on who would set such a cruel trap.

He never solved that part of the mystery.

Burton and Marion, along with all the parents, heard about the cruel trick and interrogated their children. No one owned up and no one dobbed in anyone else.

Chapter 49

For Burton and Marion, there was worse news than a penny bomb in a toilet.

Ginger rang one evening on April 1st. At first, Burton thought he was playing a silly April Fool's trick. He was crying and mumbling until Burton shouted down the line, "Pull yourself together man and tell me what is going on."

Ginger, with difficulty, explained that Madeline had been hospitalized and that she was in a coma.

"We'll come straight away. Now boy you stay strong, you hear me?" said Burton.

When the family arrived at the Atherton Hospital the matron took them aside and told them a harrowing story of Madeline's last 12 hours.

She had been feeling unwell and had taken herself off to bed.

Ginger had stayed by her side until his beloved had fallen into a deep sleep.

He had gone off to finish the ploughing the back field of their farmlet.

He returned an hour later to check on Madeline and found a horrifying scene.

Madeline had awoken to pains that were emanating from her stomach and her back and knew that these were signs of kidney failure and the onset of the birth of the baby. The doctor had explained that these pains would occur at full term. With careful management in the hospital, he believed all would be well. Now Madeline was confronted too early by everything the doctor had described.

Madeline threw the sheets off and noted the wet patch that covered a wide area and the red staining of blood. Her waters had broken and she was bleeding.

Madeline hauled herself out of the bed all the time calling Ginger's name.

She tried to walk but fell and lay sobbing.

She called to her beloved again and again but he didn't appear.

She dragged herself towards the kitchen where the telephone was located.

The red stream of blood followed her.

She felt the convulsions as the baby prepared to be pushed out and she tried desperately to stop these. It was too early and she knew that he wouldn't survive. The pain in her back felt like a white hot iron and she lost consciousness.

After finishing the ploughing, Ginger entered the

house from the back door and went to see how Madeline was feeling.

He collapsed to his knees when he came upon her body. "Madeline what has happened?" he asked.

He lifted her head and cradled it not knowing what else to do.

He looked to the trail of blood and then panic set in.

He lay Madeline back on the floor and rushed to bring her a pillow.

He grabbed the receiver of the telephone and rang for an ambulance.

He rang the hospital and tried to explain what he had come upon.

Madeline lay in the hospital in a coma. She had tubes from her mouth and a mask over her face.

A large plastic sheet covered half the bed and prevented Marion from taking her in her arms. The nurses were fussing around check this and that.

Burton sobbed when he saw his daughter looking so pale, drawn and still.

The doctor came in followed by Ginger.

He motioned to them all to follow him out into the corridor.

"I'm so sorry, I'm so sorry," Ginger kept repeating looking from Marion to Burton.

The doctor said, "Madeline is gravely ill and I'm afraid she will not awaken from the coma. Her kidneys have collapsed and her other vital organs are failing. We will keep her comfortable until she passes."

He turned and left the grieving trio.

Madeline Whittaker nee Johnson passed away on 6th April 1936.

Burton was inconsolable.

His demons had returned and he could see no other way to shake them than to run.

He began selling up and readying to leave the valley for good.

Even the appearance of Lucas-Hughes didn't stop him. "I offer my heart felt condolences to you and your family Burton. I hear you are thinking of pulling out. That would be a shame and a waste as you've been one of the most innovative farmers I have ever had the privilege to work with. May I ask that you give yourself more time to reconsider?"

To Burton, the end had come and so he packed the family in the Ford and after saying his farewells to the Hayden family, Francis family, the Osbornes and every-one else he took the Mossman Road and headed south.

They all shed a tear as they crossed the Barrett Creek Bridge and Isobel summed up their feelings, "Gone but the fun memories will always be with us. Farewell to the Daintree."

Acknowledgments

My special thanks to my partner Deborah Johnson who inspired me to write and gave me the interest in the story *Daintree Reflections*. The people in the story are her ancestors. She has been at my side as we followed in the footsteps of Marion and Burton Johnson and their family. Starting in northern New South Wales we followed them into the Daintree. Deborah has also been photographer, editor and offered ideas and changes throughout the writing process.

I also acknowledge the following for their assistance; Tyalgum community for being so welcoming when we visited and the Daintree Village folk who looked after us when we spent four days there.

I need to mention Peter and Jodi Grabasch who live in Cawarral, Queensland and operate a business called Little Aussie Encounters. They have been keenly interested in my writing and offered assistance with marketing.

Finally, a thank you to all the cousins and family we met on our journey through northern New South Wales and Queensland for their hospitality and sharing.

It has been an exhilarating journey.

About the Author

Anthony Buirchell was born in Kojonup, West Australia, in 1949.

He toiled on the 'Wheat Bins' during Christmas holidays to pay his way through high school and college.

Anthony was the Head Boy of Kojonup JHS in 1964 and again at Katanning SHS in 1966.

After studying at Claremont Teachers' College, he graduated and taught for 45 years in large primary schools and as a Principal in small country schools.

Through part time studies he attained a Bachelor of Social Science at Curtin University and a Bachelor of Education at Murdoch University.

He has a daughter, Stephanie and grandsons, Kale and Dylan.

His partner is Deborah Johnson and she was the inspiration for his books in the Destiny in Disguise Series.

The first book in this series was *Destination Daintree*.

Anthony has also researched and written the non-fiction: *The Restless Danish Immigrants: The Johnson Family*.

Blog: *www.anthonybuirchell.com*

Online shop: www.criccroc.com